In the Shadows of Sarah

June Kraholik

Table of Contents

Dedication

To my dad who always encourages me to never stop
and keep going.

Chapter 1:

The Promise

Tears ran down Hayley's face as she sat in the front row in silence. Everyone had already left while she sat motionless, staring at the casket that was draped with an American flag. The only thought that was crossing her mind was: How could this have happened? This can't be possible.

Eric was only in his 30s, and they had been married for only 5 years. Eric had done the job since they met; he knew what he was doing. This had to be a mistake—Eric wasn't gone.

"Hayley, we have to go. We are going to take Eric to the cemetery now. Hayley..."

"Yes, okay, I'm ready," she replied.

The truth was, Hayley wasn't ready. She just wasn't ready to say goodbye yet, but she got up and walked to where Eric was lying. She touched the flag that draped the casket before leaning down to kiss where Eric's head would be lying. "*I* love you, Eric."

Hayley turned away, "I am good," she said, wiping tears away from her face. Hayley walked to the back of the church to where Christian, Eric's friend/partner, was standing. Christian had stood at the back of the church watching over Hayley as she sat in silence.

"You ready, Hayley?" Christian said as he put his arm out for Hayley to grab.

"Yes, I am ready," she replied.

The two walked out of the church to Christian's vehicle. Christian opened the passenger side door to allow Hayley to climb in before closing the door. The two waited as Eric was loaded into the back of the hearse. Both watched in silence.

Hayley: "I just don't get it, Christian. I mean, I know the story, I understand what happened, but I can't see Eric not being prepared for something like that. He knew the danger, and he was always so careful."

Christian: "Hayley, it caught us off guard. No matter how well you prepare, sometimes bad shit happens. We took the precautions, we knew the house layout, and we knew the plans. I wish it were different, Hayley. We tried our best to save him.

Hayley: "I know, sometimes I wish I were there that day. Just to be there for him."

Christian: "Hayley, it was just a matter of an instant; you were there shortly after it happened. You saw it yourself, Hayley."

"I know," Hayley replied as she looked at the sea of police vehicles lined up to take Eric to the cemetery.

Hayley remembered the last time she spoke with Eric. It was right before they went to serve the search warrant on the residence.

"Hey, love. We are headed to do this search warrant. When we are done, you want to grab lunch with us?" Eric asked.

Hayley: "Humm, call me when you get done, I am right in the middle of yesterday's homicide case. I will find a stopping point when you get done. Only for you, though."

Eric laughed, "Well, I feel special, and I will take it. I love you and will see you soon."

Hayley: "I love you too. You should feel really special, you know I don't like cops."

Eric: "Yeah, you have told me that since day one, but I got you."

Hayley: "Bye, Eric."

Eric: "Bye, my Hal."

Ten minutes had gone by, and Hayley was listening to the radio traffic.

"We're 10-23," the radio said, meaning they were at the scene. The air went quiet for a moment, then the radio came back on, filled with the sharp sound of gunshots.

"Shots fired, shots fired. I need more units, I need EMS, now. Officer down."

It was Christian on the radio.

Hayley jumped up from her desk and ran to her vehicle. Starting her vehicle, she raced out of the department parking lot, headed to the search warrant residence. Hayley continued to listen to the radio to know who was shot.

Christian was yelling on the radio, "TELL EMS TO TURN RIGHT WHERE THEY ARE STOPPED. I HAVE TWO SHOT, SUSPECT DOWN, OFFICER DOWN. GOD HURRY."

Hayley mashed the gas down to the floorboard. As she turned on the road, several units had already made it to the scene. Hayley could see that the crime scene tape was already up and people had started to gather on the street. Hayley parked her vehicle as close as she could and began to run towards where Christian had told EMS to turn. As Hayley came closer to the location, one of the other officers grabbed Hayley as she was almost around the corner, where Christian was.

"Hal no. Stay back," said Lieutenant Varchetto, the shift commander.

Hayley: "Is it Eric? Please say it's not Eric."

Lt. Varchetto: "Hal stop, just calm down."

Hayley began to get upset. "Is he gone, Varch? IS HE GONE? VARCH TELL ME."

Lt. Varchetto: "Hal, I haven't been around there. Let them do their job, Hal."

Hayley broke away from Lt. Varchetto and ran around the corner. Christian and EMS were surrounding Eric, who was lying on the ground.

"CHRISTIAN."

Christian turned, tears running down his face. He just shook his head in a no motion.

"NO, NO!" Hayley cried, running toward Eric. She fell to her knees, grabbing Eric's face in her hands and laying her head on his chest. Hayley was crying uncontrollably. "Oh my God, Eric, no, no, please no." Hayley grabbed on tighter to Eric, blood smeared on her hands and arms and into her clothing.

Eric was gone. The shots were fatal; there was nothing anyone could do.

Hayley heard as Christian put the vehicle in drive, who was looking straight ahead with his Oakley sunglasses on, hiding his eyes. Christian looked over at Hayley and grabbed her hand. They followed the processional lights and sirens. It consisted of their own department and departments from all around the United States. They all came to honor Eric as Eric was their brother in blue.

Even though they didn't know him personally, the brotherhood and sisterhood were always bound together.

As they reached the cemetery, Hayley and Christian got out of the car. They walked to their seats, arm in arm. Christian's wife, Kelsey, was already waiting for them. Kelsey hugged Hayley and sat on the other side of Christian. As everyone filed in, the pastor began the ceremony.

"Ladies and Gentlemen,

We gather here today with heavy hearts, united in sorrow yet bound by a profound sense of duty and respect. We come to honor Eric, who made the ultimate sacrifice in the line of duty. Today, we stand together to remember Eric, a hero whose life was dedicated to protecting and serving our community.

In the quiet moments of reflection, we can hear the echoes of Eric's commitment, courage, and selflessness. The badge he wore, the oath he took, and each call he answered were a testament to his unwavering resolve to uphold justice and safeguard our way of life. Eric was more than an officer; he was a husband, a son, a brother, a friend, and a mentor. He was the embodiment of our highest ideals.

As we stand here, we are reminded of the words from John 15:13, "Greater love hath no man than this, that a man lay down his life for his friends." Eric lived this scripture daily. His love for his community, his dedication to the law, and his willingness to face danger for our safety will never be forgotten. He was the thin blue line that stood between chaos and order, darkness and light.

To Eric's family, we cannot fathom the depth of your loss or the pain you endure. But know this: Eric's bravery and sacrifice have left an indelible mark on our hearts and our history. He did not die in vain. His legacy lives on in every life he touched, in every child who sleeps peacefully, and in every community that thrives because of his vigilance.

We must also remember that the journey of a law enforcement officer is not traveled alone. It is shared with families who support them, communities who depend on them, and colleagues who stand shoulder to shoulder with them. The bonds formed in this journey are unbreakable, forged in trust, camaraderie, and an unwavering commitment to justice.

Let us honor Eric's memory not just with our words, but with our actions. Let us strive to uphold the values he cherished, to continue his mission with integrity and honor. In our daily lives, let us remember his sacrifice and be inspired to serve others with the same dedication and compassion.

Let us bow our heads in a moment of silence, offering our prayers and thoughts to Eric and his family. May they find peace and comfort in the knowledge that Eric's sacrifice has not been in vain, and that he is forever remembered as a true hero.

May God bless Eric, his family, and all those who continue to serve. And may we always hold his memory in our hearts, lighting our path as we move forward together. In God's name we pray, amen."

Silence was heard throughout the cemetery until broken by dispatch for Eric's final call.

"355." Silence.

"355." Silence.

"355 Officer Eric Dolce is forever 10-42. He gave the ultimate sacrifice on June 17, 2024. Eric, we will forever watch over your family. Rest in peace, my brother. We have it from here."

An honor guard member said, "Present Arms". Hayley watched as the Honor Guard lowered the American flag. 7 members of the Honor guard stood close by with rifles in their hands.

"Attention!"

Seven soldiers snapped to position, boots striking the ground in perfect unison. Rifles rested firmly against their shoulders.

"Ready!"

Metal clinked as seven bolts slid back. The sound echoed sharply, slicing through the stillness like a final heartbeat.

"Aim!"

Seven rifles rose as one, barrels glinting beneath the pale light. Every movement was precise, practiced, reverent.

"Fire!"

The first volley cracked through the silence. Seven shots exploding into the sky. The sound lingered, hanging heavy in the hearts of everyone present.

"Ready! Aim! Fire!"

The second volley followed, then the third—each one sharper, colder, final. Smoke curled upward, dissolving into the gray morning air.

"Present arms!"

Seven rifles lowered to the center, held tight against trembling hands. The soldiers' faces stayed forward, their eyes fixed ahead.

Then came Taps.

All at the ceremony were already upset, but Taps always had a way of making things hurt a little more. Once Taps concluded, the pastor stated, "This concludes the ceremony. The family will remain seated if you would like to give your condolences. Thank you."

Hayley, Christian, and Kelsey stayed seated as people approached to offer their condolences. They hugged each person and thanked them for coming.

When everyone was gone, Christian turned to Hayley, "Do you want us to give you a few minutes?"

"Yeah, I'll be with you guys soon," Hayley said.

"Okay, we will be in the car," Christian said, grabbing Kelsey's hand and walking off.

Hayley sat looking at all the flowers and the casket in front of her.

"Eric, I'm so sorry I couldn't save you. I'm so sorry, I should have gone with you. I shouldn't have changed units. I should have been there. I will never forgive myself. I am so sorry I wasn't there."

Tears ran down Hayley's face.

"How am I supposed to do this now? We were supposed to do this together."

Hayley sat in silence for a few more moments and stood up, looking at the casket one more time.

"Bye, Eric, you will always be with me." She laid her hand on Eric's casket one last time.

Hayley turned around and started walking towards Christian and Kelsey. When she reached them, Kelsey asked softly, "Do you want to come home with us?"

Hayley shook her head replying, "No, I think I just want to go home."

"Okay, home it is then," Christian said as they all got in the car.

As Christian pulled up to Hayley and Eric's home, he turned back to Hayley asking, "Are you sure you want to stay here tonight?"

"Yeah, I will be fine, I promise," replied Hayley.

Hayley got out of the vehicle and waved as Christian and Kelsey drove away. She turned around and started walking towards the front door. As she walked inside, she was greeted by Emma, the little dog she and Eric had bought before they got married.

"Hey, Emma, my girl," Hayley said while throwing her keys away. She walked over to the couch and flopped down on it. Resting her head on the armrest, she looked towards the entertainment center. There were picture frames that contained pictures of the two of them and pictures of Christian, Kelsey, Hayley, and Eric together. Christian, Hayley, and Eric all worked together and were in the same division for years. Kelsey joined the trio once she had married Christian. So many memories flooded Hayley as she sat in that spot. It was still hard to believe that one of them, whom she loved the most, was gone forever.

Although Hayley and Eric had only been married for 5 years, they had been working together for 10 years. Eric, Hayley, and Christian all worked at the same department on different shifts before going to the drug unit eventually. They worked side by side, working undercover and doing many search warrants.

When Hayley and Eric began to see each other as more than partners, the two hid it for a long time. Christian knew but never said anything until the two finally told him. They all agreed not to say anything within the department because Hayley and Eric knew that one of them would be moved. Things stayed quiet for three years until Eric decided it was time and knew he wanted to marry Hayley.

Eric: "Hal, you know you're my girl, right?"

Hayley: "Well, duh. Why, what's wrong?"

Eric: "Nothing is wrong. I think it is time."

Hayley: "Time for what, Eric?"

Eric: "Time to tell everyone we are together."

Hayley: "Hell no, I don't want to move units. Where are you going to move to? If you tell it, you have to move." Hayley said, laughing.

Eric: "Hal, we've got to tell them eventually."

Hayley: "Well, let's wait because I'm not ready to leave, and I know you aren't either."

Eric: "Let me show you something. Come here."

Hayley got up from where she was sitting on the couch and walked to Eric. When Hayley walked towards Eric, Eric was holding a box with a ring inside. He proposed to Hayley, "Hal, marry me."

Hayley: "What. Are you serious right now!?"

Eric: "I'm dead serious."

Hayley was shocked, "I don't know what to say."

Eric: "Hum, for starters, a yes would be great."

Hayley said, "Yes, I'm sorry, of course yes." She threw her arms around Eric's neck and hugged him tightly. "Oh my God, yesss."

Hayley turned from her side to her back and closed her eyes. Eric and she had many conversations about the what-ifs of the job. They both promised that if anything happened to one of them, the other would move on, keep going, and find happiness.

Hayley could not imagine it at this point. It had only been a week since Eric's passing. Her heart was so heavy in her chest. It felt like it was a weight that put pressure on her lungs, and she could barely breathe. The deep breaths that usually helped to calm Hayley seemed not deep enough, and they didn't help. She closed her eyes to calm the burning that came from all of the tears shed. Before she knew it, she was already asleep.

Chapter 2:

The Move

"So, what do you want to talk about today? What's on your mind?" Mark questioned.

Mark had been Hayley's therapist since Eric had died 6 months earlier. She immediately consulted Mark as he was well known in the law enforcement community where she lived. The last 6 months flew by but yet Hayley felt it had been a lifetime since Eric's death.

"Nothing much, just working a lot and trying to keep my mind off of things. I just, I still just can't move on. I feel like there is something holding me back, and that as time goes on, there is always the deep regret and heartache that I wasn't there for him. I could do everything I could, but I couldn't save him, and it's crushing," Hayley said, beginning to break down.

Mark handed Hayley a tissue, "It is good to feel like this, Hayley, and it is good to work also. It's not something that is going to go away altogether. It is going to take some time. Have you thought about moving out? I know you talked about that the last time we talked."

"Yeah, but to tell you the truth, that isn't going to help. I am still reminded of Eric every time I go to work, every time I look around the house, or go into the city. I can't even imagine putting myself out there to do anything. It is as if I do, somehow it will be tied back to Eric. Somehow, it will remind me of him, and I know I'll be looking for Eric in everyone I meet. I just can't fathom it.",

"Well, right now it is too soon. When you are ready, things will start to fall into place; it is just not the right time. Yes, you will always have memories of Eric here which will never go away. Do you think changing your department might help."

Hayley sighed, "No, you know I have trust issues. Other agencies around here knew Eric, too. I'm really thinking I just need to pick up and start over. Just a different place and a different identity. Not in a shady way, obviously but I don't think I want to do law enforcement anymore. I mean, Eric has been gone for only 6 months, and everyone has moved on with their life. Eric's position was filled almost the same day he died. I just can't, and there is nothing to keep me here anymore. I feel as if I have no ties left to this place."

Mark stared at Hayley, listening to every word as she looked down and pulled at the tissue Mark had handed her. "Well, I want you to keep that option open but make sure you do it because you want a new start and not running, so you don't have to feel everything. How much have you thought about this? You are not the person to mention something without totally thinking it through."

Hayley smiled, "I've been looking at houses in St. Johns County, in Florida."

Mark: "Okay, and that is by where?"

Hayley: "Saint Augustine, Florida, Jacksonville area. There is a community called Beachwalk I am looking at. It's like the beach without the house being destroyed when a hurricane comes through."

Mark: "I hear you. Living near the beach has its appeal, but it's important to remember that in a really strong hurricane, any house could be at risk."

Hayley: "I know, but it just feels safer, or at least that is what I am telling myself."

Mark: "Are you still writing and reading books?"

Hayley: "Yes, I am actually! I finished a book the other day. It was pretty good; still trying to figure out myself as a widower and single again. It just doesn't seem real still."

Mark slowly pushed back his chair and stood, a clear sign that the session was over. He straightened his shoulders and gave a small nod. "Well, keep doing that."

Hayley got up too, "Yeah, I will, I'm good though."

Mark: "Stay strong, and I will talk to you next week."

"Okay," Hayley said as she walked out of the room. Although Hayley thought she wasn't making progress, she did like speaking with Mark. It seemed to help with all of her thoughts.

Hayley left Mark's room heading back to the department. The department had been great to Hayley, allowing her to take therapy sessions during work hours. As Hayley pulled up, she parked and stared at the patrol officers as they were changing shifts. They were all laughing and talking amongst themselves. They were the younger officers, most of them in their first year or two of policing.

Hayley remembered when she first started, how excited she was. She felt she was going to make the community in which she lived so much better because she cared. Hayley thought that no one could touch her; she had made it through the police academy, and she could carry a gun. She felt safe and like she was on top of the world.

Quickly, she learned differently the first time Hayley went to arrest someone, and the fight was on. She ended up getting the person to the ground by grabbing onto their sagging pants. Once he was on the ground, she held one hand behind his back, lying on top of him with her knees in his back, until she saw another officer come around the corner. She called for the officer, and he came running over and helped Hayley put handcuffs on the person. It was a defining moment in Hayley's career.

Hayley was not your typical officer. She was petite, with a small frame and blond hair—an average-looking woman, not what most people would picture as a law enforcement type. She had always been a tomboy. She was feisty and could hold her own in any situation thrown at her.

As the department learned more about Hayley, they understood she could raise her tone and awareness depending on the situation she was in. No one had to worry about what they said with Hayley around, and she could joke around with the best of them. She was considered one of the guys by all.

Hayley walked up the stairs to the department and to her desk. Christian was at his desk, which was a rare occasion as the drug unit was always out doing something.

Christian: "Hey Hayley, how was your session?"

Hayley: "It was good."

Christian: "We still going to see you tonight?"

Hayley: "Yeah, I will see you tonight."

Christian and Kelsey had invited Hayley for dinner. It was a Friday and usually Hayley didn't hang out much since Eric's death. Christian and Kelsey were hosting several officers at their house for food and drinks. Ideally, it would be good for Hayley to get out of the house, but she was dreading it.

Hayley sat down at her desk and looked over at the picture of her and Eric. It felt like forever since she had seen Eric. She missed snuggling up close to him and his kisses on her forehead.

"Hayley, are you finished with that Vincent homicide case file?" Her supervisor asked.

"Yeah, let me print it out for you." Hayley turned on her computer and started to pull up the case file. Hayley had moved to the detective division as a homicide detective when Eric and she announced their engagement. She was good at the job, and it challenged her, which Hayley loved, as she got bored quite easily.

As Hayley was printing up the case file, Steve came over to her desk, "Are you coming to Christian's tonight?"

Hayley: "Yeah, I will be there."

Steve: "Awesome, it will be good to see you outside of work. You know?"

"Yeah, I will see you there." Hayley said, not giving Steve's comment a second thought.

Hayley walked over to her supervisor and handed the case file to him. "Here you go."

"Hayley, can you please close the door and sit here for a moment," her supervisor requested. Hayley knew what was next: her supervisor was going to evaluate her to see if she had a level head or if she was a safety issue.

Hayley closed the door and sat down.

Supervisor: "So, how are you doing?"

Hayley replied, acting all peppy, "I am good."

Supervisor: "I know it has been 6 months. I just want to make sure your head is in the game. I don't want anything to happen. I don't want you to get out on one of these scenes and not be able to handle it, or God forbid another officer's death."

Hayley: "No, I have been doing well. I'm going to therapy and making quite good progress. I am having no issues. The job is actually helping, being with so many people I know."

Hayley knew she was lying, but she didn't like people watching over her, waiting for her to make a mistake so they could blame it on Eric's death. She had seen it way too many times within the department.

Supervisor: "Now you know we are all here for you. If you need more time or help, we will get it for you. All you have to do is let me know. We are all here to help you."

Hayley thought, *yeah, right, you would throw me back down to patrol if you knew what's really going on in my head.* "Yeah, of course, I will let you know. Really, I am good. I promise."

Supervisor: "Okay, that was all Hayley. I just wanted to check on you."

"Okay, thanks for checking on me," Hayley said with a fake smile.

As Hayley walked out of the office, Christian was looking her way. They made eye contact while Hayley rolled her eyes. Christian smiled and kept working with the other detectives in his unit.

At 6 in the evening, Hayley rang Christian's doorbell, holding onto some cookies that she had picked up at the store before arriving. The desert was always what she and Eric brought to a party at Christian's place. Hayley was never much of a cook, so whatever she and Eric brought was always store-bought.

Kelsey opened the door. "Hayley, it's so good to see you."

Hayley leaned in and hugged Kelsey, "It's so good to see you, too."

Kelsey: "They are all in the back, doing what they do best."

Hayley: "Ahh, seeing who has the bigger set, huh."

Kelsey laughed, "I have missed you. An actual girl's opinion that gets it."

Hayley walked to the back porch, where several co-workers and Christian were sitting around a table. They were telling what Hayley called, "War Stories", things that they had done as an officer. It always was about who could one-up the other. Most already had their favorite adult beverages in hand, and some were smoking cigarettes to pass the time.

"HAYLEY!" Hayley could tell some of them were already under the effects of their adult beverage.

"What are you drinking? What can I get you?" Christian asked.

Hayley laughed, "A Dr. Pepper."

Christian: "Oh, come on Hal, take one for the team."

Hayley: "I am good Christian; I'm just going to laugh at you guys as the night progresses."

Hayley had her wild, drunken days years earlier, before she and Eric dated. In fact, it was during one of those drunken parties that Eric and she had shared their first kiss.

Hayley sat with her Dr. Pepper, listening to the stories that the co-workers told. Steve came and sat next to Hayley, which was not uncommon. Steve had tried to be there for Hayley since Eric died. Hayley always stayed distant from him as she did not want anyone to get the wrong impression. The department loved gossip, and Hayley did not want to start any that she could help.

"You guys remember when Hal took down that hood rat in the projects?" Steve said, looking at Hayley. Her co-workers started to laugh.

"How can one forget," Christian told the story about Hayley's first encounter with a person she was trying to arrest.

Christian: "Yeah, when I took him to jail, I told him he got taken down by a girl."

Hayley and her co-workers began to laugh. "That was my one and only claim to fame." Hayley never liked talking about what she had done at work or been through. She did not care much for "War Story" conversations.

"Hal you a damn lie girl." Christian said, laughing. Everyone laughed, but Hayley never mentioned anything she had done. That was not part of her personality.

As the night progressed, Hayley, tired of all the stories, grabbed her Dr. Pepper and walked down to the pond that was in the back of Christian's subdivision. Hayley sat on the ground looking into the water with her arms around her knees. It was quiet and peaceful away from the loud, drunken situation that was progressively getting even louder.

Hayley heard someone coming up behind her, and she turned to see who or what it was. "Do you mind if I sit with you?" It was Steve. He saw Hayley get up and watch her walk to the pond. After a few moments, he got up to join her.

"No, not at all. It was just getting pretty loud with all of you guys. I think someone is going to call the cops." Hayley said, smiling.

Steve smiled and sat down next to Hayley, setting his beer beside him. "I think we will be alright if they call on us."

Hayley: "You think?"

"Christian has it covered," Steve replied. They both smiled, sitting in silence, looking out into the lake.

Steve nudged his body into Hayley's shoulder, "Are you okay?"

Hayley: "Yeah, I am alright. I'm getting used to my new norm. Just going to take a little while."

Steve: "You will get there eventually, Hal. You know we all adore you and want to see you happy again. We will do anything for you."

Hayley: "I know, I'm getting there."

Steve reached over and grabbed Hayley's hand. Hayley looked at Steve as he said, "When you are ready, I would like to take you out sometime."

Hayley slowly pulled her hand away from Steve, "Well, thank you. I am not ready for all of that right now. You know I love all of you and appreciate everything you guys do for me."

Steve: "I know you're not right now, but I wanted to put that out there for you."

"Ahh, I'll remember that. Thank you for letting me know," Hayley replied. Steve smiled, and the two changed the subject. They talked for another 10 minutes until Hayley said, "They are probably wondering where we are. We should get back."

Steve said, "Yeah, we don't need them talking crap."

Hayley: "Yes, of course we don't. Now that they are drunk, it will be even worse."

By the time Hayley and Steve got back to Christian's house, music was now playing even louder as some of the co-workers had taken to dancing with the dates they had brought.

"Geezus Christ," Hayley said as they went inside Christian's house. Steve laughed, "Wow."

"Where have you two been?" One of their co-workers yelled.

"Away from you, sloppy drunks." Hayley piped back.

Hayley walked inside, and Christian followed her.

Christian: "You okay, Hayley?"

Hayley: "Yeah, I am good. I just walked down to the pond to take a breather."

"Steve?" Christian said in a questioning manner.

Hayley: "No, I went alone, and he came down there. And before you ask, no, I am not interested, and nothing happened."

Christian: "I didn't say anything, and even if something did happen, that would be okay too, Hal."

Hayley looked at Christian, "I said nothing happened! I am not ready yet."

Christian: "Okay, Hal damn."

Hayley: "Christian, I think I am going to move."

Christian: "Well, that will be good. Like a new start, some place without so many memories."

Hayley: "I'm planning to move out of state for a completely new beginning."

Christian set his drink on the counter, "Are you kidding me, Hal? Why would you do that? All your friends are here. Where would you even go?"

Hayley: "I've been looking at a place called Beachwalk in Saint Johns, Florida. I've been looking for a few weeks. I am going to call a realtor on Monday and get the process started on selling our house. Once that is started, I am going to contact a realtor in Saint Johns and have her start looking for houses in Beachwalk."

"Wow, I am shocked," Christian said as Kelsey walked in, asking, "What are you two talking about?" "Well, Hal here has just told me that she wants to sell her house and move to Saint Johns, Florida," replied Christian.

Kelsey looked shocked, "Oh, really? That will be a change and a new start."

Hayley: "Yes, finally, someone who understands Christian. Please just don't say anything yet. I don't want anyone saying anything until it is finalized."

Christian: "We will keep it quiet. Now, can we go have some fun the rest of the night? It's a PAR-TA."

Hayley rolled her eyes and joined the rest with Christian.

Chapter 3:

The Offer

As Hayley said she would, on Monday morning, she called a realtor.

Hayley: "Yes, my name is Hayley Dolce, and I am planning to list my house for sale."

Realtor: "Yes, ma'am, what type of residence is it?"

Hayley: "It's a single-family home with 2 bedrooms, 1 ½ bathrooms."

Realtor: "Are you the person on the house?"

Hayley: "It is my husband and me. He passed away about 6 months ago. That is why I am selling."

Realtor: "Ma'am, I am sorry to hear that. We will have to have a copy of his death certificate at closing, but that is fine."

Hayley: "Yes, ma'am, I have all the paperwork that might be required."

Realtor: "Okay, I will have one of our agents call you, and we will get your home listed as soon as possible."

Hayley: "Okay, thank you."

Hayley hung up the phone. She had started the process, but she knew it would take a while for the house to sell. The housing market was terrible, and interest rates were sky-high. Hayley thought she would have at least a year before actually moving.

Within a week, Eric and Hayley's house was listed. Once listed, Hayley was questioned daily at work about selling the house. Hayley would always answer, "Yeah, too many memories," or "I just need a clean slate."

None of her co-workers, other than Christian, knew the depth of Hayley's plan. Secretly, Christian did not want Hayley to move. Hayley felt like a part of Eric, and now she would be gone. He liked having Hayley around to remember all the times the four of them shared.

"So, have you had many people look at the house?" Mark asked. It had been 6 months since Hayley had listed the house.

Hayley: "Yes, there have been a few. All seemed interested, but no bites yet. I am hoping soon."

Mark: "So, you are sure you still want to move to Florida?"

Hayley: "Yes, I am sure."

Mark: "Does anyone know at work yet?"

Hayley: "Only Christian. No one else knows."

Mark: "How did you handle the first anniversary?"

Hayley: "I was hoping you forgot about that. It was alright, just me, Christian, and Kelsey reminiscing on some of the memories. Then, I went home and packed some stuff away. Just stayed busy and tried not to think about it much."

Mark: "And the emotions?"

Hayley: "It wasn't that bad. I mean, I cried if that is what you are asking, and I was upset, but not where I was a year ago. I don't think I will ever be that dark again."

Mark: "Well, that is good. Are you still not seeing anyone? What about Steve?"

Hayley: "No, I just don't want to go there. Steve is Steve. If I want to go out, all I have to do is say yes. I am good for now, though."

Mark: "What's wrong with Steve?"

Hayley: "Nothing! He's just not Eric, and I don't feel completely ready yet."

Mark: "Steve doesn't have to be the one; it just will break the cycle, and it will motivate you."

Hayley: "No, I think I'm good."

Mark: "I see you are still stubborn. I guess it fits you."

Hayley laughed, "Yes, that never goes away."

Mark stood up, "Keep being stubborn, but it is okay to go out with someone on a date. It's not going to hurt you."

Hayley: "I will keep that in my mind."

Mark: "You are so full of it."

Hayley laughed and walked out of Mark's clinic, "I don't think head doctors are supposed to talk to clients that way."

"Girl, I will see you next week," Mark laughed.

Hayley went straight home. She had taken the day off to relax. It was busy at work lately, and the summer heat seemed to always make people angrier, which in turn led to more homicides for Hayley to work. Plus, in the back of Hayley's mind, she knew she needed to use up her vacation time as it could not be taken when she resigned. She had hundreds of hours she never took but recently had taken the days she needed.

Hayley opened her computer and typed, *Beachwalk homes for sale, St. Johns, Florida.*

Hayley started browsing through the home listings. She clicked on one of the houses. A box opened, "To see pictures, please enter your email address and phone number." Crap, Hayley had managed prior times to see the pictures without having to put in an email address or a phone number. She did not want the phone calls, but she put her email address and phone number in the box.

Hayley began scrolling, thinking, *okay, I'm looking at 500k for a house that is the perfect size in this community.* Hayley kept scrolling. *I like that one. Eww, it has carpet.* As she scrolled, her phone rang. Unknown number, Hayley let it go to voicemail.

A text message came in, "*Hi Hayley, this is Julie. I saw where you asked to see listings from Beachwalk. I can definitely help you with that. When are you thinking about moving?*"

Hayley texted, "*Not in the near future. Probably about a year to a year and a half. I don't live in Florida right now. I am looking to relocate.*"

Julie replied, "*I relocated 3 years ago from Virginia to Florida. It was the best decision.*"

To which Hayley replied, "*Oh wow, that is awesome. My family lived down in Florida at one time. It is just hard looking at jobs down there. I have been in law enforcement for years. It's hard to find a job when my job skills are arresting people. I'm still looking, though.*"

Julie reassured Hayley, replying, "*I changed careers when I moved here, too. It was scary, but it was the best decision I made. Have you ever been to Beachwalk?*"

Hayley texted, "*That's good to know. No, I haven't, I've only seen pictures of it online. Do you know anything bad about Beachwalk?*"

Julie replied, "*No, I haven't. Everyone seems to be happy out there. I don't know any crime.*"

To this, Hayley messaged, "*I like the idea of living in the community. I am not old, but as I get older, I would like to have a community around me. It's only me, so I just like the idea. Plus, I like the beach without the worries of a hurricane taking my house out.*"

Julie replied, "*I can understand that. Is there anything that would make you move any sooner?*"

Hayley typed, "*Well, not really, I am waiting on my house to sell, and then I am trying to find one that would be perfect for me. I have a dog, and I am allergic to carpet, so it would depend on how much I had to add or change before I leave. But please keep sending the listings.*"

Julie reassured Hayley, writing, "*I will and I will cater them towards you.*"

"*I appreciate it, Julie,*" replied Hayley, as she browsed the house listings a few moments longer.

Later, she decided to get some work done for her online store. Hayley had started an online store to try and get her mind off of Eric a year earlier, and it was doing okayish. She was hoping for the store to start doing well so she could stay at home in Florida instead of venturing out. Or at least if she got a job, she could supplement her pay with the store profits. She really was looking for a job she could stay at home doing so the store bit was actually a part of her plan.

Hayley's phone rang again. She recognized the number as the realtor trying to sell her house.

"Hello?" answered Hayley.

John: "Hey Hayley, it's John. We are going to have someone come by and look at your house. It's a family. They are moving here in about 2 months. They are relocating from South Carolina. He just got a job at, well, surprisingly, at the department you work for. I guess they were looking for a slower pace and a safer place to live. Can I bring them by around 8 A.M. tomorrow?"

Hayley: "Yeah, of course. I will be at work, and I will lock Emma up in the cage."

John: "Okay, sounds good. I will let you know once the showing is over."

Hayley: "Sounds good, thank you."

The next day, Hayley sat at her desk. It was 8 A.M. on the dot. She tapped her pen, wondering about the showing. She still wasn't completely sure about the move as there was no actual progress in selling the house. Hayley had started packing, but that was all for herself, really. She didn't want to rush packing her things when the house was sold.

What if this time it does, she thought. *I'm overthinking this. There have been several people that looked at the house. Why am I so worried about it now?*

Hayley just had a feeling; she just knew that this was the couple who would buy her house. They just seemed so perfect. For starters, the house was in a neighborhood with other officers that the husband would be working with and there were also young kids in the area. It would be the perfect spot for any officer to live.

I haven't even really been looking for places in Beachwalk. I mean, I guess I know the area, but I haven't even gotten serious with Julie yet about it.

"Hayley," her supervisor interrupted Hayley's thoughts.

"Yeah," she answered.

Supervisor: "There is a stiff on Stillwater. They think an overdose."

Hayley: "Alright, text me the address. I'll be on my way."

Hayley drove to Stillwater Road. The area was populated by middle-class with labor jobs. It was a quiet neighborhood at night, but Meth had taken over the area. Hayley pulled over in front of the yellow caution tape that stated: "Police Line Do Not Cross!"

Hayley: "What do you have, Varch?"

Lt. Varchetto: "Tyler Randall, 25. Parents last talked to him about a week ago. They had not heard from him, and they asked for a welfare check. When we looked in the windows, we could see his legs. Opened up a window, went inside, and he was lying on the ground. No response, EMS was called and confirmed. The coroner has been called and will be here in about 20 minutes."

Hayley: "Was the door open?"

Lt. Varchetto: "No, once inside, we unlocked and opened the front door to allow EMS access. We kept the door open because he's got a smell already. Might need a mask."

"Alright," Hayley replied as she reached into her glove box and grabbed a jar of Vicks. She dabbed her finger into the Vicks and smeared it under her nose. A trick she had learned to help with the smell of decaying bodies.

Hayley unlocked her trunk and grabbed her camera and a notebook. When Hayley got to the door, she could smell the decay already. She turned to Varchetto, "No one in the neighborhood smelled that?" Hayley asked.

Varchetto replied, "Yeah, they thought it was his garbage."

Hayley shook her head, "Damn, I'm glad these people aren't my neighbors, what the hell."

Varchetto grinned, "I was thinking the same thing."

Hayley placed her stuff down on the outside of the door frame and began taking pictures of the whole room. She walked over to where Randall was lying. "Can you take that notebook and write down what I am saying so I don't have to take off these gloves each time I touch him?" requested Hayley.

"Yeah, sure," Varchetto agreed.

Hayley: "Right arm rubber-like material wrapped above the elbow, midway between the shoulder and the elbow. The needle lying between the arm and the torso looks like a diabetic needle used for insulin. Empty piece of sandwich bag with what appears to be white power-like residue."

"Varch, do you have a drug test kit with you? I want to see if we can get some of this powder residue to test for meth. It looks oily, so I think that is what it is," Hayley commented as she continued to take pictures.

Lt. Varchetto: "Yeah. I'll get you one. Sutton, go get Hayley a drug test kit for meth."

Minutes later, Sutton came back with a test kit.

"Thanks," said Hayley, cutting a piece of the sandwich bag off and placing it in the test kit. After popping the vials in the test kit, the results were immediate.

"It's meth! Varch, can you note the time and that it tested positive?"

Lt. Varchetto: "I got it."

Hayley: "Write down, there appears to be one track mark in the crease of his elbow, almost dead center."

The coroner arrived on scene. Hayley looked up, asking, "Hey Bill, can you help me roll him?"

Bill, while putting on rubber gloves, said, "Damn, I came too early."

Hayley smiled at Bill, "You're the coroner."

Bill: "That doesn't mean I like touching smelly ones."

Hayley and Bill rolled the body over.

Hayley: "Varch, lividity is on the back side, body is out of rigor mortis, defecated and urinated. No signs of trauma to the body can be seen."

"Got it," Varchetto said, writing in the notebook.

Hayley looked at Bill, "You good? He doesn't have any trauma to his head; he must have been sitting on the floor doing this."

Bill: "Yeah, I am good with that assumption. I guess an autopsy will tell the whole truth."

"Yeah, let's get him in the bag and get out of here," Hayley said.

Bill and Hayley lifted Randall and placed him in the black body bag. Hayley stood up as Bill zipped the bag up.

Hayley: "Too young to be zipping him up in a bag. He had his whole life ahead of him. Varch, can you get Sutton to come in here and help Bill carry him out?"

Bill: "Yeah. Sutton, come get this body."

Sutton came running in. Bill had already grabbed the feet, as it was the lightest side. Sutton grabbed the other end, and Randall was placed on a gurney.

Bill: "I'll see you next time, Hayley."

Hayley: "Hopefully not too soon, Bill. I do like sleep."

Hayley walked to her phone, taking off her rubber gloves. She grabbed a napkin and wiped the Vicks from her upper lip.

Hayley: "You know as much as they say Vicks works, you can still smell that shit."

Varchetto smiled at Hayley, "Are you good at clearing the residence? I have family here."

Hayley: "Yeah, we are good. Here, give them one of my cards and tell them to call me if they need anything."

Hayley picked up her issued phone and dialed her supervisor.

Hayley: "Hey, boss, it's going to be another meth overdose. All evidence is collected, and pictures taken. Units are leaving the scene; unknown when an autopsy will be performed at this time. Bill is going to call when he finds out."

Supervisor: "Okay, sounds good, Hayley, thank you."

Hayley: "I am going to leave from here and head home to change. I will be back in a few once I change."

Supervisor: "Alright, Hayley."

Hayley got back in her car and picked up her personal phone. She had a missed call from John, but John had left a message. Hayley played the recording, "Good news, Hayley, the family really liked your house, and they were going home to think about it. I expect an offer sometime this week. Congratulations."

Wow, the house is sold, that's great, but I have nowhere to live in Florida.

Hayley texted a message to Julie.

"Hey Julie, I am going to need to start looking at a house soon. I am going to go home tonight and pull up some houses I want to view. Can we possibly see all of the houses in one day? My work doesn't know I am leaving yet, and I am just going to take a vacation day. I can do whatever day we can see all of them at once."

Moments later, Julie messaged back, *"Absolutely, just send me a list tonight and I will set it up sometime tomorrow. I will let you know what day is available to see all of them at once."*

Hayley started to feel her stomach drop. It was starting to get real and fast. Hayley made it home, jumped in the shower, and changed clothes, heading back to the department. Once she arrived, she caught Christian in the parking lot. She grabbed his arm, saying, "I have a family going to put an offer on the house probably tomorrow. It looks like a sure thing."

Christian: "That's great, Hayley. Are you okay?"

Hayley: "Yeah, I think so. I mean, this just happened."

"Well, I am happy for you. Did you go and take a shower? You still stink," said Christian, pulling away with disgust.

Hayley laughed, "Yes, you know you can never get the smells out."

"God, I don't know how you handle that," Christian said, walking with Hayley inside the department.

Chapter 4:

A New Start

As Hayley told Julie, when she got home that evening, she emailed 5 different listings that she would like to see. The next day, Julie told Hayley that all of the houses would be available by next week. Hayley told Julie she would be there. She would meet Julie at her office, and they would go together.

"Are you sure you really want to do this?" Christian asked one night while lounging with Hayley and Kelsey.

Hayley: "Yes, I am sure. I was so confused, and I didn't know if I could leave everyone and the career behind, but I am ready for it. I have to start over."

"I am going to miss you. You are leaving me with all these egoistic men," Kelsey said, smiling at Christian. Christian smiled and grabbed Kelsey's hand.

Hayley: "Well, it's not goodbye forever, you two know that, right? We will always be connected through Eric and the department. We both can visit each other. I'll be living by the beach so it's going to be like a bonus for you guys."

Christian put his hand out for Hayley to fist bump him, "Yeah, brothers sisters for life."

Hayley fist bumped Christian, "You got that right."

The week went by fast for Hayley. She had several homicides and several case files she was trying to close. She took off as she told Julie she would and drove down to Julie's office in Florida.

"Hey Hayley, it is so good to finally meet you," Julie said, hugging Hayley.

Hayley: "It's good to see you too."

Julie: "So, are you ready?"

Hayley: "Yes, I am nervous and excited all wrapped up in one."

Julie: "It will be a fun day, no pressure at all. If we don't find anything today, you can find some more, and we will do this again."

Hayley: "Sounds great."

Julie and Hayley drove to the first residence and got out. Hayley looked at the house, and her heart started pounding. *Am I really doing this?* Hayley thought to herself.

Julie: "This is the address on Clifton Bay. It's 3 bedrooms and 3 ½ bathrooms."

Hayley walked inside with Julie, but she did not get the sense of home in the house. Like it wasn't her home. The black kitchen cabinets and carpet in the bedrooms did not help.

Hayley: "It's alright, I am not feeling this one though."

Julie: "Okay, no point in staying here then. We have 4 more houses to go to."

Hayley and Julie pulled up at the next house.

Julie: "This is the one on Killarney. 4 bedrooms and 4 ½ bathrooms. Bigger than the last house but still in your price range."

Hayley: "I don't know if I like how close the houses are together, but let's look inside."

Hayley walked into the house and immediately saw carpet on the stairs.

Hayley: "This isn't going to be it, Julie. I am sorry, I don't even need to look further."

Julie: "Okay, it's not a big deal, no point in wasting time if you know from entering the house."

The search for the houses continued until they reached house number 4 and pulled up. Hayley looked out the window at the house. She loved the way it looked from the curb.

Hayley: "I really like the way it looks from the outside."

Julie: "That's a good thing, let's go inside. This is the house on Blue Shark. It's 3 bedrooms, 3 ½ bathrooms."

Hayley walked in the front door. She loved the entry to the front door. The kitchen was perfect for her. She walked upstairs, "Ughh, carpet in the bedrooms."

Julie: "Yes, most homes will have carpet in the bedrooms."

Hayley: "I'm going to have to change that. It's okay, though, I like what I have seen so far."

They walked out the back door of the residence.

Hayley: "Oh yay, they have a fence and it's by the water. Julie, this is it, I know this is the one. Is it way over my price range?"

Julie: "No it is right in your price range, a few thousand over, but we will make an offer in your price range. I am sure they will take it as it is not that much under what they are asking."

Hayley: "Yes, this is it, Julie. I feel it."

Julie: "Okay, let's do it then."

Hayley: "I love the porch out the back too."

Hayley walked back inside and admired the house. This was going to be her house, her new start; the one she wanted since Eric passed. She felt relief come over her, like a weight was lifted off her. She was starting to get excited.

As Hayley walked outside, she looked to the right and left of the residence. On one residence, it appeared as if no one was home, but on the other side, a big black pickup truck that sat high was in the driveway.

Hayley thought to herself, *Well, I guess I can live next to someone country. I'm coming from the country. Hopefully, it is a nice family.*

Hayley and Julie got into the vehicle. Julie turned to Hayley, "This is it?"

Hayley looked out the window at the residence, "Yes, this is it for sure."

When Hayley and Julie got back to the office, Hayley filled out the paperwork and signed what was needed. It was done, Hayley's house was sold, and she was buying her first house alone, for her new start.

Hayley: "Thank you so much for showing me the houses today."

Julie: "Oh, you are so welcome, Hayley. I am glad you found one on your first time out."

Hayley: "Me too."

Hayley started the drive back home. In a matter of a month, she would have a new house, and her old house would be sold. It worked out perfectly as if it was a sign that this is exactly what she should be doing.

Once Hayley got home, she got on the computer and pulled up the listing for the house on Blue Shark. She looked at the images again. It was perfect and better in person. The excitement took over the fear; she could do this, and she would be fine. This is what she wanted, and it was okay to start over, not knowing anyone.

Hayley picked up her phone as it began to ring, "Hello."

It was Christian, "I got a minute and I had to call. Did you find one you liked?"

Hayley: "Yes, it's perfect, Christian. I absolutely love it."

Christian: "Send me the pics of it, I want to see it."

Hayley: "I will send them right now. I was just looking and admiring them again, actually."

Christian: "When are you going to tell at work?"

Hayley: "I don't know yet. I guess within the next few days. I just want to make sure everything is set and done before I tell them. You know how they are when people leave."

Christian: "Oh yeah. I have to go, we are about to head out. I am happy you found a house, Hal."

Hayley: "Thanks, Christian."

Hayley hung up the phone and leaned back in her chair. She had so much to do within a matter of a month. Hayley started to think about when she would actually put her two weeks' notice into the department. She had enough time that she could take time off and get paid for it before she left. Hayley did not know what to do, but she definitely knew she needed to take time, so she did not have to rush when it came to getting out of her house and moving into her new house.

She knew the people buying her house would be working at the department where she currently was. She definitely needed to tell them before the new person got there.

Maybe I should just go in tomorrow and give my notice, Hayley thought.

Screw it, I am starting over anyway, and I am not going to be in law enforcement anymore. So even if they did give me a bad recommendation, I would still be okay. There were other people in my unit who could do the job I do. I need the break anyway.

Weeks had passed, and as brave as Hayley thought she was the day after she agreed on a house in Florida, she had cold feet ever since. She couldn't do it. Every time she thought she could, she just froze. It was so hard, and every possible disaster that could happen came to her mind. She had to do it. She was closing on her house in 2 weeks and had to be out in a month. Furthermore, she was closing on the house in Florida in a week and had to take a day off for that. She already had the date and time, September 15th at 10 A.M...

Hayley pulled up to work and motivated herself.

I got this. I am doing this first thing because if I don't, I won't do it again today. It's going to be fine; I am going to be fine. I have to train someone anyway. Screw it, I am doing it now.

Hayley walked upstairs and into her supervisor's office, walking past Christian.

Hayley: "Can I talk to you for a minute?"

Supervisor: "Yeah, Hayley, what do you need?"

Her supervisor was still typing at his computer as Hayley sat down.

"I've got to tell you something," said Hayley. Her supervisor turned to look at Hayley as she continued: "I have bought a house in Florida, and I will be moving down there within a few weeks." Shocked, Hayley's supervisor just looked at her as she continued, "My house here has already sold, and I will be closing on it soon. I will have to go down to Florida to finalize things there sometime within the next few weeks too. I was thinking that I want to take some of my vacation time until I move, to get things backed up and move them a car full at a time. So, I guess I want to give you my two weeks' notice."

After finishing whatever she had to say in a single breath, Hayley looked at her supervisor, "Say something, you are just looking at me."

Supervisor: "I mean, Hayley, I am just shocked. I was not expecting it. I mean obviously, you have really thought this out, but is there anything I can do to keep you here? The department depends on you, and everyone loves you here."

Hayley: "I know, but it is something I have been thinking about for a while, and I just need the change with everything that has happened in the past year plus."

"Okay, let me think here for a minute," Hayley's supervisor paused and later added, "Can you give me two weeks so we can train Moss. I think Moss would be the best person to take over your caseload and job fast."

Hayley: "Yes, I can give you two weeks. When do you want me to start training Moss?"

Supervisor: "Well, immediately, let me tell the chief, and I'll call Moss in tomorrow and let him know the plans. Just keep it to yourself until tomorrow, please."

Hayley: "I will do so, sir."

Supervisor: "Okay, let me go talk to the chief. I hope you find peace with this move, Hayley. I know Eric was a special person. I know it has been hard on you. You know I will give you a great recommendation, just have the department call me."

Hayley: "Actually, I think I am going to get out of law enforcement completely."

Supervisor: "You're kidding me, right? You are great at it, Hayley."

Hayley: "Thanks, but yes, I think it is time."

Supervisor: "Wow, that's another shock. If you ever decide to go back to it, let me know, and I will make some calls."

Hayley: "Thank you, I really appreciate that."

Hayley and her supervisor walked out of the office. Hayley headed towards her desk, and her supervisor headed downstairs to talk to the chief. As Hayley passed Christian's desk, Christian looked up. Hayley winked at him and kept walking. Christian knew Hayley had finally told the department she was leaving. Christian glanced back down and resumed going through the paperwork.

After work on Hayley's ride home, Christian called saying, "So, tell me what he said. I've been dying to know."

Hayley: "Well, you disappeared and I couldn't find you."

Christian: "We had to go serve a warrant, and it was a cluster."

Hayley: "Oh, okay! Actually, he didn't say much. He asked me to reconsider and requested me to stay 2 weeks instead of leaving right away. He also wants me to train Moss."

Christian: "MOSS?"

Hayley: "Yeah, he can do the job, Christian."

Christian: "Oh my God! Moss is an idiot. You can't be serious."

Hayley: "Christian, he can do the job, he's just different."

Christian: "Right, he's an idiot. I guess it doesn't matter; I'm not in that unit and have no urge to be. Horrible choice."

Hayley laughed, "Be nice, Christian."

Christian: "I will be, I'm just not going to talk to him, that's all. Let me go, I just made it home, and I am going to take Kelsey out tonight."

Hayley: "You in the doghouse?"

Christian: "Yeah, kind of. Last week I worked late every night and she was pissed."

Hayley laughed loudly, "You better make up for it, she's good for you."

Christian: "Yeah, I know, I will talk to you tomorrow."

The next 2 weeks flew by for Hayley. As it came closer to her last day, her heart began to get heavy. She had spent 11 years with the people at the department—11 years of dedication and hard work to get where she was. Everyone at the department had known Eric, but where she was headed, people would only know him through the stories she chose to share. Hayley didn't know if she even wanted to mention she was in law enforcement or that she was ever married. She decided not to say anything to the new people she met until maybe one day they asked about her previous jobs or why she wasn't married.

Hayley worked daily on finishing her case files and training Moss. Christian kept true to his word and said hello to Moss when he saw him with Hayley. Moss was learning and was doing a good job.

"Why are you bagging her hands?" Moss quizzed.

Hayley: "Because she has broken fingernails, which is indicative of a struggle. There may be DNA under her nails. The crime lab can check it."

Moss: "Why are you pulling open her eyes?"

"I'm looking for petechia. Because of the fingernails being broken, I would say there was a struggle, right?" Hayley asked.

Moss: "Yes."

Hayley: "During a fight, they could have hit each other or choked each other, right?"

Moss: "Yes"

"Petechia indicates strangulation," Hayley said, looking in the eyes, "Right here, you see that?"

Moss: "Yes."

Hayley: That is what petechia looks like. I have seen it worse, but if you notice this amount, you will see it in other victims."

Moss: "Okay. I got it."

Hayley: "Although tomorrow is my last day. You know you can call me anytime, Moss. I am working from home, so I'll be available."

Moss: "Thanks, Hayley. I will try not to bother you."

Bill walked into the room. "Are you really leaving us, Hayley?"

Hayley stood up, saying, "Yes, Bill, I am. Tomorrow is my last day."

Bill: "You are going to be a beach bum, I heard."

Hayley smiled, "I guess you could say that."

Bill: "Well, I am sure going to miss you, Hayley. We have had some great years."

"With us getting woken up in the middle of the night and," Hayley paused to glance at her watch, "seeing each other at 3:34 a.m."

Bill: "Well, yeah, you're going to miss this."

Hayley: "The hell you say, Bill. I am not going to miss this one bit."

Bill was right, though. Hayley was going to miss it. She was going to miss the adrenaline and the complexity of solving a homicide. She was going to miss the people and the comfort of being and doing the same thing.

Hayley: "Bill, I am going home and getting a few hours of sleep. Then I am going to drag my ass into work and go to my farewell party. Are you coming?"

Bill: "It depends on who dies tomorrow."

Hayley laughed, "Okay, Bill, see you later."

In the morning, Hayley pulled into the department parking lot. This was the last time she would be doing so. All these thoughts were crushing her. Hayley still believed she made the best decision possible. As she got out, she heard someone running up behind her. As she turned, Christian hit her, knocking them both to the ground.

"Damn you, Christian," said Hayley as Christian and his unit laughed hysterically and Christian helped her get up.

Hayley: "Shit, I was up all night, dude. I wasn't paying attention."

Christian: "You always got to pay attention, girl."

Hayley: "Where are you guys going?"

Christian: "We are going to head out for a few. You know these things aren't for us; we are the outcasts."

Hayley: "Well, not with me, you guys better be there."

"We will be there towards the end," Christian winked.

As Hayley got to her desk, her desk was trashed with silly string and banners wishing her well.

"Thanks, guys! I guarantee I know who did this," Hayley said as she knew it was Christian and the drug unit.

Hayley worked with Moss during her last shift at the department. At 4 P.M., she went downstairs where people had gathered to wish Hayley well.

Her supervisor began to speak, "Hayley, I never thought I would be saying goodbye to you. I thought I would be passing the reins over to you when I retired. It has been an emotional year and a half. We have all felt it, but you being here was like a piece of Eric was here with us."

Hayley heard the door open and caught a glimpse of Christian and his division walking in from the corner of her eye.

"Thank you, guys, for joining us," Hayley's supervisor said to Christian. Christian smiled and waved.

"As I was saying, a piece of Eric was always with us. We all watched as the love between the two of you grew; we all knew it way before you said anything. When you came to the homicide division, I did not know if we could tame you enough."

The room laughed. "As you settled in, I was so glad you decided to come over. I don't believe we will ever be able to replace you and the work you do, but we are going to try to with Moss, right, Moss?"

Moss replied, "Yes, sir."

"When you came to me and told me it was your time to move on, I was shocked and crushed. You have become family to all of us, and you will be missed dearly. We all wish you the best in your new endeavors. Know that if you ever want to come back, there is always a place for you here. Congratulations."

The entire room was filled with the sound of applause.

"Thank you, guys," said Hayley and became quiet for a moment, trying to contain her emotions. She then added, "This department has become home to me. All of you are my family, and I appreciate all of you who have stood by me. Eric's passing was hard on all of us, and I don't think any of us in this room will ever forget it. I thank all of you for the support you gave me during that time. My life changed drastically from what I thought it would be to what it is today. It's my time to make changes in my own life and follow a path that I did not know was possible for me. I told Christian I wasn't going to cry, so I am going to leave it at that."

Everyone laughed while Christian smiled at the back of the room. "Thank you all for everything. You are always welcome to Blue Shark Drive anytime," Hayley concluded. The room filled with applause once again. Christian came over to Hayley, "We are going to get out of here. I'll see you later, okay?"

"Okay, be safe," Hayley replied, hugging Christian before he walked away.

Hayley spent the last two hours at work saying goodbye. As everyone left, Hayley walked back upstairs and started packing her things. She placed all of her pictures and personal belongings into one box.

Once finished, she placed the lid on the box and started walking towards the door. She turned around one last time and looked at her desk. She turned to her right and looked at Christian's desk and Eric's old desk. Tears filled Hayley's eyes, so many memories. She pushed against the door and walked out, never turning around again.

Chapter 5:

The Meeting

Hayley was woken by her phone. Hayley looked over at the time, it was 7 a.m...

"Hey girl, what are you doing?"

It was Christian.

"I'm sleeping, remember I don't work anymore," Hayley said with her eyes closed.

Christian: "I was just wishing you good morning and letting you know I was going to work."

Hayley: "You're such a pain in the ass, Christian."

Christian: "I know. So, you are going to take some stuff to the new house today?"

Hayley: "Yeah, that was the plan. I was going to get up at 8, but I guess I am going to get up now, thanks to you."

Christian: "Haha, I will talk to you later. Drive safe."

"I will thank you," said Hayley, hanging up the phone and sitting up in bed. She smiled, thinking about Christian's call. Hayley knew he was going to miss her being around and was already missing her at work. Hayley had worked with Christian for years, and she was tied to Eric, whom Christian knew was special. She knew it was hard on Christian with her moving away.

Hayley got up, putting on a pair of jogging shorts, a t-shirt, some tennis shoes, and pulling her hair back in a ponytail. She started packing small boxes into her car. Movers were coming to move the big stuff, but Hayley wanted to bring some small stuff to the new house, put pictures on the walls, and items she would need in the next few weeks while she was staying at both locations.

Hayley grabbed the last small box she was bringing to the house and walked out the door. She locked the door and placed the last box in the trunk. She began the drive to the new house on Blue Shark Drive. Hayley had received the keys to the house a week earlier from Julie.

Hayley pulled up in the driveway. She looked at her new house and was very pleased with her decision. It was the perfect location and the perfect house for her new start. Hayley got out of the car and looked over. The big black truck was parked in front of her neighbor's house again. She wondered if the person ever worked; they had not been out either time Hayley had been at the house.

Hayley opened her car door, grabbed the two boxes, and walked towards the door. She went inside, placing the boxes on the counter before walking back outside. Hayley reached over the seat and grabbed two more boxes. Out of the corner of her eye, she could see movement. When she grabbed the boxes, she turned quickly to see who was coming up beside her car.

"Hi there."

Hayley turned to see a male with sandy blonde hair standing between her house and the house with the big black truck.

"Hey there to you," Hayley replied while closing the door of her car.

The man then said, "I guess we are going to be neighbors."

Hayley set the boxes she had in her hands on the car hood.

"Yes, it looks like it," replied Hayley. She already could tell the man was cocky.

"My name is Jordan Voss."

"Nice to meet you, Jordan," Hayley said, collecting the boxes she had set on her car hood.

"Do you have a name?" Jordan asked, shockingly, as Hayley had not told him her name yet.

Hayley: "Hayley, my name is Hayley."

Jordan: "Nice to meet you, Hayley. Do you need any help?"

"No, I've got it!" Hayley said, walking towards the house.

"I was in the military, and now I am a cop," Jordan said, trying to impress Hayley.

"Oh yeah, that is nice," Hayley said, walking inside the house. Hayley placed the boxes on the kitchen counter and turned to go back outside to get more boxes. As she did, Jordan was standing at the door with two more boxes for Hayley.

Hayley: "I said I didn't need your help."

Jordan: "I know you did, but I am being neighborly. Are you always this nice to people who try to help you?"

Hayley: "Sometimes I'm nicer."

Jordan began to laugh, "You have jokes."

Hayley stopped and looked at Jordan. She noticed his blue eyes for the first time and the fit statue he had. "Do you always stalk women who pull up next to your house? Don't you have a wife or girlfriend to impress?"

Jordan was taken aback by Hayley's comment saying, "Damn your feisty."

Hayley: "Damn, you're an idiot."

Jordan: "Look, I was just trying to be nice and welcoming to the neighborhood. I will let you be Hayley. It was nice to meet you. Maybe next time you won't be such a crotchety bitch."

Hayley: "Maybe next time I won't have to deal with an egotistical ass hole."

Jordan laughed, "Oh, this is going to be fun," adding "And no, I don't," as he walked off.

"No, you don't what?" Hayley questioned.

Jordan: "No, I don't have a wife or kids. You are stuck with the egotistical ass hole by himself."

Great. Hayley thought. I am living next door to a cop, and not just any cop, a cocky one at that. *Just what I need. I thought I was going to get away from it.* One thing Hayley did know was the cocky cops. She watched as several of the males would chase multiple women at the same time. Usually, they only stopped when they got one pregnant or the badge bunny suckered them into marrying them. Even then, some of them still chased after women. It was part of the lifestyle for some of the departments she worked at.

It was every department, Hayley always thought it was the adrenaline of the chase, and the "badge bunnies" as they called the women, throwing themselves all over anyone in uniform. The male officers often married nurses or teachers, if they ever did, while the female officers usually married other officers or military men. It was just the way things were.

Hayley locked the house up and walked back to her car. Jordan had since left, and Hayley did not see him outside. Hayley headed back to her old house to grab more boxes and drive back to the new house. She pulled up in the driveway of the new house and got back out. Jordan was outside working under his truck when Hayley got out of the car.

Jordan: "Hey Hayley, glad to see you back."

Hayley looked over at Jordan, replying, "Hi to you."

Jordan slid from under the truck and looked at Hayley, saying, "I am not a bad guy, Hayley. I could protect you."

Hayley glared at Jordan, "It's comments like that that make you an idiot. I am sure you just can't keep the ladies away."

Jordan: "Actually, I don't have a problem one bit. I'm sure with your upbeat, chipper attitude, you are single, and no dates lined up."

Hayley did not comment back to Jordan. Jordan smiled and slid back under his truck. *Oh my God, I am living next to a douche bag; a freaking idiot.* Hayley thought as she walked back outside to grab more boxes from her car. Her blood was boiling.

Hayley: "You know, if you would stop being so cocky and actually realize that just because you are a cop and were in the military, that doesn't mean crap. You might find a high-quality lady and not badge bunnies to circle in and out of your house like a used car lot."

Crap, Hayley thought as not many people use the phrase badge bunnies.

Jordan slid from under the truck, shocked, "Badge Bunnies? What do you know about Badge Bunnies? Did a cop hurt your feelings one time? Hayley, what do you do because I am beginning to think that you do something in the criminal justice field."

Hayley: "No, I don't, I'm an entrepreneur, I run an online store."

Jordan: "Oh, so you're unemployed. Who bought you the house, your daddy?"

Hayley: "No, Jordan, how did you pay for your house? You buy it with the money you are given for being corrupt."

Jordan sat up, "Hey, this is where I draw the line. Call me anything, but one thing I won't tolerate is being called corrupt. I have integrity and I'm not dirty."

Hayley got in her car, saying, "Like the integrity you have with women. Have a nice day, Jordan."

Hayley was pleased as she got the last word.

Jordan continued working on his truck, thinking about the conversation. *How the hell does she even know what a Badge Bunny is? Man, she is feisty for being so little. She's cute, though, but mean as hell. Someone has done her wrong. I am a cop and a military vet. Who does she think she is? She's going to be a pain in the ass to live next to. I'll calm her ass down. I'll show her a used car lot; she will be in the rotation for sure.*

Hayley made it back to her old house. She threw her car keys on the counter and called Christian.

Christian: "Hey, how was it?"

Hayley: "Christian, I am living next to a cocky, egotistical cop who used to be military."

Christian laughed hysterically, "Oh, I am sure you two got along so well already. Oh man, I want you to record these conversations next time. I needed this laugh."

Hayley: "God of all people to live next to, I picked a house with him next door."

Christian: "Does him have a name?"

Hayley: "Jordan, his name is Jordan. What kind of name is that anyway, Christian?"

Christian: "I don't know. Some kind of Florida name, but it sounds like he got under your skin, Hal. You do like fighting with the people you end up dating and marrying."

Hayley: "No, he's such an idiot already, Christian. You know he is going to have women all up in his house all hours of the night."

Christian: "Hayley, what does it matter? Stay inside and don't talk to him."

Hayley: "You're right, I was just hoping for a quiet family beside me. Not a single cop."

Christian: "You are going to be fine and will hold your own, I know."

Hayley: "I know, but I am getting away from all of that. I didn't want to deal with it here."

Christian hung up with Hayley. Kelsey looked at Christian and asked, "What happened?"

"Hayley met her match, who also happens to be her new neighbor," Christian replied, laughing hysterically.

Kelsey's eyes got big, "Oh boy."

"Yeah, this is going to be fun to hear about," said Christian, and they both laughed.

Chapter 6:

An Eventful Day

It had been a month since Hayley had moved into her new home. Her online business was still doing great, and the anxieties of her needing to get another cop job had subsided. Hayley was living a peaceful life where she had time to work on her business and had time to just sit outside, admiring the Florida sun in peace. Everything had started to fall into place as she wanted it to.

Her weekends were usually spent tending to the small yard she loved. This particular Saturday, Hayley was mowing. Dressed in a tank top, hat, and listening to her favorite music, she was busy in her own little world. A 6-foot privacy fence lined her yard as she mowed peacefully.

The front yard was always a different story as Jordan would always be out, and even if he wasn't, he made it a point to come out and irritate Hayley by revving his truck engine or sitting on his front porch watching what she was doing. It was a game to Jordan, and it would irritate the crap out of Hayley. Jordan still did not know anything about Hayley, especially about her law enforcement career prior to moving.

As Haley continued working in her garden, she smelled something familiar. It was the smell of a burning dead body. As she tried to downplay the smell as a memory and her imagination, she became more and more curious. Hayley stopped the mower. She knew it was coming from the back of her property in the wooded area behind her house. She walked to the gate at the back fence and opened it, looking along the fence and by the wood line. She could not see anything, but her curiosity got the best of her, and she began to follow the scent.

Hayley made it to the wood line and looked back. No one was around as she stepped into the woods. She followed the scent to where she felt it stopped. Hayley began looking through the brush and up in the trees. Hayley knew she was smelling a dead body and wasn't going nuts.

"What are you doing, Hayley?" someone said from the back. Hayley jumped and screamed. It was Jordan who also got scared as Hayley screamed, "What the hell, Hayley?" he shouted.

Hayley: "What the hell, Jordan. Are you following me?"

Jordan: "No, I am out here for a reason. What are you doing out here?"

Hayley, trying to play off said, "I smelled something funny, and I was coming to see what it was."

Jordan, not convinced, looked at Hayley, trying to make her confess, "Hayley, there is only one thing that smells like what we are smelling, and we both know what it is. How the hell do you know what a dead body smells like? Not just a dead body, a burned dead body."

Hayley knew she had to make something up and fast, so she replied, "I have dealt with a dead body before. Something I don't talk about, but I never forget the smell."

Jordan, curious about the depth of that statement but wanting to get to Hayley, smiled and said, "Is that how you killed your husband?"

"Yep, the exact way," Hayley said, not looking up.

Jordon: "Why don't you go back to the house. I've already informed the respective authorities, and there are some officers coming to look."

Hayley: "No, I am not going anywhere until I am convinced there is nothing out here. Why are you telling me what to do?"

Jordan: "Hayley, if you are here when they get here, they are going to ask you a million questions, more than I am asking you. If you find something, there are going to be even more questions. Just go, I will tell you if we find anything."

As Hayley took a step towards Jordan to bark back at him, she tripped and fell. As she looked back towards what she had fallen over, she was taken back. She started scooting backwards, "Shit."

Under the bush, just like she had thought, there was what remained of a charred body, covered by only a few limbs. Hayley stood up, "There is your body. I'll be at the house when they want to ask questions." Hayley turned around and started walking back to the house, not fazed by what she had just seen. Jordan took out his cell phone to call back and tell the officers he had found the body he was smelling. Jordan watched as Hayley walked away, placing her earbuds back in her ears, messing with her phone like it didn't bother her much.

He yelled, "You know you just found a body, and you are just going to walk away like nothing happened?"

Hayley kept walking, throwing up her hands in the air as if to say, "Oh well." Jordan thought to himself, *Oh hell no, she is going to answer some questions about this later. How can she just walk away like it is no big deal? She is hiding something. Who am I living next door to?*

30 minutes after Hayley left, Detective Johnson came and knocked at her door, as she knew they would.

Detective Johnson: "Hayley!"

Hayley: "Yes, I am Hayley, you can call me Hal."

Detective Johnson: "I am Detective Johnson. Can I talk to you about today?"

Hayley: "Yeah, sure, come in."

Hayley led Detective Johnson to her living room area and motioned him to sit down on the couch.

Detective Johnson: "Hal, it was an eventful day for our department, and I am sure for you."

"Yes, it sure was," Hayley replied, trying to understand how in-depth Detective Johnson was going to get into her knowledge about dead bodies.

Detective Johnson: "Can you tell me today how you came across the person in the woods?"

Hayley: "Yeah, I was mowing my grass in the back yard, and I smelled something bad. I opened my back gate and looked around and didn't see anything. I continued to mow, but the smell didn't fade. So, I stopped mowing and decided to find out where the smell was coming from. I started walking in the direction from which it was coming. This led me to the woods. When I was trying to find where the smell was coming from, that is when Jordan walked up on me. When Jordan and I were talking, I tripped over the person and fell. That's when I came back to the house."

Detective Johnson: "You didn't see the person before tripping over them?"

Hayley: "No, the bush had grown up, and I was talking to Jordan, not looking where I was walking."

Detective Johnson: "So, did you and Jordan go out there together?"

Hayley: "No."

Detective Johnson: "Are you and Jordan friends?"

Hayley: "I wouldn't call us friends, but we are neighbors."

Detective Johnson: "How long have you known Jordan?"

Hayley: "Hmmm, since I moved here. I am sorry, but did Jordan have something to do with this? I mean, as his neighbor, I would like to know."

Detective Johnson: "Hal, no, not at all. I am just trying to get the details for the report. I think that will be it, Ms. Hayley. Are you going to be alright, are you alright?"

Hayley: "Yes, Detective Johnson, I am fine. A little bit of a weird day, but I am good."

Detective Johnson: "Well, here is my card. If you need anything, please feel free to contact me, okay?"

"Thank you, I will," Hayley said, smiling.

As Detective Johnson opened the door and walked away, Hayley rolled her eyes and closed the door behind him. He wasn't even a good detective, Hayley thought. *Why would you not ask anything about the smell or how I had smelled it before? Why wouldn't you dig deeper? I could have had a boyfriend dump the body there.*

Hayley was relieved that no other questions were asked, but she still felt the detective should've asked her more questions. She then wondered why she did not hear anything. How could someone pull a truck back there and get a body out, in silence? For the rest of the evening, Hayley thought about how the person who dumped the body could have done it. It made no sense; she lived in a great neighborhood. She had a cop for a neighbor; someone didn't obviously know that. Hayley pondered it until she fell asleep.

As Hayley was deep asleep, she was woken by something. She sat up in bed and looked around, trying to fully wake up. She didn't know what she had heard that woke her up. Hayley slid to the side of the bed. Was she thinking she heard something because of the day's events? As she listened, she heard it again. It was as if someone was walking through the side yard between Jordan and her house.

Hayley got out of bed, sliding on a pair of shorts and listening. It was as if the person was just walking back and forth. Hayley tiptoed back to her nightstand and grabbed her Glock handgun out of it. She made her way to the back of her house and to her back porch. She slid the door open softly before sliding out. She listened and could still hear someone on the side of her house.

Hayley walked along the side of her house towards the corner where she heard the sounds. Hayley picked her arms up, holding her gun at her chest. Hayley, still hearing the sound, stood at the back corner of her house. Her heart was pounding, and Hayley knew whoever was standing on the other side of the house might be the person who dumped the body in the woods.

Hayley thought to herself, one, two, three, and she spun around the house, raising her gun, only to find another gun being pointed straight at her. Hayley swung her right hand, slapping the gun out of her face. At the same time, her own gun was being slapped away. It was Jordan.

Jordon: "Jesus Christ, Hayley, what are you doing? My God, you almost shot me."

Hayley: "Oh, I didn't almost shoot you. Stop being dramatic. You just had a gun pointed in my face as well. What the hell are you doing out here on the side of my house?"

Jordon: "Hal, I wasn't on the side of the house. I was sleeping. I heard something and came out to see what the heck it was. What are you doing, and why the heck do you have a gun? You could have shot me; thank God your finger wasn't on the trigger."

Hayley: "What, because I am female, you think I can't have a gun?"

Jordon: "No, I didn't say that, and how did you know to slap away my gun from your face?"

Hayley: "It was just a reaction. When did you start hearing the sounds? Did you get up right away?" Hayley asked, looking around.

Jordon: "I don't know, probably 5 minutes before I came out, a total of 10 minutes before you were poking a gun in my face."

Hayley, holding her gun down, was still looking around.

Jordon: "Why don't you go put that gun up. And why do you have a Glock and not something smaller?"

Hayley looked at Jordan and said, "Why are you telling me what I should or should not be carrying? It's none of your business, Jordan, and why are we talking about this right now when someone may or may not be around our houses? Let's just check the yards and be done with this."

As Hayley walked off, Jordan said, "You're going to check your yard alone?"

Hayley turned back around and whispered, "Yes, and on the other side of the fence. What are you scared of? Do you want me to go first?"

Furious by Hayley's remark, Jordan said, "Just meet me here when you're done so we're both okay." Hayley waved to say okay and walked off with her weapon held towards her chest. Jordan watched as she walked off and thought, *she is tactically searching. Who the hell is she? There is something up with her.*

Jordan turned and searched his backyard before returning to the spot. As he waited for Hayley, he thought about how she intrigued him. She was different in many ways. For one, Hayley didn't take crap from him as so many women had and did. Hayley wasn't afraid to speak her mind and all of the strange things, like the body, her having a gun, and her tactically searching her yard. She was a mystery to Jordan, and he wanted to discover more about her. Hayley finally came back to the location and stated, "I am guessing you didn't find anything?"

Jordan: "No."

"You want to go check the woods?" Hayley said, wondering to herself if someone had come back to see if the body was gone.

Jordan: "Hell no, I don't want to check the woods right now. It's late, Hal, and if anyone was out there, we probably scared them off anyway."

Hayley thought about it and was content with Jordan's conclusion. "You are probably right. Obviously, you've talked to Detective Johnson—you're calling me Hal. Goodnight, Jordan," Hayley said, turning around to walk into her house.

"Goodnight," Jordan said, watching as Hayley walked away. *She acts like this is no big deal. Like this is just another night. There is more to her, or she is a mental case, one or the other.*

As Hayley walked to her bedroom, she placed her gun back in her nightstand. She took off the shorts she was wearing and got back into bed. She thought to herself, Jordan asks too many questions. He would make a great detective, but Hayley knew she had to be more careful with her words and actions around Jordan. He knew something was up with the events that happened.

Hayley didn't know why it was so important to keep her past life a secret. Maybe it was because of the pain she had experienced, or maybe it was because law enforcement was a whole lifestyle that she was trying to put behind her. She wanted to forget all of it, but Hayley knew by the day's events she couldn't. She knew it was still in her with the joy she felt today, investigating the smell and the sound. It was hard to put it down, but she thought she was doing a pretty good job.

Jordan made it back inside, placing his gun in his nightstand. He thought about the sequence of events the day had brought, trying to make sense of what had happened. *Man, there is something strange about Hayley. She is not friendly, she knew what a dead body smelled like, she tripped over a dead body and brushed it off as if it was nothing.* Jordan's mind spun as he tried to make sense of it.

Maybe she killed someone? Absolutely not, Jordan thought. She couldn't do anything like that. *Did she work with bodies?* No, Jordan thought, *she could not deal with death, or could she?* No matter what it was, Jordan was going to talk with her tomorrow when he saw her. He had to know the truth about everything she was up to. He didn't know what it was, but it was something.

The next day, as the sun set, Hayley was sitting on her back porch reading and drinking a glass of wine. She heard her gate open. She turned and saw Jordan walking through the gate towards her. *"So, we are just going to trespass in each other's yards now?"* Hayley said, aggravated.

Jordan: "How do you know what trespassing is anyway? We need to talk."

Hayley replayed Jordan's words in her head. Crap—a slip-up. "We don't need to talk about anything," she said.

Jordan sat in the chair directly across from Hayley. He leaned over, resting his elbows on his legs with a concerned yet confused look on his face. "You know what, Hayley," he continued, "most people don't know what a dead body smells like. You followed the smell to the woods, and you actually fell over it. You did not flinch when you did."

Hayley knew Jordan knew something was going on, but he was still confused as to what. "I never said I knew what a dead body smelled like; I was following the smell, Jordan," she said, sipping the wine she was drinking.

Jordan: "Most people, women, would have reacted a lot differently than you did. I can't wrap my head around it. Well, it is strange. You acted like it was just another day for you, that it was no big deal."

"Well, Jordan, I am not most people, women. Stuff like that just doesn't bother me. But if you are thinking I am some crazy ex-murderer, I am not," Hayley laughed.

Jordan smiled, "No, I don't think that, well, it did cross my mind, not gonna lie, but I don't think you could deal with all of the gore."

Hayley laughed, "Yeah, you are probably right, it would be nasty".

"What about last night? Why do you have a gun, a Glock, and why were you searching your backyard tactically?" Hayley thought about it; she didn't even realize that she had. It was ingrained in her to search the way she was.

Calmly, Hayley replied, "Well, Jordan, I always wanted to make sure that I could protect myself. I wanted to make sure that if anything was to happen, I could handle it. I took some classes and did some shooting. Just to make sure I could do it without a man since I am such a man-hater." Hayley smiled and rolled her eyes.

Jordan laughed, "Where did you take the classes?"

Hayley: "What is this 21 questions? I took classes where I used to live. You know they do have those classes; I am sure your department has them. Do you want a glass of wine? I am going to get another glass."

Jordan: "Yes, I guess they do. Yeah, sure."

Hayley opened the sliding door and asked, "You want to pick which one you want?"

Jordan stood up, "You have more than one kind?"

"Of course I do, the kind of wine depends on the mood," Hayley said, smiling.

Jordan walked inside. Hayley's house looked like a Bohemian refuge. As Hayley poured the glass of wine, Jordan looked around. On the mantle in the living room, he could see an American flag folded in a shadow box. He had seen many flags like that; someone Hayley knew died in the line of duty, either in the military or as a police officer.

"Which one do you want? This one is what I am drinking, and this is a red. If you are more into red wine, this one has more of a sweet taste." Jordan stared at the wine; he wasn't a wine drinker. "Well, in that case, give me the red to be different," he replied after giving it much thought.

As Hayley poured the glass of wine, Jordan pointed to the flag in the shadow box, "Is that one of your family members' shadow boxes?" Hayley looked up at Jordan and then to Eric's flag that she placed on the mantle and replied, "Yes, it is!" After handing Jordan the wine, the two sat back outside on the porch.

Hayley: "How long have you lived here, Jordan?"

Jordan: "I've been in the house about 2 years. I wanted something somewhere in the city but away from excitement. If that makes sense. How did you end up here?"

Hayley: "It does. I needed a change, and who wouldn't want to be at the beach? I had nothing holding me back from where I am from, so it was a good time to move. My business was doing good, and it allowed me to move and not work but on it. I am a simple person and don't need much."

Jordan sipped the wine. It was horrible and so bitter. He was going to drink it anyway, just so Hayley didn't know he had never tried wine.

Jordan: "Is this your final move or just a stopping point?"

Hayley: "No, I think this is it. For the most part, when you aren't around or having one of your drinking fests, it's pretty quiet. I am not old by any means, but I want to settle somewhere where I can grow old."

Jordan took a big gulp of wine, trying to finish it, then asked, "Do you want a family?"

Hayley: "Not really sure about that. Don't think that is in my cards, but we will see. What about you?"

Jordan: "I am liking being single right now. The drunk fests are fun, and I like hanging out with the guys. And by the way, Friday we are getting together to have fun at the house; don't be surprised."

Hayley rolled her eyes, "You know alcohol is addictive, and you being in the military and a cop, you are susceptible to getting addicted because of this lifestyle of yours."

Jordan, irritated by the comment, gulped the last little bit of wine and set the glass down, standing up and saying, "Hayley, it's called being responsible. You know nothing about the military or law enforcement. You should stay in your lane."

Hayley felt anger throughout her whole body as she replied, "I don't need to be in the military or law enforcement to see the epidemic with our military and law enforcement. They use it to shield the PTSD."

Raising his voice, Jordan said, "Oh, so I got PTSD?"

"Oh, I am sure of it," Hayley snapped back. "You also have anger issues," she added.

Jordan: "I see, a woman scorned by her last military or cop boyfriend; now we are all the same. If you weren't a badge bunny, you wouldn't have to worry about it."

Hayley: "I am not a badge bunny; I would refuse to date any of you."

Jordan walked off, "Goodbye, Hal. I may need to change your nickname to BB."

Hayley piped back, "AH is your new nickname."

Jordan had forgotten his suspicion of Hayley. He was too aggravated with her putting him in the category of an alcoholic, like she understood what the military or cops went through on a daily basis. He was not an alcoholic; he was young and just wanted to have fun.

Hayley got up and poured another glass of wine. Jordan was so typical—it was exactly what she'd expect from him. He was just like all cops, an arrogant idiot. No brains at all. She thought, *Man, he has anger issues, too. Why would someone get so mad over a simple comment? He is one of those cops who, though all the women wanted him, believes you should fall all over him. What an idiot. He needed to grow up.*

Chapter 7:

The Party

As Jordan stated, Friday came, and people began to show up at Jordan's house. She had not spoken with Jordan since their disagreement. Hayley was outside finishing some planting when the first people started to arrive.

Dan, one of Jordan's friends, considered his best friend, walked up to Jordan. Dan knew Jordan's history—he'd known him both before and after the move to the house. He'd been there through all of Jordan's ups and downs, witnessing everything over the past three years. Jordan confided in him. Dan clasped Jordan's hand and leaned in close.

"Jordan, who is that fine piece right there?" Dan asked. Jordan looked in the direction of where his friend was looking. He was looking at Hayley, who was working in her yard.

Jordan: "Don't bother with that one. She is a shrew and about the angriest woman I've ever met. She believes all military and cops are alcoholics."

Dan continued to stare at Hayley as they walked into the house. Jordan, seeing him stare, said, "Dude, she is off limits."

Dan smiled, "Okay, okay, since when did you care anyway?"

Jordan, realizing he sounded defensive, said, "I have to live next to her. I already have to deal with her on a daily basis; I don't want to make it worse."

Dan said, "I get it," and the conversation dropped.

Hayley completed what she was doing outside and went inside. As it began to get dark, Hayley could hear more people arriving at Jordan's house. Hayley peeked through the blinds and saw Jordan outside talking to two females with one of his friends. Jordan was smiling at the female. Jordan looked towards the window Hayley was looking out from, like he knew she was looking at him. Jordan looked at Hayley, grabbed one of the women, and kissed her while staring at Hayley. Hayley closed the blinds and was irritated by Jordan.

Hayley, lying on her couch, watched TV, listening to the laughter outside. She thought back to the parties that she had with those she worked with, and she began to miss them. Hayley got up from the couch, grabbed a book, and walked to her back porch. She sat down in the chair, acting as if she was reading, but she was intentionally listening to the laughter, reminiscing on the parties she had attended. As time passed, she heard her gate open. She looked towards the direction of her gate, and it was Jordan.

"Why are you just walking in my yard, Jordan?" Hayley asked.

"I am coming to see you," Jordan replied. Hayley could tell Jordan was pretty intoxicated.

Hayley: "Jordan, you are having a party, go back home."

Jordan: "What are you doing? Wouldn't it be quieter inside, reading if that is what you really are doing?"

Hayley: "I can read with other things going on."

Jordan: "What were you looking at me earlier for?"

Hayley: "Jordan, I was looking out the window because you guys were being loud."

Jordan: "Louder than we are now?"

Hayley looked at Jordan and asked, "What do you want? You have something on your mind; you don't just come over to hang out with me. All your boys are over there. What are you doing here?"

Jordan: "Why are you so standoffish with me? How come you don't like me? All girls like me."

Hayley: "Well, I think you just answered your questions, but you are cocky and you think you are a gift to every female that walks. You're not at all. You are drunk, aren't you?"

Jordan: "No, I've had a few, but I am fine. Why are you so secretive, too? There is something you are hiding from me. What are you not telling me? What happened before you moved here?"

Hayley: "You are asking too many questions. We are neighbors, not best friends. You don't have to tell everyone all of your business. I like to keep my world to myself."

Jordan: "God, you are a pain in the ass. You act like a cop at times."

Hayley's heart just dropped, but she instantly responded, "You are drunk, me a cop? Are you serious?"

Jordan: "Maybe not, but something is up with you."

Hayley: "You are just mad because there is a woman who does not think you hung the moon."

Jordan thought about it. Maybe that is why he liked her so much. She did not like him, which made him obsess about her at times because of it. He was going to tell her she intrigued him, he was drinking, and he could play it off if she didn't like him.

"Hal, look…" Jordan and Hayley heard the gate open. Two of Jordan's partners, Mike and Nick, came in. "What are you two doing back here?," one of them asked. Hayley could tell both of them were pretty intoxicated.

Hayley: "This is my house and all of you are trespassing."

Nick: "Trespassing? People actually say stuff like that, Jordan, who are you neighbors with?"

Jordan got up from the chair, "An old shrewd, retired badge bunny. Let's go."

Hayley: "You are a crappy drunk, Jordan. It's rough when you realize you are not as irresistible as you think you are with women."

Mike and Nick looked at Jordan, "Damn, Jordan, what did you do?" The three began laughing as they walked out of the gate.

Hayley sat in the chair, irritated. She could hear Jordan return to his house and start howling and talking. She couldn't help but think again that Jordan was on to her. He knew something was going on with her, and she hoped he wouldn't figure it out.

Jordan, back at his residence, held a glass up, "To the badge bunnies!" The crowd roared and laughed.

"So, what is going on with you and your neighbor?" Dan asked as things started to calm down.

Jordan: "Hayley? Absolutely nothing."

Dan: "Why are you letting her get to you?"

Jordan: "Dan, there is something about her. She is hiding something, I know it. She found that body, and she was so calm about it. The gun incident. I just can't put my finger on it. I mean, you met her; do you think she is a cop? Some kind of undercover thing?"

Dan laughed, "No, not at all. You think too much. Just be careful."

Jordan looked at Dan, "Be careful? What do you mean be careful?"

Dan: "Well, I just don't want to have a revisit of three years ago. I didn't think you were going to get past that dude."

Jordan: "No, I am good, not that one. I will never go there again, you know that."

Dan threw his arm around Jordan and said, "It's a party, dude. Why are we talking about her?"

Jordan: "Exactly."

Dan and Jordan continued to talk. The party went through the night until the morning hours. Hayley had managed to fall asleep with all of the music and the loud speaking. As she walked to the kitchen, she looked out of the window. There were still a bunch of vehicles in the driveway. Hayley remembered how at all the parties, there were always people sleeping over and sleeping on couches, the floor, and outside. She missed the bond she had with her co-workers, but she did not mind waking up without a hangover.

Hayley picked up the phone and dialed Christian.

Christian: "Hey, Hal. What are you doing? Hey, Kelsey Hal's on the phone."

Hayley: "Nothing, I was just thinking about the two of you and wanted to see what you were up to."

Christian: "Nothing, we had a little gathering last night. It was fun, got a little wild; you know how that is with these guys."

Hayley laughed, "Yes, I remember. How is everyone?"

Christian: "Well, they are good. Steve asked about you the other day."

Hayley: "Mmm, did he find anyone yet?"

Christian: "No, no one wants him. He is too needy."

Hayley laughed, "Ain't that the truth."

Christian: "What did you do last night?"

Hayley: "Well, I read, and my neighbor had a party with a bunch of cops and dimbos."

Christian: "You two still don't like each other? I figured you two would have ironed things out by now."

Hayley: "No, he is an idiot and a drunk."

Christian laughed.

Kelsey came into the room, "Hal did Christian tell you we are planning on coming to see you in about 2 weeks?"

Hayley: "What? Christian, why didn't you say anything?"

"I was going to ask you before I told you we were coming," Christian said while smirking at Kelsey.

Hayley: "I would love for you to come and see me. I am missing all of you."

Christian: "We will plan to be there. When it gets closer, I will let you know what days. It has been busy at work, so I have to find out what weeks would be best. I would like to come for more than just a day."

"Of course, come and stay a week or two," Hayley said, smiling.

Christian: "I will remember that."

"Can't wait to see you, Hal," Kelsey yelled so that Hayley could hear her through the phone.

Hayley: "Tell her I can't wait to see her too, Christian."

Christian: "I will. So how are you, Hal? I can tell something is brewing in you."

Hayley: "I don't know. I'm missing Eric this week. Nothing big, no crying, just thinking a lot about him. I miss talking to him; he was my best friend, not just my husband. And then the party last night, just thinking about all of you I left up there. I don't miss the job, but I miss the family, the camaraderie. I haven't met anyone here I trust like that."

Christian: "Hayley, you have a cop living right next to you. Why don't you talk to him? I know you could get a job there in law enforcement. It may help."

Hayley: "No, I don't want to work as a cop here. I am getting too old to prove myself again and work my way back up to being a detective. Plus, I would have to go to their academy, and Christian, I am not doing another police academy. I like sleeping through the night, and I like making my own schedule."

Christian: "I get that. Nothing has changed; overworked all the time, no sleep, and the bosses are still wanting more. Have you talked to Mark?"

Hayley: "My head doctor, Mark?"

Christian: "Yeah."

Hayley: "No, not in a while. I have an appointment next week over the phone. I am not that sad, not depressed."

Christian: "I know, but sometimes it is good to talk to people."

"Isn't that what I am doing now?" Hayley said, laughing.

Christian: "Yes, you are, but I don't have the degrees or certifications."

Hayley: "I better go, Christian. I have some stuff to do around the house."

Christian: "Okay, Hal, we will see you soon."

Hayley: "Okay, Christian, bye."

Hayley sat down on the couch, putting her head back, resting it on the back of the couch. She needed to see Christian and Kelsey. She missed them; they were her tie to Eric. Maybe that is why she missed him so much this past week.

"She doing alright?" Kelsey asked Christian as he hung up the phone, walking into the kitchen.

Christian: "I really don't know. She said she was missing Eric and all of the guys. I mean, she has a neighbor who is a cop. She just won't tell him, and you know they would hire her down there in a minute with all of her experience."

Kelsey: "She is hardheaded and stubborn like all of you are."

Christian walked to Kelsey and hugged her, kissing her on the forehead.

Christian: "I must not be too hardheaded. I made you fall for me."

Kelsey: "It was the alcohol, I am sure."

Christian: "I love you, Kelsey. I can't imagine having to do life without you."

Kelsey: "I feel the same. Maybe us going down there will help her."

Christian: "I may tell the neighbor that she was a cop when we go down there."

Kelsey: "Hayley will be so mad with you, especially if she does not like the boy."

Christian: "I will get a feel from him, but I just think he would be good for her in more ways than one, Kelsey."

Kelsey: "Yes, probably, but we are talking about Hayley."

Christian: "I know."

Chapter 8:

A Storm Brewing

The week for Hayley flew by as it normally did. Even though she worked from home now, she felt it was busier than when she worked for the department. Hayley felt she worked harder as it was all up to her; she didn't have a paycheck if she didn't work.

Hayley's weekends were made up of cleaning and working around the house and in the yard. She barely got sleep most weekends due to Jordan and his parties. Like usual, last night was an all-night ordeal with loud music and talking.

Jordan and Haley hadn't spoken since he told her she was a shrewd badge bunny. It had worked out well; both would avoid each other when they could. It allowed Hayley to let her guard down, since Jordan was the one asking all the questions.

Hayley looked at the clock; she had another 30 minutes before she met with Mark. It was the first time she would be talking to Mark over the internet. She had always met him in person. She wondered if it could even help her because it was not the in-person kind of meeting.

Hayley grabbed her computer and walked out to the porch. She placed the computer down on the table and walked back inside to grab a drink before she spoke with Mark. As Hayley walked inside to get a drink, Jordan walked out to his back door. He looked at his backyard, which was covered with cans and trash. Jordan couldn't help but wonder if he really wanted to party every weekend anymore. He felt it was getting out of hand.

At first, it was great, and he enjoyed living his wild life, but now, it was too much. Each weekend, the next day after everyone left, he was picking up after adults who, the night prior, were so intoxicated, they couldn't even clean up after themselves. Jordan, with a bag in one hand, began picking up the cans and trash in the yard. Hayley walked to her porch and set her drink down. She looked at the link that Mark had sent her and clicked it, waiting for it to connect. She did not hear Jordan outside picking up his yard. Jordan did not hear Hayley outside until he heard, "Hey Mark!" The excited sound in Hayley's voice intrigued Jordan, and he began to listen.

Mark: "Hey Hayley, wow, you look like you are doing good. How have you been?"

Hayley: "I'm good. I know you can't imagine this, but I have been busier than I was when I was working up there. I do sleep at night now, though."

Mark laughed, "Well, that is good."

Jordan, still listening, wondered, *Why didn't she sleep at night?*

Mark: "Are you still just running your business online?"

Hayley: "Yeah, that is all I am doing, me and Emma."

Mark: "I forgot you took the dog you two had."

Hayley: "Yes, Emma has been great."

Jordan again began to think, *the dog you TWO had, what the hell. More than one person, where is the other person?*

Mark: "So, what is on your mind, Hayley? What do you want to talk about today?"

Hayley: "I don't know. I've been thinking about Eric a lot lately. Not sad, just all the memories. Sometimes I still think I am going to wake up, like it's a really long bad dream. I mean, I know I am not, I know it happened, but maybe I am still hoping."

Jordan, still listening, *Who's Eric and what happened?!*

Mark: "Hayley, that is normal when you have a spouse who was killed the way Eric was. The whole incident, the funeral, the friends, the move, you have been through a lot. The job change is a big thing, too. Have you got out and met people?"

Hayley: "I found a body. I didn't tell you about it. That was hard, and it brought me back to all of the bodies, all of the times I had to deal with them. It was so natural and like I was back at it, doing exactly what I had done for years. No emotion, it was just another "job". And no, I haven't met anyone besides my annoying neighbor. I just don't feel like it. I have been enjoying my peace."

Oh my God, who am I living next door to! All the bodies? Just a job! Jordan could not believe what he was hearing. *Did this Eric person get murdered? Was he part of the bodies?*

Mark: "Annoying neighbor? You have to tell me about him."

Hayley: "His name is Jordan. He is a cop, and he is so nosy. I think he is on to me; he actually is a pretty good investigator. Typical cop parties and women, not going to settle down until one of the bunnies sinks their teeth into him or he gets one pregnant."

"He seems like your kind of person, sounds like Eric," Mark said, laughing. "Hayley, he could help you. You don't think you could look past his annoying habits like you did with Eric? I mean not to date him or anything like that, just as support," he added.

Hayley: "Absolutely not."

Mark: "Why, tell me why. I think there is more to it than what you are saying."

Hayley: "Eric and Jordan are two different people but have similar personalities. We could have good conversations if he would stop his egotistical ways; we would probably be pretty good friends, joking and laughing."

Hayley's voice began to crack, and tears started to form in her eyes as she said, "But I can't shake the thought of getting used to him being around and then him getting shot and killed in the line of duty. Becoming close to his friends and then once everything is over and done with, they move on, and I am forgotten."

Mark: "Hayley, you still have Christian and Kelsey. They have stuck with you, and so many others wanted you to stay and would enjoy talking to you. You pushed them away."

Hayley: "I know I have pushed them away, but it just hurts. Eric lived for the job; he loved every minute of it. It just seems the career he loved replaced him the minute he was over. Like he didn't exist. And I'm not playing the victim, or I don't have the victim mindset, but it hurts."

Jordan was in shock. He sat down and put his back up against the fence and continued to listen. Oh my God, her husband died in the line of duty. Jordan's heart was heavy. Even though he did not know Eric, he was one of his brothers in blue. *Why didn't Hayley say anything?* he thought. She knows all law enforcement take care of each other when a spouse is killed in the line of duty or not. It was the unspoken word of all who served; the family will always be supported and always be protected.

Mark: "Hayley, with your past and Eric's death, can I ask you something?"

Hayley: "Yeah."

Mark: "I want you to think of everyone in your life now, or everyone who has been in your life. Can you name anyone stronger than you are?"

Hayley: "Well, I don't know, I would have to think about it."

Hayley sat in silence, trying to think of someone who had been through what she had.

Hayley: "I can't think of anyone right now. I will have to think about it."

Mark: "Get back with me on that. I told you that to get your mind working. You are stronger than you know. You could have given up after Eric died. You could have sunk into a deep depression, and everyone would have understood. Some would have tried to get you out of it, but others would have been okay with it. You didn't, though, Hayley; you decided to fight and get out of the darkness. You decided what was best for you and where you wanted to be, and you took a pretty big leap of faith, quitting your job and moving to a different state. You are following the dream of being a business owner. Don't think what you have done is easy, you should be proud of yourself."

Hayley: "I am, I just feel like I am still missing something. Like I need to do more, or I need to be more."

Mark: "Why don't you start by getting out more. Go to the beach, go see the shops by the beach; I don't know what there is to do there, but get out a little. You know what I mean?"

Hayley: "Yeah, I guess I can. I'm still picking myself up. I will get there."

Mark: "I have no doubt in my mind you will, Hayley. I've to go now; I have a client coming in. I have an appointment with you in two weeks. Are you still good with it?"

Hayley: "Yeah, I am good with it."

Mark: "Alright, I want to hear about everything you have done the next time."

Hayley: "I am going to be full of surprises, partying it up over here."

Jordan smiled at Hayley's joke to Mark. Mark laughed, "I will talk to you then, bye."

Hayley: "Bye, Mark."

Jordan could hear Hayley get up and walk into the house. Jordan couldn't believe what he had heard. Hayley had lost her husband in the worst way. His life was cut short by probably a piece of crap that was trying to get away from him. And she sat in silence, not telling anyone.

She was stubborn, so many times she could have told Jordan, so many times she could have told him she knew the game he was playing, but she didn't. Jordan knew he had to talk to Hayley, but he could never tell her that he had listened to her conversation with Mark. He was drawn to wanting to help her, but he knew Hayley would not take any help. Jordan knew he had to talk to her, even if she gave him backlash. She would come around eventually.

Hayley walked inside and sat down at her computer. She opened a folder of photos of her and Eric, her heart tightening as she began to scroll through. She stopped at one that Eric had taken after a huge drug bust that she, Christian, and Eric had done. Eric was smiling and holding up some of the money that was seized. Hayley thought about how much Eric loved the job, how he lived for it every minute. It truly was his calling.

Hayley whispered; *I am lost, Eric; I don't know what to do without you. Why did you leave me? Help me figure this out.* Hayley clicked through a few more pictures before closing the folder. Hayley knew she had to keep pushing through; she had to keep going. Everything had to work out in the end.

Hayley worked online, completing order requests and approving items to be shipped. As she looked over, time had slipped away from her. At least she was caught up, and tomorrow, she was going to go to the beach. The beach always had a way of clearing Hayley's mind. It was one of the reasons she chose to move to Florida.

Hayley started to collect the trash; it was trash day tomorrow. She walked outside and threw the trash bag into the can before rolling it to the street. As she got the can to the street, she heard Jordan's door open. She looked over to see Jordan throwing several bags into his garbage can before rolling it towards the street. When Jordan spotted her, Hayley was looking at him.

"Hey Hal, it's been a while, how are you doing?" Jordan said sincerely.

"I'm good. I see you had another drunk fest over there last night," sounding clearly unamused by him talking to her.

Jordan, irritated by the comment, sincerely said, "Yeah, we did. It is kind of getting old. I am sorry if we kept you awake."

Hayley wondered why he was being so nice to her. She replied, "No, you didn't, but it is not good for you to drink so much, or them. Not a great lifestyle to be living."

Jordan: "Yeah. I have heard that. Look Hal, maybe we should start over. I am really not that bad of a person. You never know, you might just like me."

"Like you? I doubt that will happen. I am not one of your lady friends, you're not getting in my pants," Hayley replied defensively.

Jordan: "No, I didn't mean it like that. I meant it as a friend. My God, Hal, why are you so defensive all the time? I am trying to extend a welcome, and I'm sorry."

Hayley: "How about you just keep it quiet at your house. That is all I want."

"Christ Hal, you are so stubborn," Jordan said, finally sounding irritated himself.

Jordan began to walk back to his house, saying, "By the way, it's hurricane season. A few storms are brewing, so you might want to keep an eye on them." Jordan walked back into his house and slammed the door.

Hayley, proud of herself for irritating Jordan but thought about his comment about hurricane season. She had not even thought about it. When she sat down at her computer, she looked up the hurricanes. There was one coming straight for them, Sarah. An interesting name for a hurricane, Hayley thought. It would be a few days away and may turn by the time it reaches them.

Only time would tell.

Chapter 9:

A Lucky Catch

As Hayley had planned, in the morning she would pack up all of her beach items into a bag and head towards the beach, and that is exactly what she did. Once Hayley got to the beach, she unpacked her beach chair and placed her towel on it before sitting down. She breathed in the smell of salt water, and a sense of calm surrounded her. She watched as the waves crashed onto the shore.

She wondered, specifically about what Mark had said, "Do you know anyone stronger than you are?" What a question Mark had asked her, but the truth was, she couldn't think of anyone. She knew there had to be people that have suffered way more than she had.

Hayley's mind drifted back to the day Eric had died: being on the scene, finding Eric, and lying on top of him, Christian being there, and how upset he was. The funeral, sitting at Eric's casket and Christian being strong, telling her it was time to go. She didn't feel strong; she felt weak. Weak for not being able to hold it together on the scene or at the funeral.

Maybe that was one of the many reasons that she wanted to start over. Her co-workers had seen her at her weakest point. A point only Eric had seen. She didn't want to be the damsel in distress that everyone had to monitor, like she felt before leaving. Hayley still believed it was the best decision she had made to leave everything and start over.

Hayley's mind then drifted to Jordan. She disliked him so much. Why? He was a cop, a person whom she previously would have joked and laughed with on her shift. He was a person with whom she would have a lot in common. She pushed him away, possibly to keep from living that lifestyle again. Maybe she was jaded to the career field that had so easily replaced Eric. Jordan was nice to her the last time he talked to her, but she was rude and nasty to him. He surely was up to something, being nice to her. Her mind then went to what Mark and she had talked about. He could be a friend, a friend who understood what she was going through. Jordan would understand a line-of-duty death. Hayley did not believe she could be nice to him; he was such a typical cop.

Hayley leaned back in her chair. She grabbed her newest book and opened it to the current page she was on. She lay back and began to read, only looking up to watch the waves and to watch people for a few moments. She was at peace, and before Hayley knew it, she had finished her book and a few hours had passed. Hayley placed the book back into her bag, watching the waves one last time.

Hayley started to pack things up. She wanted to see some of the shops before it got dark, and everything started to close down. Hayley made her way back to her vehicle and placed her beach bag in it. She slid on a cover-up dress over her bathing suit and slid on a comfortable pair of sandals. Hayley looked in the mirror, fixing her wind-blown hair. She grabbed her purse before locking her vehicle up. She began walking towards a little district of shops on the beach she had found.

As Hayley made it to the shops, they were filled with shell décor and wooden wind chimes. She could smell the various types of sunscreens in each shop. The shops were lined with bathing suits, towels, and surfboards. All hoping that the tourists would have forgotten one of the items they stocked.

Most days would be filled with customers getting those items they forgot and buying souvenirs to take back home from their vacation. Hayley loved shells and wooden chimes; it was something about them that was calming. The loud metal ones always had annoyed her, but she had started collecting several of the wooden and shell ones since coming to Florida. Hayley purchased a set of each, a pair of wooden and a pair of shell wind chimes.

As Hayley moved to the next shop, she admired the items made from shells, taking in the craftsmanship, when a familiar voice caught her attention.

"Yes, because what I wanted to do today was deal with you. That was my goal. Where did you put the bag?" As Hayley turned, she could see it was Jordan. He had a skinny white male standing in front of him with handcuffs on.

"I don't know what you are talking about," the guy replied.

"I saw you Brad, we do this every week. Where did you throw it? You didn't swallow it, did you?" Jordan questioned.

"I didn't swallow anything; I don't know what you are talking about," the guy continued to argue.

"Dan, can you grab him so I can look for this bag?" Jordan requested. Hayley could see Dan, whom she had seen at Jordan's house. Dan was dressed in plain clothes like Jordan.

Hayley watched as Dan grabbed the man that Jordan had called Brad and walked off. Jordan could be seen looking around the ground, moving things on the tables that were closest to him. Hayley started to walk closer to where Jordan was, hiding enough that he could not see her. She had played this game many times with the criminals she had arrested. She knew the hiding spots and how hard it could be to find a small baggy or dope. She looked around while keeping out of eye distance from Jordan.

As she walked, she saw the bag. It was sitting barely visible halfway under one of the displays. Hayley looked around for how she could get Jordan's attention. She turned to the rack of shirts and grabbed one before turning around.

"Jordan, are you following me? Can't you let me be?" Hayley said, holding on to one of the shirts, not moving from where she was.

Jordan, who was concentrating on looking for the baggy, looked up to see Hayley standing a few rows away from him.

Jordan: "No, Hayley, I am working. Stop bothering me."

Hayley: "What are you looking for?"

"You wouldn't even understand. What are you doing here?" Jordan asked, panning the area while talking to Hayley.

Hayley: "I went to the beach and bought some new wind chimes. Want to see them?"

"No Hayley, I am busy," Jordan said as he panned the area, making his way back towards Hayley.

Hayley stayed where she was, pointing one of her toes in the direction of where the baggy was and asked, "What does it look like? Maybe I could help you."

"No, just don't walk over this way, I know it is here somewhere. He threw that crap as soon as we came in here," Jordan said, making his way to Hayley. "There it is," Jordan said while leaning down and picking up the baggy.

"What is that?" Hayley said, acting like she did not know.

"That is what you call methamphetamine. I got him now," Jordan said, amused.

Hayley saw the excitement in Jordan's face. The excitement she had seen on Eric's face many times. Hayley put down the shirt that she had grabbed to get Jordan's attention.

Hayley: "Sounds like a bore to me, looking for little bags. Have fun, Jordan. I am going to finish shopping."

Jordan watched as Hayley walked out. *How is she always in the middle of the weirdest things? She was standing right by it, and it was as if her foot was pointing to it. He only noticed it because he was looking at Hayley's legs.*

Hayley drove home after shopping at a few more stores. As she got home, she grabbed a hammer and nails and went to her back porch to add her newest wind chimes she had bought. The wind had started to pick up from the hurricane heading their way.

After hanging up the wind chimes, Hayley walked inside, grabbed a glass of wine, and sat on the back porch listening to the chimes. It had been a good day; it was a relaxing one; one that she needed and should have taken earlier.

As Hayley settled in her thoughts, her phone rang. It was Christian.

Hayley: "Hey, Christian."

Christian: "Hey Hal, what are you up to?"

Hayley: "I just got back from the beach and was sitting on the back porch."

Christian: "That's got to be nice not to work like the rest of us."

Hayley: "I do work Christian; I just have more freedom when it comes to when I work."

Christian: "Oh, I see. I need to find one of those jobs. Hey, I was looking at the weather. It looks like you are going to get that hurricane, I think they are calling it Sarah. Are you prepared?"

Hayley: "Well, I have plenty of supplies. I bought those when I first got here. I still have to put boards up on the windows. I think it is only going to be a category 3 when it hits, so I am not sure if I am going to board up the windows yet."

Christian: "Huh, Hal, you need to watch the news more. It is picking up speed; they think it is going to be a category 5, if not almost a 5."

Hayley: "Really? I guess I am going to board up tomorrow, then. We still have a few days; the wind is picking up, but we've got 2 more days. Not supposed to be here until Tuesday or Wednesday night."

Christian: "Do you need me and Kelsey to come and help you? We can come down for the day and then come back. We are going to get a little bit of rain here but not like you."

Hayley: "No, I will be good. It's only plywood and a few sheets. They were already cut to size, just haven't had to use them yet."

Christian: "Do you think it is going to be okay for us to come the week of the hurricane? Do you think it will be okay and the damage will be okay?"

Hayley: "Yeah, it will be fine. Come and spend the extended weekend. The tourists will be away, so fewer people will be here. It will be fine."

Christian: "Okay, how about we play it by ear, and I will call you."

Hayley: "Okay, Christian, but I am going to tell you, you and Kelsey better be here."

Christian: "Alright Hal. Let me go. I'm glad you had a good day, jealous but happy for you."

Hayley: "Talk to you soon, bye."

Christian: "Bye."

Hayley was surprised by the hurricane. She turned on the computer and started looking at the hurricane paths. *Crap*, she thought, *it is headed right for us*. Hayley got up and walked to the garage to get the plywood.

As she started moving it around, she looked at the writing on each board to see which part of the house it belonged to. It looked like she had all of the pieces she would need. She checked the screws, yep, she had everything she needed. She was going to be okay. Tomorrow, she would get all the boards up and everything tied down. Everything would be ready for Hurricane Sarah.

"Good job today, Jordan. Hopefully, Brad will get something besides being released again," Dan said, walking in where Jordan was typing his report.

"Yeah, I found where he threw it this time. I got him," replied Jordan.

He went quiet for a moment then said, "Hayley was in the store when this went down."

Dan: "Hayley? Your neighbor?"

Jordan: "Yeah, it was really weird. I was looking for the bag and there she was standing right next to it."

Dan: "Hmm, that is weird. What did she say?"

Jordan: "Nothing much, she was giving me a hard time, and then she asked me what I was looking for, and then there it was, right beside her."

Dan: "Strange."

Jordan: "You know her husband was a cop."

Dan looked surprised, "She was married? She told you that?"

Jordan: "I will neither deny nor confirm that I was outside, and I may or may not have heard a conversation that she was having with what appeared to be a shrink named Mark."

Dan: "How did he die?"

Jordan: "He was shot in the line of duty. From what I understand, that is why she moved here. To start over again."

Dan: "So, you think she was a badge bunny, and now she has changed her ways?"

"I don't know. Obviously, if she were, she definitely isn't now. She is angry with all of us," Jordan said, laughing.

Dan: "You're not getting soft on her because of it, are you?"

Jordan: "Hell no, but her husband was one of us, and he got shot on the job."

Dan: "Do you know what he did at the department?"

Jordan: "No, I didn't hear her say. I mean, why wouldn't she say anything? I mean, she is part of the law enforcement family. We should take care of her; it's a brotherhood and we take care of our own."

Dan: "Maybe they didn't have a good relationship. Maybe she wants to forget."

Jordan: "I don't think so, the way she was talking about him. It seems like there is a little bit more than I heard."

Dan: "Here we go, conspiracy thing again. Her husband died, so don't get attached to her. She is broken, Jordan."

Jordan: "I'm not going to get attached to her, Dan. I will never let anyone get to me again, you know that. I am going to find out more, though."

Dan: "You like mystery. I am just going to leave that there. Are you ready for the hurricane?"

Jordan: "I got to put the plywood up still, but yeah, I will be ready. Are you on call too?"

Dan: "Yeah, I will be out and about most of the time. No point in sitting at home. Are you going to stay at the house until you are called?"

Jordan: "Yeah, I just want to relax until the electricity goes out. You know we are going to be all over the place once it hits."

Dan: "Yeah, you are right."

Jordan had finished his report and hit submit. "Alright, I am done, I'm going home," Jordan said while getting up.

Dan: "Good, I am headed out too."

Jordan and Dan walked outside the station and to their vehicles, both waving to each other before driving off. Jordan began to think about everything that he had to do when he got home. He only had a few days before the hurricane. He wondered about Hayley; *Does she even know what to do for a hurricane? Would she be alright by herself?*

Then Jordan thought, *why does it matter?* She wasn't his responsibility, but maybe he felt she was. Her husband was in the brotherhood. He decided he would help her only if he noticed that she was going to have damage to her house or if she asked for his help. Hayley wouldn't, but if she asked, he would help her with whatever she needed.

Chapter 10:

Sarah's Beginnings

Hayley got up in the morning. She knew she had a long day getting ready for Hurricane Sarah. Hayley turned on the television. The hurricane was already being broadcast on most channels. It was definitely going to hit them, but it looked like late afternoon tomorrow, not the evening like they thought.

As Hayley walked outside, she could hear Jordan moving around in his yard. She began to screw the boards over her windows. As she walked to the front, she grabbed the biggest board. It slipped from Hayley's hands, hitting the porch. Hayley grabbed the board and held it with her leg as she tried to screw the board up. As she did, she reached the top of the board, trying to balance the board correctly and screw it in at the same time. Hayley felt the board getting picked up, so she looked up. It was Jordan. "I got it," Hayley said.

"Stop. Let me help you," Jordan said.

Hayley finished screwing the board up and turned to Jordan, "Thank you."

Jordan looked at Hayley, "It's not a problem. So, are you staying here for the hurricane?"

"Yes, I will be here. What about you?" Hayley knew Jordan would be gone or on a call rotation because of the hurricane, but she acted clueless.

Jordan: "Yes, I will be home. I am on call in case something happens, but I will be home."

Hayley: "It looks like it will be okay. We are safe here, I think."

Jordan: "Yeah, for the most part. The wind is what will hurt us. The trees falling, electricity going out, and stuff like that. We don't have to worry about flooding here."

Hayley: "How long do you think our electricity will be out for?"

Jordan: "It is hard to say. I think the longest it has been off since I have been here is about 5 days. BUT there were a lot of trees down and a lot of things going on with that hurricane."

Hayley: "Well, this will be a first for me. We will see how it goes."

Jordan: "Give me your number. I will check on you, and we can keep in contact during the storm."

Hayley thought for a while about giving Jordan her number. So long that Jordan said, "Hal, it's not a big deal. I am not going to call you or bother you. I am just strictly getting your number for emergency purposes."

Hayley was nervous about the hurricane but was not going to show it to Jordan. She finally said, "Okay," before giving Jordan her number. Jordan called Hayley's number, "That is my number, save it, and if you need anything, just let me know."

Hayley: "I should be fine but thank you."

Jordan: "Hal, don't be stubborn, really, if you need me, call or text me."

Hayley, not wanting to give in to Jordan's snappy attitude, said, "Okay."

Jordan walked away, back to his house to finish putting up the boards for the hurricane. He was happy he got Hayley's number but could not think of how he could start speaking to her regularly without her catching on to what he was doing. He wanted to know more about Hayley. He knew there was more to her than the attitude and persona that she put off at times. He had seen a softer side of Hayley and heard a softer side of Hayley the day he learned of her husband's death. Jordan often wondered why she wouldn't open up to him. He felt she was still hiding something from him.

Hayley continued to check all of the items she had for the hurricane: candles, water, food, flashlights, extra batteries, and everything she learned she should have. She placed the book she had just purchased on the coffee table. Hayley had planned on reading while the electricity was out. She made sure the boards were secure on her house; she made sure that everything was perfect. It was not a big deal; she was ready.

As Hayley was finishing up, her phone began to ring.

"Hello."

"Are you ready for the hurricane?"

It was Christian.

Hayley: "Yes, I am ready to go. About to turn the TV on and leave it on until I lose power."

Christian: "I'm worried about it for you. What if something happens?"

"Oh, Christian, I am fine," she replied and paused, "If I need anything, I have Jordan's number."

Christian about dropped the phone, "You got Jordan's number. What…How did you get his number?"

Hayley: "Oh, Christian, it's not a big deal. It is just in case something happens, we can help each other. I will be fine, and he will be fine, I am sure, but just in case."

Christian: "Hmm, that is interesting. I think you like him."

Hayley: "Absolutely not. It is in case of an emergency. We are the only ones around. Everyone else is leaving town."

Christian: "He is going to be home and not out?"

Hayley: "He said he is on call but will be home unless it gets really bad."

Christian: "Interesting that you had a conversation with words together."

Hayley: "Stop. We are about to have a hurricane; it's nothing special. I can't deal with you right now. I am nervous as hell about it."

Christian: "You will be fine, I am sure. And we will see you later in the week, and we will help you if things are all over the place. Just let us know. If we need to, we can bring something to you or do something for you before we get down there."

Hayley: "I will let you know. It should hit in a few hours, so I will let you know once we are done with it. It is supposed to be a fast storm."

Christian: "Yeah, but a strong one. From what I have seen, it is tearing a bunch of stuff up. Do you have many trees around your house?"

Hayley: "No, I don't. Jordan has a few, but I don't think they can reach my house. They could crash into his, but not mine, so I am good."

Hayley flipped on the TV when Christian said that the hurricane was tearing up cities. She could see the damage in some cities, and trees fallen on roads and houses.

Christian: "Just let us know, Hal. We will be thinking about you."

Hayley: "Thanks, Christian, I will do."

Christian: "Talk to you soon, bye."

Hayley: "Bye."

Hayley sat down on the couch and watched the storm. It was flooded in places, and the trees down were an eye-opener to Hayley about the damage heading her way. She was glued to the TV watching it over and over again.

As she watched it, she got a text message from Jordan, *"Are you seeing the damage on TV?"*

Hayley texted back, *"Yes, it seems crazy how strong and how much damage it is causing, and it is moving fast."*

"Yeah, it is the wind. Makes me wish I had taken down the trees around my house lol," Jordan replied.

"Right, might need to get that done after this storm," Hayley texted back.

"Agree," Jordan wrote. Jordan thought, okay, I am not going to text anything else, but I have opened the lines of communication. Maybe she would not feel weird about texting now. It seemed there was always an endgame for Jordan.

Hayley watched the video of the storm for another hour. She was mesmerized by the damage. Her heart pounded, hoping that within the next few hours, her home would be okay. She even hoped that Jordan's home would be okay. Hayley got up and looked outside. The sun was starting to fade behind the clouds. As she looked at the trees, she could see the wind picking up. The rain would be starting soon. Hayley hoped that she would be prepared as much as she thought she was.

Within an hour, it started to rain. Hayley walked onto her porch and watched the rain. It was not raining hard yet, but it was coming. Hayley could see the wind blowing the trees around. The rain with the wind was blowing sideways onto the porch. It was not too bad, Hayley thought to herself. As Hayley walked back inside, she heard her phone ping, telling her she had a message. It was from Jordan.

"It is about to start. Are you doing okay? Why were you on your porch?"

Jesus, Hayley thought. She texted back, *"I am fine. Why are you watching me?"*

Another ping, *"I'm not watching you. I was looking outside and saw you standing on your front porch. Daredevil, I see."*

The comment made Hayley laugh. She replied, *"Yeah, I live on the wild side over here all the time."* Jordan, reading the message, laughed.

As time went on, Hayley could hear the howling of the wind and the rain hitting the plywood she had placed across the windows. Every so often, she could hear the cracking of trees and something hitting the side of the house.

"Can you hear the howling of the wind?" Hayley texted Jordan.

"Yeah, I hear it," Jordan replied.

"Can you hear things hitting the house? Is your house okay?" Hayley asked.

"Yeah, I have heard it," Jordan replied.

"What do you think the wind speed is, to hear it howling like that?" Hayley asked.

"Well, it depends. At least 25 miles per hour, I would think," Jordan replied.

"That's not too fast," Hayley texted.

"No, it's not too bad, probably," Jordan replied to her text.

As Hayley remained glued to the TV, she started to see the damage in her area. She was happy to still have electricity, until she wasn't. As Hayley was excited to have electricity, it went out. *Oh no,* Hayley thought. *Here we go.*

Hayley stumbled around to find the candles she had lying around the house. Hayley lit each one, illuminating the house with a yellow glow. Hayley sat down on the couch and picked up her phone after hearing a ping on her phone. *"Did your electricity go out?"* Jordan texted.

"Yep, sitting here with my candles lit," Hayley replied.

"You lit candles?" Jordan asked.

"Yeah," Hayley replied.

"Oh, I have a flashlight," Jordan texted.

"How come we still have cell phone service?" Hayley asked.

"I don't know, but enjoy it while you can," Jordan replied.

"Have you been called yet?" Hayley asked.

"No, I won't be called until the eye of the storm or after," Jordan replied.

"Oh," Hayley texted.

Hayley pulled out the book she had purchased and started to read. 20 minutes later, she received a ping from her phone. *"What are you doing?"* Jordan was obviously bored.

"I am reading," Hayley replied.

"You read? What are you reading?" Jordan asked.

"Yes, Jordan, I read. I'm reading a book called Whispered Promises by June Kraholik," Hayley replied.

"What is it about?" Jordan asked.

"It's about two people who met when they were kids and reunited throughout the years. Years later, they come back together and have to make a decision to be together or walk away forever," Hayley replied.

"Love story stuff. Sounds boring," Jordan texted.

Jordan couldn't believe that Hayley was reading or reading a love story. After losing her husband, Jordan couldn't imagine wanting to read a love story. Jordan thought maybe Hayley did have a sensitive heart; maybe she actually had a heart under the tough exterior that she gave off to everyone.

"It would be boring for you because you refuse to have a relationship or feel anything, and I am guessing if you ever would feel anything, you would walk away from the person," Hayley texted.

"That is fair to say, but aren't you the same way? You seem far from wanting to be nice to anyone, much less a dude that actually liked you," Jordan replied.

Hayley laughed. Jordan was right with the way she had acted towards him, or any male figure that acted remotely interested in her. *"Fair enough to say, but I do believe that there are people who stay together forever,"* Hayley texted.

"Really?" Jordan asked.

"Yeah, of course. You don't?" Hayley replied.

"I don't know. With the career I am in, I see a lot of divorces, but I do see some relationships that stay together. I believe that for some people it is true," Jordan replied.

"But not for you?" Hayley asked, wanting to know Jordan's thoughts.

"Well, Hal, this job is hard on relationships. I am very independent, and the job takes up a lot of time. Most women I have met don't understand it, and it ends up with drama. So, I have found it is easier not to deal with the ladies, but on the surface level. I guess I figured eventually they would walk away. Why share myself with them if I already believe that they are going to walk away? Does that make sense?" Jordan explained.

"It does, but don't you think that you are already deciding it is not going to work with these women before the relationship even starts? And I think you picked the wrong women. They are pretty bimboish, and they are all badge bunnies," Hayley replied.

Jordan laughed; Hayley understood Jordan more than Jordan thought. Hayley continued, *"Plus, how can you have anything work where you put on the persona of a 'player' attitude. No good women would want to be with you. You are attracting what you are putting off."*

Jordan joked with Hayley, *"Easy there. What are you trying to do? Make me rethink all of my life decisions. Hal, you know you have issues, too. You won't let anyone help you. You refuse to allow anyone close to you. Like you have to hide something. You have to do it all yourself because you fear you may owe someone, or someone may start to like you or want to help you more. You don't have to do that; people might just want to help you without any other intentions."*

Hayley read what Jordan wrote. He was right, she had been exactly like that with him. That wasn't her, though; she was fun and was a happy person, and she knew what love was. But she couldn't. Instead, Hayley replied, *"I am just as independent as well, and I like the way I live. I like being able to do whatever I want whenever I want. It's easy."*

"I think we are both on the same page that way. It looks like we are about to go into the eye of the storm. Want to go see what outside looks like when it stops?" Jordan texted.

"Yeah, that sounds like a plan," Hayley replied.

As the eye of the hurricane came over the city, the sun gleamed through the clouds, and Hayley could see the light coming through the plywood where her windows sat. Hayley walked to her front door and opened it. She stepped out on her porch and looked in front of her. The grass was soaking wet, and, in some places, water was flowing through it. Green tree leaves and small branches were scattered as far as Hayley could see. She could not see trees fallen from her view, but the leaves and branches were a reminder of the hurricane that they were going through.

Hayley walked back inside and grabbed her rain boots to come back outside. As she put the rainboots on, Jordan walked out of his house. Jordan looked around; it was the typical look of the hurricanes he had been through.

Hayley saw Jordan. Seeing him, she felt weird. It was like she was seeing him in a different way. The person she was looking at was the same person she was texting. It was like they were two different people. Jordan could see Hayley looking at him out of the corner of his eye as he looked out at his front yard. He felt strange, like he didn't know what to say to Hayley. Their interactions in person had always been intense, but the text messages they exchanged were friendly and different.

He looked over at Hayley, "Well, not too bad right now." As Hayley was pulling on her last rainboot, she said, "No, I figured there would be more trees down."

"Well, we still have the second half of the hurricane. The trees start to come down once the ground is soaked, and the soil loosens. The wetter it is, the more they will fall. It is coming," Jordan warned Hayley.

"I'm going to look in the back, you coming?" Hayley said.

Jordan started walking in the grass, trying to miss the big puddles. Hayley smiled, "You don't have rainboots?"

"No, I am going to get my shoes wet. I don't know why I think I am going to keep them dry," Jordan replied.

"Hayley laughed, "How are you in law enforcement and don't have rainboots?"

"I don't know, I think they are ugly," Jordan replied.

"And that is a reason to get your shoes wet? Because you think they are ugly?" Hayley judged him.

Jordan realized how dumb his comment sounded. He looked over at Hayley, "Shut up."

They walked first to Hayley's backyard. The fence was leaning, but there was nothing that would be too hard to fix. "I'm good with only having to fix the fence," Hayley commented.

"Yeah, we can lean it back after the storm." Surprised at the comment that came out of his mouth, Jordan froze, waiting to be yelled at by Hayley.

Hayley did notice what was said by Jordan, but instead of anger, Hayley said, "Yeah, I would appreciate the help. It's probably going to be heavy. You want to look at your yard?" Hayley asked.

"Yeah," Jordan replied.

As they walked into Jordan's backyard, they could see branches down from the trees around his house. Jordan turned and looked at a tree. "What's wrong?" Hayley asked, looking at the tree Jordan was staring at. "That's not good. You see how it is leaning?" Jordan replied.

"Yeah, do you think it is going to fall?" Hayley asked.

"I hope not," Jordan smirked and looked at Hayley," I might need to get that tree taken down when the hurricane is over."

"Yeah, it might be a good idea," Hayley said, looking at the tree. Jordan was right; it was leaning towards his house, not bad enough to worry at that moment, but enough to wonder how the rest of the storm was going to influence the tree. Jordan could only hope that the tree would not come down. If it did, it would crash into his house, and he would have more damage than he wanted. He was worried but did not want to appear worried to Hayley.

As the two looked at the tree, it started to lightly rain again. "Well, here it comes again. We should get inside," Jordan said, walking toward the front of the house.

Hayley walked to her porch, and Jordan stood on his porch. "I will see you in a few, I guess," Hayley said, looking over at Jordan. "Yep," Jordan said, walking inside. Jordan was nervous after seeing the tree leaning towards his house, but there was nothing he could do at this point.

Chapter 11:

The Rescue

Soon, the wind and the rain began again. Hayley picked up her book again, soon losing herself in its pages. When her phone pinged, it startled her. She picked up her phone, it was, of course, Jordan, *"How is the book?"*

Hayley: *"Are you that bored, Jordan?"*

Jordan: *"Pretty much."*

Hayley laughed, *"lol, yes, it is getting good. It's like you are there in the situation."*

Jordan: *"Hal, it's fiction. It's not real."*

Hayley: *"I know, but it is a story that you could imagine happening."*

Jordan: *"You are a romantic."*

Hayley: *"No, I just like happy endings."*

Jordan: *"You know it is going to be a happy ending?"*

Hayley: *"No, but they always turned out good."*

Jordan: *"Everything is not always a happy ending in life, Hal. I hope you know that."*

Jordan thought about his own past when texting those words to Hayley.

Hayley: *"Oh, Jordan, stop being so dang negative. Yes, I know that the real world is totally different and has a lot of pain. It is good to be engrossed in the imagination sometimes."*

Jordan: *"If you say so."*

With Hayley reading that, for the first time, she wondered what Jordan had been through. She wondered what he might be hiding from her. It was the first time Hayley began to think about his actions with women and his words. *He went through something he hadn't said. He is hiding something from me. I mean, why would he tell me? We haven't been really friendly.*

Hayley: *"Sounds like you have something in your past you don't talk about to me."*

Jordan: *"Everyone has a past, Hal. Some things we are proud of, some things we are not."*

Hayley: *"I get that. You have never been so close to someone you wanted just them?"*

Jordan: *"I have, but it just never worked out. What about you Hal? Have you ever been in love? Did you think you found the one?"*

Hayley thought again about telling Jordan. She was finally ready to tell him, *"Yes, I have been in love, but it is complicated. I've been married….."*

As Hayley wrote those words, she heard a tree crack and a big crash. The crash and what Hayley thought was a tree shook the ground. She erased what she had written. *"Jordan, are you okay? What the hell was that?"* Hayley texted as she walked to the window in the direction from which she heard the crash. She tried to peer through the little slit in the board. Whatever it was had to crash into Jordan's house.

Hayley texted again, *"Jordan?"* Hayley checked, and she still had service. Hayley's heart began to pound. Jordan is in trouble. He would have messaged back. Hayley texted Jordan again, *"Jordan, answer me?"* Nothing.

Jordan could hear his phone going off, but he couldn't move. The crash Hayley had heard was the tree that the two had looked at earlier. It had snapped, and it came through his house, crashing into the room where he was sitting. Jordan heard it coming and jumped up to leave the room, but it happened too fast. His leg was pinned under what was his roof and the floor on which he was sitting.

Jordan tried to reach for his phone, but it was just out of reach. He tried to move the debris from the roof and roll the tree to get his leg from under what had fallen. But he was not strong enough compared to the size of the tree...

I am freaking stuck, and I think my leg is broken.

The pain in Jordan's leg made him feel that his ankle was pretty messed up, and his leg might be broken. Jordan leaned his back up against the wall where he was trying to make it to when his leg was pinned under the debris. Jordan wondered if Hayley was thinking about why he hadn't messaged her. Maybe she didn't care. Maybe she hadn't even heard the crash. Jordan then thought she had to hear the crash; it was loud as it came crashing through the house. As he sat in his thoughts, he could hear his phone pinging. Jordan hoped it was Hayley and that she would know to get help.

Hayley paced the room she was in. It was pouring outside, and the wind was whipping badly. *I have to check on him. OMG, I know this is not smart, but I can't let him be in his house hurt if that is what it is.*

Hayley put on her jacket.

This is not smart. This is dumb. Why am I going to do this? Hayley thought. Hayley opened her door, and it flung open. Emma jumped up. "No, Emma, you stay," Hayley shouted as she grabbed the door and put all of her body weight on the door. She pushed slowly, closing the door with all her body weight. Emma lay down at the door, whimpering.

She ran to the back door running outside. It was pouring and the wind was strong. Hayley hesitated, put her hood over her head, then took off running towards the gate to open it. The rain beat down on her so hard it felt like tiny pins striking her arms and legs. She grabbed the gate and pulled—it flew open with the wind as Hayley dashed through, splashing through the standing water that filled her rainboots and soaked her clothes. Reaching Jordan's porch, she banged on the door and shouted, 'JORDAN!' She hit it harder. 'JORDAN!' Still no answer. She tried the doorknob, but of course, it was locked.

Hayley ran off Jordan's porch to the side of his house. That's when she saw the huge tree through the back of Jordan's house. "Oh God!" she exclaimed. She ran to where the tree was through Jordan's house. "JORDAN, JORDAN."

Jordan had closed his eyes and was trying to relax, waiting, just waiting for someone to come and check on him. While he had his eyes closed, he thought he heard banging on his front door, but he thought it was something hitting the front door. Jordan began letting his mind wander, and then he heard, "JORDAN, JORDAN." It was Hayley. He yelled, "HAL, HAL, I'm over here."

Hayley stopped at the point where she heard Jordan and asked, "Are you okay?"

Jordan: "No, I need help getting my leg out."

Hayley: "How can I get in? Can I get in the back way?"

Jordan: "No, you are going to have to come through the front of the house."

Hayley: "Okay, I am coming."

Hayley started to run back to the front of Jordan's house to his porch. As she reached the concrete, she slipped and fell. "Damn it," she shouted. Hayley rolled to her side, sitting up. She grabbed her knee. It hurt, it hurt badly, but Hayley didn't believe it was broken. She stood up and grabbed the doorknob, turning it and throwing herself into Jordan's door. She did it several times, but the door was not budging. Hayley grabbed Jordan's porch railing with both arms and started kicking the door with her foot. The door was moving. Hayley kicked harder. It budged more; Hayley kicked harder. Finally, Jordan's door flung open with the force and the wind.

Hayley walked into the house, closing the door the best she could behind her. "JORDAN," she shouted.

Jordan: "Hal, I am back here."

Hayley went towards Jordan's voice in a back room. In the shadows, she could see a dim light coming from a back room. She walked towards it.

As she went to open the door, the door would not open all the way because of the tree in the room. "Jordan, do you have tools?" she asked.

"Yeah, go back through the house and to the kitchen. There is a door going into the garage, and there is a toolbox in there," he replied.

Hayley turned around and ran towards the front of the house, looking for the kitchen. Finding the kitchen, Hayley saw the door Jordan was talking about. She opened the door and began looking frantically for the toolbox. It was in the corner of the garage. She looked through the toolbox, a screwdriver and a hammer, just what she needed. She grabbed the toolbox and ran back to where Jordan was.

As she made it back, she put the toolbox on the floor. She took out the screwdriver and hammer. Hayley put the screwdriver in the hinge holding the door at the top. She started to bang on it. Jordan could not see what Hayley was doing, but he imagined what she might be doing. Jordan sat listening to whatever Hayley was doing.

The pin to the top hinge popped out. Hayley stuck the screwdriver in the bottom hinge and began hitting the pin out. Once it popped out, Hayley threw down the screwdriver and the hammer. She grabbed the door, moving it away from the door frame. Once removed, Hayley and Jordan could see each other.

Jordan looked at Hayley. She was soaking wet, and he could read her face; she was worried. "You are full of surprises," he said, trying to joke. "I need some help getting my leg unpinned." Hayley looked at Jordan. He was pale, probably from the pain, but he assured Haley that he was going to be okay. "You think?" Hayley asked. Jordan smiled.

Hayley walked to where she could see Jordan's leg better. His leg was caught under the roof, which was under the tree. Hayley began to try and move the tree off the roof it was lying on.

"STOP STOP, that's killing me," Jordan yelled in pain.

Hayley froze, hearing Jordan yell. Hayley looked and examined the situation, "Let me get some more stuff from the garage." Hayley ran to the garage and grabbed Jordan's carjack and his chainsaw. She ran back to where Jordan was.

"Oh, this does not look like it is going to be fun for me," Jordan said, his heart pounding while looking at the chainsaw. "Have you ever used a chainsaw before?" he asked.

"No, but I have seen them being used before," Hayley replied. Jordan's heart started to beat even faster. "Do you know how to use that jack you brought?" he asked Hayley nervously.

"Yes, a little, but I'm going to jack everything up a little off your leg. Maybe we can slide your leg out. If that doesn't work, we will cut the tree. That's only the last result because I would have to stand on the roof that is on your leg to cut it. I got this! Why don't you trust me?" Hayley said, smiling, trying to lighten the mood.

Jordan looked at Hayley, drenched. The smile, as Hayley joked, took away some of the pain Jordan was feeling at the moment. "Hell, no, I don't trust you, but let's try it," Jordan replied.

Hayley looked for the perfect spot to place the carjack. "Jordan, where should I put it?" Hayley asked.

"Try right there, Hal," Jordan replied, pointing to a piece of the roof that appeared to be where his leg was pinched under it. "I think if you put it there, you can lift it enough where I can get my leg out and the tree won't roll," Jordan added.

Hayley slid the jack under a small part of the roof. She began pumping up and down on the handle, and the roof began to rise.

"Slow down, Hal, slow down, I don't want the tree to roll," Jordan exclaimed. Hayley slowed down to a slower pace. Jordan put his hands on his legs right above the knee and started trying to pull his leg out from under the debris. "Keep going Hal," Jordan shouted. Hayley kept pumping the jack as Jordan asked, periodically stopping to check if Jordan could pull his leg out. "DAMN IT," Jordan yelled. "What, what is it?" Hayley asked anxiously.

"I can't pull my leg out. I should be able to by now. Can you come look and see what is keeping my leg from moving?" Jordan told Hayley.

Hayley walked towards Jordan. She got down on her knees and looked under the roof to where Jordan's leg was pinned. "You are going to have to slide back with your leg, or I've got to jack it up more."

"No, don't jack it up anymore. Let me try backing up," Jordan said while placing his hands behind him and scooting backwards. Hayley, still watching, instructed, "A little bit further, Jordan, and you will be good."

"Hal, I can't, I'm totally pushed up against the wall," Jordan replied.

Hayley looked. She could slide his leg out from the side of the debris. All she had to do was grab Jordan's leg and jerk it towards the opening. "I think I can get your leg out," Hayley said.

"Okay?" Jordan said, questioning what Hayley had on her mind.

"It's probably going to hurt," Hayley told Jordan. Jordan leaned his head back, "Just do it. Just do it fast," Jordan shouted.

Hayley: "Do you want me to tell you when I'm going to do it?"

Jordan: "No Hal, just do it."

Hayley grabbed Jordan's leg and began to slide it through the small opening. She had to pull hard and in a jerking motion to get his leg out. Jordan began to yell, "AHHHHH!" Hayley didn't stop; she kept jerking his leg out until it was finally free. "Got it," Hayley said.

"Holy shit, that hurt. Oh my God, I am in pain," Jordan shouted as he pulled his leg toward him. He could not bend it. Jordan looked at his leg; his ankle, knee, and foot were swollen. "My ankle and knee are screwed, but I don't think my leg is broken," he said. Jordan was breathing heavily from the pain; he was also pale as a ghost.

"Do you want to try and walk out of here?" Hayley asked, trying to see how confident Jordan was about his leg. She didn't know if he believed it, but they had to get out of that room and somewhere where they could see better to examine Jordan's leg.

Hayley: "Come on, lean on me."

Jordan: "I don't think you can hold me."

Hayley: "Jordan, stop thinking and grab on. Don't ask any questions, just come on."

Hayley had trained tactically while she worked for the department she came from. She knew it would be slow-moving, but she could help Jordan walk. Jordan stood up, not asking any questions.

Hayley: "Throw your arm around my shoulder."

Jordan put his arm around Hayley's shoulder, and Hayley grabbed Jordan's waist and onto the belt he was wearing. She then grabbed Jordan's hand, which was not wrapped around Hayley's shoulder. Jordan took a step, feeling out Hayley's strength. Slowly, the two walked in the dark towards the front of Jordan's house. When they reached the living room by the front door, Jordan said, "Okay, give me a minute." Jordan pointed to the couch, and Hayley helped him to sit down on it. "You're a lot stronger than you appear," Jordan said, out of breath.

Hayley: "I am full of surprises."

Jordan: "What other surprises do you have?"

Hayley (smiling): "I told you no questions, Jordan."

Jordan: "I hear you. I guess I will discover them the more I know you. Thank you, Hal. I know getting out in the storm sucked. I truly thank you. I thought I was going to be sitting there until work couldn't get a hold of me."

Hayley: "I knew something was wrong when I heard the crash and nothing else from you."

Jordan: "Damn, I don't know what to do. I guess the insurance company will help me find a place to stay while my house is getting fixed. I just hope they realize I am not going to be able to do stairs. Tonight, I can just sleep here on the couch and will be fine. When the storm stops, can you help me get to the hospital? I can't go all night and wait. I don't want to trust that EMS can get through all of the roads."

Hayley: "Jordan, you're not staying here tonight. I have a guest bedroom, and you can stay there. I will get you to the hospital as soon as the storm stops, and I will wait for you to bring you back home."

Jordan: "Hal, no, you don't have to do that. I will be fine."

Hayley: "And how are you going to get around when you get back from the hospital? You are at least going to have crutches."

Jordan: "I am a survivor Hal, I will get it."

Hayley: "Stop being stubborn. What do you need? I will get it for you, and we can go. It's not raining too bad now. We can make it and get some ice for your ankle and knee until it stops."

Jordan: "I am not having you get what I need."

Hayley: "Okay, hardhead—so you're just going to wear the same clothes and smell like death? Just tell me where a bag is and where to look for things, and I will get the stuff. Don't make me punch your knee or step on your ankle."

Jordan sat in silence. Hayley was right, he couldn't do it himself, and it drove him crazy.

Jordan: "The first room down the hallway to the left. There is a big duffel bag in the closet. In the dresser are my clothes, and pants are in the closet. The next room on the left is the bathroom. The soap, shampoo, and all other items are in there."

Hayley: "Okay, where was the flashlight you had?"

Jordan: "I left it in the room where I was."

Hayley grabbed her phone, "I'm not going back there. I will be right back."

Hayley turned the light on her phone and walked down the hall into the first room. Jordan's room was clean. He had a pair of work pants sitting on the chair by the window, but it was organized. Hayley opened the closet door and found the duffel bag Jordan had mentioned. She grabbed it and walked to the dresser. Hayley opened the top dresser. "*Hmmm, he's a boxer guy,*" she thought. Hayley grabbed all of the underwear that Jordan had in his dresser.

As she was taking them out to place them in the duffel bag, Hayley noticed a picture on the dresser. Hayley picked it up and looked at it. It was a picture of Jordan smiling with a baby. Hayley set the picture back down, wondering who the baby was. Hayley continued to look into the other drawers. She grabbed some shirts and pajama bottoms, then went back to the closet for shorts and pants for Jordan, unsure what he'd want to wear.

"Are you good in there?" Jordan asked nervously. He didn't know if Hayley was going through his stuff.

Hayley popped out of the room with the duffel bag full, "Do you have a gun we need to take?"

"Yes, check the nightstand. It is in the one closest to the window," Jordan replied. Hayley went back into the room and opened the nightstand. She pulled out Jordan's gun. Under the gun, there was another picture, this time it was Jordan and a little girl who was around one. Again, Jordan was smiling, holding the child. Hayley closed the drawer and walked out of the room. "Okay, bathroom stuff, and that is it," she said.

Jordan, still sitting on the couch, said, "Wonderful."

Hayley laughed, "Am I making you feel uncomfortable going through your stuff? Such a typical cop thing."

After the comment came out of Hayley's mouth, she knew she shouldn't have said it.

"Typical cop, huh? How would you know?" Jordan said, smiling.

"I told you not to ask questions. That's the rule," Hayley replied, walking into the bathroom. Jordan had a clean bathroom as well. She grabbed all of the items she could find in Jordan's bathroom that she thought he might need: shampoo, soap, deodorant, toothpaste, toothbrush, hair gel, and everything. Hayley stuffed it in the duffel bag and walked to the front of the house.

Jordan: "Geezus Hal."

Hayley: "I didn't know what you would need, so I packed a bunch. I have to bring this to my house before I can help you. I can't do both. I will be right back."

Jordan: "Hal, it is still storming pretty bad."

Hayley: "I got it. I will be fine."

With that, Hayley opened the front door and slammed it behind her. Jordan, still sitting on the couch, was embarrassed and felt completely helpless. Jordan got up from the couch and swung his leg to the ground.

Damn that hurts so bad, he thought. All Jordan had were his thoughts, waiting for Hayley to come back and help him.

What a turn of events, he thought. All he wanted to do was talk to Hayley more, and now, she had come to help him, helped him free himself, and now she was allowing him to stay with her until he could get to a hospital.

Plus, she was going to drive him there and wait for him. He wondered what Hayley had seen in his house. He wondered how much explaining he would need to do, but he thought maybe she would not ask questions since he agreed not to ask her questions. Jordan smiled and laughed a little. He thought, *this is such a messed-up situation.* Jordan shook his head and continued to wait for Hayley.

As Hayley made her way back to her yard, she managed not to slip and fall like she did the first time. Again, she was soaking wet. She threw Jordan's clothes down and walked back out, heading towards Jordan's house. Hayley began to hear a tree crack. She looked in the direction of the cracking, and it was a tree falling. Luckily, it was not heading towards her house, and it would not hit Jordan's house this time. Hayley began to run faster to get back to Jordan's house. When she opened the door, Jordan was trying to walk towards her.

"What was that?" Jordan asked, looking shocked.

Hayley: "It was another tree; it didn't hit anything. Where is your phone?"

Jordan: "Crap, it is back in the room."

Hayley: "Okay, I'll go get it."

Jordan: "Hal, you don't have to. Let's just go."

Hayley: "No, you need it."

Hayley turned on the light to her phone and walked back towards the bedroom where she had freed Jordan earlier. She called Jordan's phone and looked around. She could see it lying on the ground. She walked over and grabbed his phone. He had several phone calls and several missed messages. When she reached Jordan, she handed it to him. Jordan placed it into his pocket, saying, "Thank you."

Hayley: "You ready?"

Jordan: "Yeah, how are we going to do this?"

Hayley: "The same way we did earlier, slow and steady."

Jordan looked at Hayley, "Okay."

Jordan grabbed onto Hayley's shoulder, and Hayley wrapped her arms around Jordan's waist. They walked out of the front door and onto the porch. We're going to get soaked," Jordan said, glancing at Hayley. She was already drenched from carrying his things to her house. Jordan took one look at her and smirked. "Yeah, probably not the best thing to say right now."

Hayley: "No, not at all. Come on, Jordan."

Jordan and Hayley walked slowly outside and into the rain. For the first time, Jordan felt the rain pounding down on him like needles. He would have loved to run, but he limped with Hayley as fast as he could. As Hayley went to the backyard, Jordan asked, "We are going in the back door?"

Hayley: "Jordan, I couldn't close the front door because of the wind. So yes, keep walking."

Jordan and Hayley were silent the rest of the way to Hayley's house; through the gate, into the porch, and up the three stairs going into Hayley's house. By the time they reached the house, both were dripping wet. As they stood on the kitchen tile, Hayley looked at Jordan, "Let me get some towels, the tile is pretty slippery." Emma was jumping around, excited that Hayley was home and wondering who their guest was. "Emma down, stay down," Hayley yelled.

Hayley took a few more steps before her foot slipped out in front of her, and she came crashing down on the same knee she had slipped and fallen on earlier. "Mother fucker!" Hayley shouted. Jordan looked at Hayley, surprised that such words came out of her mouth. He began to laugh, "Hayley, I have never heard such words."

"Sorry, I did that earlier at your house, and it was the same knee I just fell on again," she replied.

Hayley stood up and took off her wet shoes and socks. She slowly and cautiously walked until Jordan couldn't see her. Jordan was still smiling at Hayley's words, and just the sight of her falling so hard.

A few moments later, Hayley walked back with several towels. She had a towel wrapped around her, and she handed one to Jordan. He dried off the best he could. Hayley leaned down by Jordan's legs and began to take his shoes off. "What are you doing?" Hayley looked up, "I am taking off your shoes, what do you think I am doing?"

Jordan: "You don't need to do that."

Hayley: "So you're going to lean down and take them off. Jordan just chill out, it's okay."

It wasn't okay with Jordan; he hated needing the help. Hayley dried Jordan's foot off.

Hayley: "Do you think you can lean on that leg long enough to get your shoe and sock off?"

Jordan: "Yeah, I got it."

Jordan didn't know if he could or not, but he was going to try. Jordan put his weight on his leg, and shooting pain could be felt throughout his whole leg. Hayley quickly grabbed Jordan's shoe and sock off. As soon as she did, Jordan took the weight off his leg. "Damn it," Jordan let out.

Hayley: "You okay?"

Jordan: "Yes."

Hayley put her arm back around Jordan and walked towards her couch. As she went to set Jordan down, she stopped. "You've got to get dry clothes on."

Jordan: "Are you serious right now Hal?"

Hayley: "Yes, if you don't, you are going to be sitting or lying on wet."

Jordan could only think, *this is going from bad to worse.*

Jordan: "You aren't going to help me with this. I can do it."

Hayley: "I didn't plan on it. I am going to change while you are changing."

Hayley went to the duffel bag and started pulling out some clothes. She brought them to Jordan. "Here, if you need help, let me know. I will be right back." Hayley walked to her bedroom and shut the door. She stripped off the wet clothing she was wearing and put on dry clothes. She grabbed a towel and wrapped her hair up to dry it. She opened her bedroom door, asking, "Are you good?"

Jordan: "Yeah, give me a few more minutes."

"Okay," Hayley replied as she sat down on her bed and waited for Jordan to tell her he was dressed. Hayley smiled, thinking about such a turn of events. Christian was supposed to be here in a few days, and one of the extra bedrooms in her house was about to belong to Jordan. Jordan, the neighbor she did not like, the neighbor she purposely went over and helped escape from the house. She knew she was never going to live this one down with Christian.

Jordan: "Alright Hal, I am good."

Hayley grabbed her wet clothes and headed back to the living room. When she reached the living room, she grabbed Jordan's wet clothing and headed to place them in the washer for now.

Jordan: "You don't have to do that."

Hayley: "Jordan, stop."

Hayley placed the clothing in the washer before returning to the kitchen area. Hayley: "You want anything to drink?"

Jordan: "What do you have?"

Hayley: "Wine, beer, coke, water?"

Jordan: "I guess get me some water. I don't want to smell like alcohol once we go to the hospital."

Haley poured Jordan a glass of water. She grabbed two-gallon-size ziplock bags and filled them with ice. She grabbed the items and went into the living room. She handed Jordan the water, "Flip your leg onto the couch. Jordan put his leg on the couch, and Hayley placed one of the bags of ice on his knee and one on his ankle, "There you go."

Jordan: "Thank you. I feel helpless."

Hayley (smiling): "Nah, when we get you fixed up, you do owe me, though."

Jordan laughed, "It is a deal."

Hayley: "How much longer do you think it will be?"

Jordan: "I wouldn't think maybe another hour or so. It's a fast-moving storm."

Hayley lay down on the other half of the L-shaped couch in her living room. Hayley: "Well, that sucks."

Jordan: "I'm not that bad to deal with Hal. You don't have to talk to me if you don't want to."

Hayley laughed, "I didn't mean anything by that."

Jordan: "I know, I am just giving you a hard time."

Hayley: "What do you think is all wrong with your leg?"

Jordan: "I don't know Hal, I know I'm going to need surgery for my knee at least. I have some torn shit in it. Not sure about my ankle."

Hayley: "Does it hurt bad?"

Jordan: "Yes, Hal, a good pain killer would be great right about now."

Hayley: "I have some Hydrocodone; you want one of those?"

Jordan cut his eyes to Hayley, "Hydrocodone? You just told a cop you have drugs in your house. Not only a cop, a narcotics cop."

Hayley: "Oh, chill out. I got them the last time I got dental work done. They are legal."

Jordan: "Not for me, I can't take that. I will pop positive, that would be the end for me."

Hayley: "They are going to give you something for pain when you get to the hospital, just tell them to give you Hydrocodone."

Jordan thought about it, and that did make sense.

Hayley got up and went to her bathroom cabinet, grabbing a Hydrocodone pill from the bottle she had stored there. She returned to the living room and handed it to Jordan. Jordan took it from her, placing it in his mouth and swallowing it with water.

Jordan: "Thank you."

Hayley: "No problem."

Both lay back on the couch, each on their own side of the couch.

Jordan stared at the American flag in the shadow box on the mantle.

Jordan: "You said that was a family member's shadow box."

Hayley looked at the shadow box, "Yes, his name was Eric."

Jordan: "How did he die?"

Hayley did not want to talk about the story, but felt it was time to talk about it. Talk about it as much as Jordan asked.

Hayley: "He was killed in the line of duty. He went to serve a search warrant and was shot and killed by one of the suspects."

Jordan: "Oh wow, I am so sorry, Hal. Where did he work?"

Hayley: "He worked for the department in the city I was living in."

Jordan: "What kind of warrant was he serving?"

Hayley: "They were narcotics warrants for trafficking. They were going to arrest them and then search the residence they went to."

Jordan: "Was he the only one killed?"

Hayley: "Yeah, it happened really fast."

Jordan: "How old was he?"

Hayley: "He was our age, in his early 30s. A little older than me."

Jordan: "Did he have a family? Kids?"

Here it was. A moment she never wanted to talk about again.

Hayley: "He had no kids, but he was married."

Jordan: "What happened to his wife?"

Jordan was wondering how far he could take it and if Hayley would actually tell him she was the person married to him.

Hayley: "I was his wife, Jordan. I left a year after it happened to start over."

Jordan turned towards Hayley to look at her. He could not believe that she actually told him.

Jordan: "I am so sorry, Hal. I hate that for you, and I hate that one of my brothers was killed."

Hayley: "It's okay."

Jordan: "How are you doing?"

Hayley: "It is day by day, better than it was last year and the year before."

Jordan: "Man, Hal, I am so sorry. I can't imagine what you went through and will go through. I truly am sorry."

Jordan did not know what else to say.

Hayley, noticing Jordan didn't know what to say, lightened the mood, "Well, now you know I was a badge bunny, and I got one trapped and married."

Jordan began to laugh, "Ahh, I see. Even got him to marry you."

Hayley laughed, "I sure did. Had to get him off the market and fast."

The two laughed. An awkward silence was broken by Jordan's phone ringing.

Hayley could hear someone talking but could not make out what the person was saying. It was Dan.

Dan: "Hey, just checking on you, are you okay?"

Jordan: "Yeah, I am good. I have a tree through my house."

Dan: "A tree through your house, do you need me to come over? Are you good?"

"No," Jordan paused before speaking again, "When the tree fell, it pinned my leg between the debris. Hayley came over and helped me free my leg from the debris. I am at her house right now. My knee and my ankle are pretty messed up. When the storm stops, she is going to take me to the hospital to have it looked at."

Dan was silent, "I am sorry, did you say you are at Hayley's house? Hayley, your neighbor Hayley's house?"

Jordan: "Yeah."

Dan: "You said your leg was pinned under some debris, and she helped you get it out?"

Jordan: "Yes."

Dan: "And now you are sitting over her house, waiting for the storm to stop so she can take you to the hospital?"

Jordan: "Yes."

Dan began to laugh hysterically, "You can't make this shit up."

Jordan: "I am glad you think this is funny."

Hayley looked over at Jordan, who was looking at her, shaking his head.

Dan: "Okay, Casanova, do you need me to help you with anything, or does Hayley have it handled. I mean, she already rescued you."

Dan began to laugh again.

Jordan: "No, I am good, but can you let the bosses know I am out of commission until further notice?"

Dan: "Of course, you don't need my help. Hayley is all the man you need."

Jordan: "Goodbye, Dan."

Dan was still laughing while Jordan hung up the phone.

Hayley: "Who is Dan? I am sure another cop."

JordanL "Yes, Dan is my partner at work. We have known each other for a while."

Hayley: "Ahh, I got you."

Jordan, wanting to change the subject, said, "So, how is your book so far?"

Hayley: "It is pretty good. I am halfway into it."

"Let's read some of it," Jordan said, knowing they had time to kill and that he was done with small talk for the moment.

Hayley: "You want to read a love story?"

Jordan: "Not really, but I will listen if you read it. I mean, we have time to waste."

Emma had jumped on the couch with Jordan. Hayley was shocked and considered it interesting.

Hayley grabbed the book and began reading out loud to Jordan. Jordan listened as Hayley read, staring in the opposite direction from where Hayley was. Every so often, Jordan would stop Hayley and ask questions, not knowing what had transpired in the book to that point. Hayley would explain it to Jordan before continuing in the book. About 30 minutes into reading, Hayley's phone rang. It was Christian. Hayley picked up the phone.

Jordan listened and could hear someone talking but could not make out what was being said.

Christian: "Hey Hal, I just wanted to check on you. Do you still have electricity?"

Hayley: "No, it went out a while ago. I've been sitting in the house by candlelight."

Christian: "Interesting, how come your phone is still working?"

Hayley: "Your guess is as good as mine, but I am grateful."

Christian: "Are you sure you still want Kelsey and me to come down later this week?"

As Hayley went to answer, Jordan's phone rang. Jordan grabbed it as soon as it rang and mouthed to Hayley, *I am sorry.*

Before Hayley could answer Christian's last question, he said, "I am sorry, was that another phone ringing?"

Hayley: "Yes."

Christian: "Who are you with? Who is there with you?"

"Well, it's a long story, but a tree went through Jordan's house. I helped him, and he is at my house right now. We are waiting out the storm, and once it is over, I am going to take him to the hospital because his leg is pretty messed up."

Christian was silent before he began hysterically laughing.

Christian: "You are kidding me, right?"

Hayley: "No, not at all."

Christian continued to laugh, "I told you. I knew it the first time you talked about him."

Hayley: "No and yes. I'd better see you and Kelsey here on Friday evening or Saturday morning."

Christian: "Oh, I can't wait to hear this story."

Hayley: "Goodbye, Christian. I will see you Friday or Saturday."

Hayley hung up the phone as Christian continued to laugh. Kelsey walked into the room and asked Christian, "What are you laughing at?"

Christian: "Guess who is at Hal's house waiting out the storm with her?"

Kelsey: "Who?"

"Jordan!" Christian replied, laughing.

Kelsey: "Jordan, the neighbor she doesn't like Jordan?"

Christian: "Yep."

Kelsey: "Oh boy, it's going to be an interesting weekend."

Christian: "Yes, my dear, it is going to be."

"So, who is Christian?" Jordan asked, turning around on the couch to look at Hayley.

Hayley: "Christian was Eric's partner."

Jordan: "So, you two are pretty close."

Hayley: "Yeah, before Eric died, Eric, me, Christian, and his wife Kelsey would hang out a lot. They were family to us."

Jordan: "And after?"

Hayley: "Christian and Kelsey took care of me for a while, and we hung out sometimes until I moved here."

Jordan: "Is this the first time you are going to see them since being here?"

Hayley: "Yeah, it will be good to see them. It' s been too long, but, in a way, I guess I was still trying to get away from all of my old life."

Jordan: "I understand that, but you don't need to lose friends like that. Just make new memories with them. Memories here."

Hayley: "Yes, you are right. So, are you ready to start reading again?"

"Oh yes, give me more of this love story," Jordan said as he turned back around to get comfortable on the couch.

Hayley smiled and began to read more of the book as Jordan listened. Jordan faced the opposite direction, asking Hayley questions as needed, but after a while, Jordan had to ask no more questions. He was vested in what Hayley was reading to him. Though he would never admit it, he wanted to know more about the book.

As Hayley read, she would periodically look over to see if Jordan was still awake, which he was, and Hayley would just smile. As Hayley read, the hurricane had moved past their city, but Hayley continued to read, as Jordan did not say anything about the hurricane passing them. Hayley got to the last paragraph in the book:

"Life is made up of moments in which we choose a direction, hoping the path chosen leads us to our purpose and our soulmate. William Shakespeare once wrote, "The course of true love never did run smooth." Love worth having is messy and teaches us lessons, preparing us for what is waiting on the other side. Trust in the journey with all its bumps and curves. With faith, you will find your fairy tale in the end. "

After reading, Hayley closed the book. She looked over at Jordan, who was staring off, but he remained silent. Finally, Hayley said, "What did you think?"

Jordan: "I think they put up with a lot of crap with each other. I also think I am ready to go to the hospital."

Hayley laughed, "Aww, did the book choke you up. I won't tell anyone. You want to take my car or yours?"

Jordan: "Let's take my work truck. It will be easier, and we won't get stopped in it. You know there are going to be cops everywhere helping, and they are not going to want people on the road."

Hayley: "You are not driving. You know that, right?"

Jordan: "You think Hal? I know that you're going to drive my work vehicle. I trust you enough to know you're not going to do anything stupid in it."

Hayley: "Where are your keys?"

Jordan: "If you go into my house, they are going to be on a hook right next to the door."

Hayley: "Okay, and do you have a garage opener in your car?"

Jordan: "Yeah, it should work. If it doesn't, you can manually open the door."

"Okay," Hayley said, "I will be right back."

Jordan: "Okay, I will be here when you get back."

Jordan joked with Hayley. Hayley smiled and walked out.

Jordan lay back on the couch, waiting for Hayley, but deep in his thoughts. I just read a romance novel with my neighbor I don't even get along with. It was the first time reading with any female, and it was the first time that he would even consider reading a love story at all. It was different, kind of a special thing they shared, but no one would ever know about it. Jordan smiled and closed his eyes, waiting for her to come back.

Hayley walked next door to Jordan's house and opened the door. His keys were exactly where he said they would be. Hayley walked to the kitchen and out into the garage. She unlocked Jordan's work vehicle and jumped inside. She pushed the garage door opener, and the door began to open. *Perfect*, Hayley thought. Hayley put the key in the ignition and turned it to start the vehicle. As she did, music began to blare, which in turn made Hayley jump and scream. Hayley turned the music down. Her heart was racing; she took a deep breath before backing out of the driveway.

Jordan could hear the music start and Hayley scream from inside the house. Jordan laughed. He wished he could have seen Hayley's reaction when the music came on. He could hear Hayley pull into the driveway of her house. Jordan pulled himself up and was sitting on the couch when Hayley walked back in.

Hayley flung the door open, "You know, you really shouldn't listen to music that loud, and you could have warned me."

Jordan laughed, "Not that I remembered at this point with everything that happened, but I would have given anything to see your reaction." Jordan pulled himself up from the couch and was standing. Hayley walked over to Jordan. Jordan put his arm around Hayley's shoulder, and Hayley put her hand around Jordan's waist, grabbing his belt. Their free hands were together to use as leverage to get him to the vehicle.

As they made it to the vehicle, Hayley stopped, opened the door, and asked, "How are we going to do this?"

Jordan looked, "I think I am just going to back up and pull myself up with my arms. I may need something to use for my good leg to push up on."

Hayley lunged her leg and said, "Just use my leg."

Jordan: "I'm not going to use your leg."

Hayley: "Jordan, just do it. Come on."

Jordan backed up to the vehicle and began pulling himself up with his arms. When he couldn't pull himself up anymore, he took his good leg and pressed on Hayley's leg slightly, worried that he was going to hurt her. Once seated in the vehicle, he swung his good leg in and pulled his hurt leg slowly into the vehicle. Hayley closed the door and went around to the driver's side. She jumped in and looked at Jordan, "You ready?"

Jordan looked over at Hayley, putting on his seatbelt, "I guess. Please don't get in a wreck."

Hayley, shrugging her shoulders, smiled, "We will see how it goes." She began to back out of the driveway onto the road. Jordan just looked at Hayley.

Chapter 12:

The Game

As predicted, getting to the hospital was almost impossible. Although they were traveling on back roads to get there, trees and power lines proved to be a problem.

Jordan: "Turn Hayley, that road."

Hayley slammed on the brakes and backed up, "Jordan, you've got to tell me to turn sooner, I don't know where I am going."

Jordan: "Hayley, stop! Stop! Stop!"

Hayley: "Jordan, I am going to go over the tree. We are in a truck."

Jordan braced, and Hayley slowed to go over the tree that was on the road.

Jordan grabbed his leg and moaned, "Damn it, Hayley."

Hayley: "Sorry, I am trying to get there."

Jordan continued to give directions to Hayley. Hayley continued to drive, scaring Jordan that she was going to get in a wreck and causing pain to his leg each time she ran over something or hit a pothole in the road.

Hayley and Jordan finally made it to the hospital. She pulled right up to the emergency room door. She jumped out of the vehicle and went to the passenger side door. Jordan opened the door and slid his legs down, "I got it." Jordan was irritated with Hayley after the driving she had just done.

"Let me help you," Hayley told Jordan as he was trying to get out of the vehicle. Hayley ignored Jordan and grabbed his hand as he tried to get out. Jordan knew he needed help and threw his arm around Hayley's neck. Hayley grabbed Jordan around his waist, grabbing onto his belt. They walked slowly into the emergency room entrance. As they entered, Hayley and Jordan walked to a chair, and Jordan sat down. Hayley went to the desk.

"Can I help you, ma'am?" The front desk clerk asked.

Hayley: "Yes, my friend needs to have his leg looked at. He had part of his roof, and a tree fell on it. His knee and his ankle look pretty bad."

The front desk clerk pushed a clipboard in front of Hayley and said, "He needs to fill this out, and we need his insurance card. Then he will need to wait for his number."

Hayley was kind of irritated by this point, "Ma'am, we don't know where his insurance cards are; he has a tree through his house. I don't think we were thinking about where his wallet was when he had a tree through his house."

"Ma'am, we have procedures at this hospital. I will need his insurance and driver's license to prove who we are treating or looking at," the front clerk snapped back at Hayley.

As Hayley argued with the front desk clerk, Dan had walked in, "Hey Jordan, you doing good?"

Jordan: "Yeah, my leg is pretty messed up, Dan. I am going to need surgery."

"What is she doing?" Dan said pointing to Hayley.

Jordan smirked, "She is arguing with the front desk clerk about my insurance and driver's license."

"You are not going to help her? You know Mandy" Dan said. Jordan and Dan both knew the front desk clerk, as they had been in the emergency room many times while working.

"Listen, why don't you call the police department and ask them for Jordan Voss' insurance information. I will even take a picture for you to send to them. He needs to be seen fast, his leg…"

As Mandy cut Hayley off, Dan said, "Jesus, she is feisty. Let me stop this." Dan walked to the desk and stood behind Hayley.

Mandy cut Hayley off, "Until you have what I am asking you for, we are not treating you."

Hayley's eyes widened as Hayley went to speak, "Listen…" Dan stepped in front of Hayley, "Mandy sweetie, how are you doing?" Dan said, smiling.

"Hey, Dan. Fine, how are you?" Mandy smiled at Dan.

Dan replied, "I am good. Hey, Jordan has hurt his leg. It is pretty bad; can we get him back in a room? He is going to need X-rays, possible surgery. You know Jordan is getting older."

Mandy laughed.

Hayley listened with her hands folded, giving a death stare to Mandy.

Mandy: "Yes, you know we can. I'll look up his stuff in the system. Is he still staying at the same address?"

Dan: "Yes, you know he is a creature of habit."

Hayley walked to where Jordan was sitting and sat down, saying, "Are you serious right now?"

Jordan looked over at Hayley, "Yeah, Mandy doesn't like people, but she loves some Dan."

"You know her?" Hayley said.

"Yeah, of course I do," Jordan said, laughing.

Hayley looked at Jordan, "You set me up."

Jordan chuckled, "I don't know what you are talking about. I am in pain."

Hayley rolled her eyes, "I am going to move the vehicle." Hayley walked outside and got back into Jordan's work vehicle and drove off. She drove around the parking lot and finally found a parking spot. It took a while, and when Hayley walked back in, Jordan and Dan were gone. Hayley figured Jordan was taken back, and Dan went with him. Hayley sat in a chair and waited for Dan or someone to tell her what Jordan needed or what to do.

As Hayley waited, it got later and later. Most people had gone from the emergency room. She lay down on two chairs and closed her eyes, waiting for Jordan or someone to tell her something. Hours went by until Hayley felt someone touch her, "Hayley?"

Hayley jumped up, smacking the person, who turned out to be a doctor, standing in front of her. Hayley, realizing she was not in danger, said, "Yes, I am Hayley."

The person replied, "I am Doctor Patel. I viewed Mr. Voss' leg. He has shattered his kneecap and torn ligaments in his knee. In his ankle, he completely tore the ligaments. Because of the damage to his patella, we had to do surgery. I did a partial patellectomy and went in and put wires and pins to place it back together. As for the ligaments, the swelling will subside. His ankle has torn ligaments or a sprain, which we call a grade 2, close to a grade 3. I did not do surgery on his ankle; I would like it to heal naturally. He is out now from the surgery and is waking up. I can take you back if you would like."

Hayley was still trying to process what Dr. Patel had told her. "Dr. Patel, what does this mean? Will he have braces or crutches? Will he need physical therapy? Like, what is he looking at for downtime? And he's in law enforcement, is he going to be able to return to duty?"

Dr Patel replied, "Ms. Hayley, he has a long road ahead of him. Yes, he will have both a brace for his knee and ankle. He will need crutches to get around, so yes, crutches. He will also have physical therapy that he will need to complete to strengthen his knee and ankle. We are looking at 6 weeks, the best-case scenario, but I think he is looking at double that time, if not longer."

Hayley started to get anxious about Jordan, "And work?"

Dr Patel replied, "Ms. Hayley, he is going to be out for a while. When he can go back, he has to go slowly. He is not going to be able to do everything that he could at one time. He needs to be careful of the knee; it will never be 100 percent again. If you're asking whether he can work in law enforcement—yes, absolutely. But could he be a SWAT officer or part of a special unit? I just don't see how that would work. Let's just get through the surgery and healing, start physical therapy, and go from there."

Hayley asked, "Does he have any medication he will need to take?"

Dr Patel replied, "Yes, he will have a prescription to fill a few different ones. He just needs to relax. He is going to need someone to help him for the first few weeks. Jordan won't be able to do things on his own."

Hayley thought, *Oh crap.* "Dr. Patel, have you told Jordan this yet?"

Dr. Patel: "Yes, he is aware. I told him before he asked me to come get you."

Hayley: "Okay. Can you take me to see him?"

Dr. Patel: "Yes, of course, this way."

Hayley walked with Dr. Patel, heading back to the room Jordan was in. Dr. Patel had told Hayley that Jordan would remain in the emergency room until the morning. Hayley's mind was in overdrive. Jordan couldn't stay by himself; he was going to need help. Hayley wondered if Dan was going to help him, but would Dan even be around, given the damage from the storm? When Hayley and Dr. Patel reached the door, Dr. Patel motioned to Jordan's room. Hayley knocked on the door before walking in. When she opened the door, Jordan was staring at the ceiling in thought. "Hey," Hayley said softly.

"Hal, I'm messed up. I don't know what I am going to do," Jordan started running his hands through his hair, looking still at the ceiling.

"Hey, it's going to be okay. You are going to be fine; we will get you fixed up, and we will get you back out there doing the job you love," Hayley said, trying to reassure Jordan.

Both were quiet.

Jordan: "I know I am going to be alright, but I don't know what I am going to do until I can get along by myself. I am going to do it, but this isn't something small like usual. I have always been down for a day or two, and then I am fine. I am back at it. The doctor said it may take longer than 12 weeks."

Hayley walked closer to Jordan, "And you are going to work on getting past the first few weeks, and then after that, you will take it day by day. You are extremely stubborn; you aren't going to let this beat you."

Jordan looked at Hayley, and Hayley smiled. "Where did Dan go?" Hayley asked, trying to change the subject and figure out where Jordan would be staying, with her or Dan.

Jordan: "He got called out, some trees down blocking the road. He had to go help."

Hayley: "How long do you think it will take to clean up, at least to get people back to somewhat normalcy here?"

Jordan: "It should be about a week or so, not too long."

Hayley thought about it. There was no way that Jordan could take care of himself, especially in the first week. He would have to stay with Hayley, and she was not going to take no for an answer. In a way, it gave Hayley a sense of helping someone again, just like she did in law enforcement. It was different, but Hayley felt it was exactly the same. She didn't want to mention it to Jordan yet but would give him no choice once it was time for him to be discharged.

Hayley looked around the room and found a chair in a corner of the room. She walked over and grabbed it, bringing it back to where Jordan was.

"What are you doing?" Jordan asked, watching Hayley.

Hayley: "Well, I am not going to stand the whole time. My feet are hurting."

Jordan: "You're not going to stay here the whole time."

Hayley: "Oh yes, I am, I'm not leaving you."

Hayley's words fell on Jordan's heart strings.

Jordan: "Hal you have done enough for me already. You don't have to stay here any longer. Dan will be back soon, and he will take me home when I get released."

Hayley: "Jordan, I will let you know when I have had enough. Until then, we'd better figure out something to talk about."

Since the two hardly knew anything about each other, they spent most of the night asking all the boring questions you ask when you meet someone for the first time. They made a game out of it, laughing at each other's responses.

Hayley, with a bubbly personality, said, "So Jordan, what do you do for a living?"

Jordan, in a cocky voice, said, "I am a drug agent."

Hayley replied, "Oh my God, that is so cool, do you like to shoot people or something?"

Jordan laughed, "Hayley, what is your favorite color?"

Hayley replied, "It's obviously pink."

Hayley followed up by, "How many siblings do you have?"

Jordan replied, "Two sisters and a brother."

Hayley said, "Oh my gosh, that is awesome."

The two continued the game until the next morning the doctor came into the room. Hayley had her head lying on her hands on the edge of Jordan's hospital bed, and Jordan had his head turned towards Hayley. Dr. Patel knocked on the door loudly, waking Jordan up.

Dr. Patel: "Good morning, Jordan. We are about to move you to a room. I want to observe you for another day."

Jordan: "Okay, Doc, I appreciate it."

Dr. Patel walked out, and Jordan looked over at Hayley. She was asleep, and Jordan put his hand on Hayley's arm. "Hal, Hal, wake up," he said, shaking her arm a little. Hayley lifted her head, asking, "What's wrong?"

Jordan: "Nothing, Hal. I am about to get moved into a room."

Hayley: "Oh, okay!"

Hayley lifted herself off the bed and sat up in the chair, trying to wake up. A few minutes later, a nurse came in and took Jordan and Hayley to the room where he would be staying for at least another night. As they got to the room, a nurse came in and checked Jordan's vitals and left after making small talk with Jordan.

"She was sweet with you," Hayley said, smiling.

Jordan replied, "No, and she also looks to be maybe 20."

Hayley laughed, "You know it's the whole drug agent thing."

Jordan laughed, "Yeah, that's it."

Hayley: "Can I get anything for you? I mean, I feel useless sitting here doing nothing."

Jordan: "How about smuggling me some good food in here?"

Hayley: "Like what is good to you? You act like I should know."

Jordan: "A greasy hamburger with everything but mayonnaise on it."

Hayley: "Okay, well, that is going to be a few more hours before I can get you one of those. How about this? I will let you get settled in here, and then I will run to the house, get a change of clothes for you, and take a cold shower. I'm sure the electricity isn't back yet. I'll pick up the greasy hamburger and smuggle it in here for you."

Jordan: "That sounds great. Where did we leave off last night before we passed out?"

Hayley: "I don't remember exactly. Maybe the best childhood memory."

Jordan: "Mmmm, that's a hard one. I guess each year for Veterans Day, we would all load up and go to this hotel on the beach called The Lodge. We would stay there through the weekend. The whole family either went swimming at the beach or we ate together. It was the only time I remember my parents and all the kids together and happy. We did that until my older brother graduated, and then it just stopped. Kind of sad, but I guess we all grew up. What about you, Hal?"

Jordan said as he was shifting one of his legs in the bed with his arms.

Hayley thought about it and was quiet for a moment.

Hayley: "When my dad left, my mom and I stayed in the house for a while but ended up moving into a smaller house. It wasn't a new house, but my mom said it was a fresh start and a new adventure. She let me pick out my room colors, and of course, I picked two different shades of pink."

Hayley smiled. Jordan's heart hurt for Hayley in that moment, realizing she didn't have both of her parents in her life.

Hayley continued, "The house my mom still lives in today. We had a sense of freedom. There were so many laughs and lots of dancing, just me and her. We made so many memories I will never forget."

Jordan: "I am sorry about your dad."

Hayley: "No, no need to be sorry. It worked out for the best, and I believe I wouldn't have had all the great memories I have of that house and those times with my mom."

Jordan: "Did your mom ever remarry?"

Hayley: "Eventually she did, but it was after I was out of the house. It was just me and her until after I graduated."

Jordan: "Wow, where is your mom now?"

Hayley: "She is still in the town I moved from; still married and happy."

Jordan: "Why do you think she waited so long to get married?"

Hayley: "I think she got burned pretty bad by my dad. She never talked about it and let me form my own opinion; I think that was part of it. The other part of it was that she wanted me to be independent. She didn't want me to believe I had to depend on some guy; she wanted me to make my own career and path in life."

Jordan: "Did she have boyfriends?"

Hayley: "If she did, I never knew about them. It was always just me and her."

Jordan: "Did you ever go on vacations?"

Hayley (laughing): "Yes, Jordan, we went on vacations. We weren't poor. She was independent before my dad. We went to the beach a lot, saw shows together, and movies. We did everything a two-parent household does."

Jordan: "Hal, I didn't mean anything by it."

Jordan was concerned he had crossed the line.

Hayley: "No, it's okay. What about your parents? Are they still together?"

Jordan: "Yes, George and Robin are still married, living the life without kids. Traveling and seeing the world."

Hayley (smiling): "Sounds like a dream."

Jordan: "From us talking, I am guessing that you are the only child?"

Hayley: "Yes, it was only me. My mom had a miscarriage after me, and then my dad left a few years later. So, it was only me."

Jordan: "Ahhh, let's stay away from that subject. What was your first car?"

Hayley (laughing): "A 1980 Chevy Camaro."

Jordan: "Owww vintage."

Hayley: "What was yours?"

Jordan: "A 1990 Toyota Tacoma."

Hayley: "Sooo typical."

Jordan (laughing): "Why do you say that?"

Hayley (grinning): "Just typical. I'd better go. Let me go get you some clean clothes, you are starting to stink."

Jordan: "You don't smell so great either, Hal."

Hayley: "Greasy cheeseburger with everything but mayonnaise."

Jordan: "You got it correct."

Hayley: "Okay, I'll be back."

Hayley walked out of the room, into the hallway.

Jordan smiled at Hayley as she walked out of the room. He leaned his head back on the pillow, looking at the ceiling, replaying the conversation with Hayley in his mind. *I can understand why she is the way she is. She didn't have a dad. Maybe there is more to her story than I imagined. Damn, I really like her; she is different.*

Jordan closed his eyes and fell asleep thinking of Hayley.

Chapter 13:

We Were Lucky

Hayley finally made it home. As she unlocked the door to her house, it felt like a sauna was hitting her in the face. Emma greeted her, happy to see her. She went into the bathroom and looked in the mirror, horrified at how bad she looked. *Oh my God, what the hell.* Hayley turned on the water; of course, no hot water, but it was good enough to use it to shower.

As Hayley got in the shower, the thought of Eric popped into her mind. Her mind wandered through different memories of her and Eric laughing together, the times when Eric and she were learning about each other. They already knew a lot about each other when they started dating, but it was the little details—like the ones she and Jordan had talked about—that made all the difference. Hayley smiled, thinking about the memories of Eric.

During the whole storm, she had not thought about Eric, only Jordan and getting him help. Now, memories of Eric rang through her mind. Hayley found herself fighting between the memories of Eric and the time she had just spent with Jordan. It felt as if she was cheating on Eric; that, in a way, she was forgetting about it. To Hayley, it was confusing as she had already made up her mind, Jordan was not a friend, he was an enemy.

As Hayley got out of the shower, her phone rang.

"Where the hell have you been? I've been trying to get a hold of you. Hal, I have been worried sick about you." It was Christian.

Hayley: "Yeah, I am fine. Service is just really bad here, Christian."

Christian: "Have you got power back?"

Hayley: "No. It has been a day or so."

Christian: "A Day or so? Hal, what the hell is going on there? How can't you remember what day it is?"

Hayley: "It's just been crazy here. There is a lot of damage, and things have been crazy."

Christian: "Are you okay? That's all that is important."

Hayley: "Yes, I am fine. Still no power, but I am good."

Christian: "Good, we are still going to come Saturday morning for sure. You know that is in two days, right> Like today is Thursday, Friday, and then we will be there in the morning."

Hayley: "Yes, I got it!"

She said, rummaging through Jordan's clothes, pulling out something for him to wear.

Christian: "Hal, what are you doing? And where have you been?"

Hayley: "Christian, I have been in the hospital with Jordan. When the tree came through the roof, it really screwed up his leg. He had to have surgery yesterday, and I stayed with him. His friend Dan is helping with the cleanup, and he is pretty upset about it, so I stayed with him."

Christian was quiet, not knowing whether to laugh at the fact that Hayley cared about Jordan or the fact that Jordan may have just lost his career as a law enforcement officer. Instead of joking, Christian asked, "How bad is it, Hal? Is he going to be able to come back?"

Hayley sat down on the couch and placed Jordan's clothes next to her and replied, "It's not bad that he won't be able to walk, but it is bad where SWAT and the drug squad may not be in his future."

Christian: "Damn. Does he know it yet?"

Hayley: "If he does, he hasn't said anything. The doctor told him to just make it through the next few weeks, and then they would talk about it."

Christian: "Man, I hate that for him. We both know that is crushing."

Hayley: "Yeah, I know."

Christian: "What are you going to do tonight? Can't be much you can do."

Hayley: "I came home to take a shower and grab some clothes for Jordan. I am going to take the clothes back to him, and I told him I would smuggle in a greasy cheeseburger, with no mayonnaise."

Christian couldn't hold the laughter this time. He laughed hysterically.

Hayley: "Why are you laughing, Christian?"

Christian: "You are going to hang out with your neighbor and bring him clothes and a cheeseburger?"

Hayley: "Yes. What else am I going to do? The good thing is that the hospital has electricity."

Christian: "Oh, that's why? You are going to hang out with your hated neighbor for electricity?"

Hayley: "Christian, it's not like that. He needs help right now. He doesn't have anyone else."

Christian (laughing): "Oh, okay!"

Hayley: "Let me go, Christian. I will see you in two days, technically less."

Christian: "Okay, Hayley. Go assist your neighbor."

Hayley: "Jordan, his name is Jordan, and goodbye, Christian."

Laughing, Christian said, "Bye, Hal."

Kelsey was sitting on the couch when Christian walked into the room. She asked, "Hey, how is Hal?"

Christian sat down and replied, "She is doing good. Heading back to the hospital to take Jordan some clothes and smuggle a greasy cheeseburger into him."

Kelsey smiled, "Oh, really?"

Christian chuckled, "Yeah. Whether she admits it or not, I have seen this before."

Kelsey asked, "With Eric?"

Christian replied, "Yeah, they fought like cats and dogs for a long time. The same thing, Hal thought he was a prick and arrogant."

"Well, I think it is good for her to have someone around," Kelsey said.

"It is just kind of weird. I never thought I would have to think of anyone but her and Eric. It was Hal and Eric for so long, Kelsey," Christian said.

Kelsey got up and walked over to where Christan was sitting and wrapped her arms around Christian's neck, "I know."

"I am happy for her if she likes him, but it's going to be so hard to see. Eric was my brother, my best friend," Christian started to tear up, but fought back the tears from falling.

"I can't imagine what you are going to feel. I know how weird it will be for me too, but we can't forget Hal is young Christian, we knew this might happen," Kelsey said, reassuring Christian.

Christian and Kelsey continue to hug, both silent in their thoughts.

Hayley had made it to get Jordan his hamburger and fries and was headed back to the hospital. Trees were still down, and Hayley was maneuvering around them. Very few were on the roads. Most people were finding somewhere open to eat or helping get trees out of the middle of the road. As Hayley looked at the damage surrounding her, her phone rang.

"Hey, I am just checking on you."

It was Jordan.

Hayley: "Why are you checking on me? I am fine. Not only did I get you a greasy cheeseburger with no mayo, I got greasy french fries too."

Jordan laughed, "Renegade, I see. Smuggling in the fries, too. Well, be careful in my truck. I just wanted to check on you."

Hayley: "Oh, so this is what it is about. You are worried about my driving in your truck. "

Jordan (laughing): "Just bring my truck back in one piece, please."

Hayley: "I got this, goodbye Jordan."

"Bye," Jordan said, setting down the phone, smiling.

"Knock knock."

Jordan looked in the direction of the room door. It was Dan.

Jordan: "Hey, man."

Dan: "Who was that on the phone?"

Jordan: "Oh, it was just Hayley. She went to get me some clothes and something to eat."

Dan: "The man-eater went to get you clothes and something to eat?"

Jordan: "Oh, stop, she is being nice, and Hal is not that bad."

Dan looked at Jordan like he had lost all his senses.

Dan: "You're kidding me, right? What has gotten into you?"

Jordan: "Nothing, dude. She just helped me out even when she didn't have to, and she slept here keeping me company."

Dan: "She slept here last night?"

Jordan: "Yeah."

Dan: "Eww, I would have loved to be a fly on the wall last night here. What did she do, read you Taming of the Shrew?"

Jordan (laughing): "You're an idiot. No, we talked."

Dan: "What did you guys have to talk about? All night?"

Jordan: "Stuff, dude. We just talked about different things."

Dan looked at Jordan, "You like her."

Jordan: "No man."

Dan: "You damn like her. Holy shit, Jordan."

Jordan: "It's fine, nothing is going on. She's not bad at all, Dan, and she is funny."

Dan: "Here we go again."

Jordan: "No, and I really don't want to talk about this with you of all people."

Dan: "When do you get out of here?"

Jordan: "Probably tomorrow sometime."

Dan's phone began to ring. He answered, "Hello, yeah, I am checking on him right now. He is doing well. Probably going to get out of here sometime tomorrow. Alright, give me about 15 minutes, and I can get there. Bye."

Jordan looked at Dan, "Duty calls."

"Yes, but I can't wait to hear all about these interesting conversations with you and the shrew," Dan said, walking towards the door.

Jordan: "Stop it."

Dan smiled and started humming, So This Is Love by Ilene Woods.

Jordan started laughing, "Get out of here."

Dan kept humming, turning around, and walking away.

Jordan, still smiling, lay his head back on his pillow, thinking to himself how much Dan loved teasing him. He was a good friend to Jordan and had been through a lot with him. Somewhere in the middle of his thoughts, he closed his eyes. He was deep in thought when he heard tapping on his door. He looked up and smiled. It was Hayley.

Jordan: "Hey!"

Hayley: "So, Dan went speeding out of here."

Jordan: "Yeah, they called him to go help."

Hayley: "Ah, well, you owe me, I broke the rules for you."

Hayley sat down and opened the backpack she was carrying. Jordan sat up as Hayley grabbed the cheeseburger and fries out of the bag.

Jordan: "You are the best. Thank you so much."

Jordan took a bite.

Jordan: "This is so good, do you want a bite?"

Hayley: "Nah, I am good."

Jordan: "What, you don't eat greasy hamburgers?"

Hayley: "I'm a vegetarian."

Chewing on the cheeseburger, Jordan looked at Hayley, "You're kidding me?"

Hayley: "No, I have been one for a while now; about 10 years."

Jordan: "What are you, an animal rights activist or something?"

Hayley giggled, "No, Jordan, I just don't eat meat. I'm not a tree hugger or anything like that."

Jordan: "How was it driving? Were there a lot of people out?"

Hayley: "No, it was pretty clear. Just people cutting things up and a few people trying to find something to eat."

Jordan: "Did you have electricity at the house?"

"No, it was a cold shower," Hayley said as she handed Jordan the fries.

"Ahh, a shower. I need a shower," Jordan said as he grabbed the fries from Hayley, passing her the cheeseburger wrapper.

Hayley: "I'm sure one of these ladies would love to help you into the shower."

Jordan: "Ha, funny, but you are right. Do you mind?"

Hayley: "I'm not helping you."

Jordan: "No, do you mind if I take a shower?"

Hayley: "I really don't! You stink."

Jordan laughed and hit the call button for the nursing station.

Nurse: "Can I help you?"

Jordan: "Yes, ma'am. Can I get some help with getting into the shower? If possible, pretty please."

The nurse giggled, "Yes, Jordan, I will be right there."

Hayley looked at Jordan, "Oh my geezus, you have got to be kidding me."

Jordan: "I got it like that."

Hayley: "You're an idiot, Jordan."

The nurse walked in, "I am here."

Hayley stood up, "I think I am going to go downstairs and get something to drink. Do you want anything?"

Jordan: "No, I am good. Do you have my clothes?"

Hayley reached into the bag and handed Jordan the clothes she had brought him.

Hayley: "I didn't know what kind of panties you wanted, so I got you ones to match your outfit."

Jordan: "Hayley, don't ever call my underwear panties again."

Hayley laughed as she grabbed the bag and walked out of the room.

Jordan turned to the nurse, "She's got jokes."

The nurse helped Jordan out of the bed and into the bathroom.

Hayley, pleased with herself, got on the elevator and headed downstairs to where the drinks machines were. Hayley walked towards the drink machine and noticed how many people were sitting in the lobby. She could tell the individuals had not showered, that the hurricane had either taken their home or they had not left the lobby since the hurricane. Hayley made it to the drink machine and started to insert the money into the machine. She could see a doctor out of the corner of her eye walking towards a female and a male who were sitting in the lobby.

Hayley grabbed her drink and turned around. She stood looking at the doctor talking to the male and female. The female started yelling, "Oh God, no, please no." Hayley watched as the female began to cry and sat down in the chair, she had once been sitting in. The male tried to comfort her as the doctor was still speaking. Hayley watched as the male began to cry and talk to the doctor. His arm was around the female, trying to comfort her. Hayley's heart was heavy watching the scene unfold. She hurt for the two, knowing someone was gone. They had lost someone in the storm. Hayley stood lost in her thoughts; she did not see someone walk up on her.

"Excuse me, ma'am, are you finished with the machine?"

Hayley looked over, lost in her own thoughts, trying to process what the person had just said.

"Yes, I am sorry!" Hayley said, stepping aside and walking towards the direction she had come from, still looking at the male and female. She stared in the direction of the male and female until she could no longer see them. She stepped on the elevator, heading back to Jordan's room. She realized at that moment how lucky she and Jordan were that they had made it out of the storm. Yes, Jordan had a tree through his house and a long recovery, but at least they were both here. As the elevator opened, Hayley walked past the nursing station, seeing the nurse that helped Jordan.

Hayley walked into Jordan's room.

Hayley: "You look a lot better."

Jordan: "I feel a lot better, but that hurt like a bitch."

Hayley: "It will get easier."

Jordan: "You were gone a while; anything interesting going on in the hospital. Did you get lost?"

Hayley: "Funny. No, I didn't get lost. In the lobby, there were two people crying. They lost someone, I am guessing. I didn't think about it, but I guess we are lucky."

Jordan: "Most people don't take the storms seriously. They probably were out in the middle of it."

Hayley: "You don't know that Jordan. Don't be cynical. You got hurt, and you were inside."

Jordan: "You are right, but more times than not, people get hurt because they were doing something they shouldn't have."

Hayley: "That could have been us, Jordan."

Jordan: "Hal, it wasn't our time."

Hayley: "You believe that we have a certain time we go?"

Jordan: "Yes, I believe that, especially in the work I do. You don't? You believe it is always accidents?"

Hayley: "I choose not to believe that my life was shattered because it was Eric's time to die. I can't believe that it was planned out and already decided."

Jordan: "I didn't think about it like that."

Changing the subject because Jordan knew there was no good going to come from the conversation, "How was my girl Emma doing?"

Hayley: "She was good, upset I didn't have her new bestie with me, but doing as good as can be expected, as hot as it is in the house. Did they tell you anything else about when they were going to release you?"

Jordan: "No, not yet. The doctor is supposed to be back in soon for evening rounds. Why are you trying to get out of here?"

Hayley: "No, Jordan! I am trying to figure out if you are going to be here over the weekend or not."

Hayley and Jordan spoke about general stuff. Both were kind of tired but continued to talk. They could talk about anything and never run out of things to say. Minutes turned into an hour when they heard a knock at the door. They turned, and it was Dr. Patel.

Dr. Patel: "Good evening, Jordan, Hayley."

Jordan looked over at Dr. Patel.

Jordan: "Hey Doc, what do you have for me?"

Dr. Patel: "Well, Jordan, I think you are recovering pretty well. I am thinking about releasing you tomorrow morning, if everything goes well tonight."

Jordan: "That's good news, Doc."

Dr. Patel: "Listen, Jordan, I need you to stay off your leg, don't push yourself for the first few weeks when you get home."

Jordan: "You got it, Doc."

Dr. Patel: "Jordan, your recovery and what you will be able to do is counting on you not pushing yourself. I know how you guys do. No work and stay off the leg. Ms. Hayley, will you make sure that Jordan does not push himself?"

Hayley: "Yes, of course. I will keep him contained."

Dr. Patel (smiling): "I will see you two before you leave tomorrow in the morning, and then we will get you released."

Jordan: "Thank you, Doc."

Dr Patel turned and walked out. Jordan looked at Hayley, "This is freaking great news, I'll get home and can-do things."

Hayley looked at Jordan, "You do not listen at all."

"What?" Jordan said, looking confused.

Hayley: "He just told you to sit down and not overdo it."

Jordan: "Yeah, but he tells that to everyone, I will be fine."

Hayley: "But what if you're not Jordan. You could make it worse."

Jordan: "Oh, Hal, I will be fine. Plus, I have you to keep me under control."

Hayley: "I am not your mother, Jordan. You need to listen."

Jordan: "Oh, thank God you aren't. It will be fine, Hal. I won't push myself, I promise."

Hayley started to move back and forth in the chair. Jordan looked at her, "What's wrong?"

Hayley said, "Nothing, I need a pillow on this chair. They are so uncomfortable."

Jordan: "Come get in bed with me."

Hayley: "You are sick. I am not getting in bed with you."

Jordan: "Oh, Hal, you are wishful thinking. I can't move my leg, remember. Geezus."

Hayley looked at Jordan; she could tell he was shocked that she felt he was hitting on her.

Hayley: "The bed is too small for both of us."

Jordan: "You're kidding me, right? We aren't big people, Hal. Come on, I'll scoot over." Jordan started to move over in the bed, and Hayley got up and got into the bed with him.

Jordan: "Better?"

Hayley: "Yes, much better."

Jordan turned on the TV, and the two sat in silence watching random shows on TV, just to pass the time. Before they knew it, they were fast asleep.

Dan, getting a moment to break away, headed to the hospital. He tried to call Jordan, but his phone went straight to voicemail. Dan wondered about Hayley. What was her intent? What did she want from Jordan? Money? Security? A baby? Dan did not trust Hayley, and he feared Jordan being hurt all over again. The two had a pact together, never to fall prey again, never to let someone get to them again. Dan knew Jordan was acting differently. He had seen it before. He saw it when Jordan had met Jessica years ago.

Dan made it to the hospital and made his way to Jordan's room. He wondered if Hayley would be there or if she had finally left Jordan alone. He was vulnerable right now; he wasn't thinking straight. It was not a good time for Hayley to be spending so much time with Jordan. Dan made it to the room door and knocked before walking in.

Dan began to say, "How is my" and stopped. Dan looked and saw Jordan and Hayley lying in the bed, fast asleep. Hayley had her head on Jordan's shoulder, and Jordan was resting his head on Hayley's head. They were turned towards each other, slightly holding each other's hands. Dan backed out of the room, looking at the two one more time. He shut the door slightly and left them alone.

Chapter 14:

Surprise Kisses

Jordan woke in the morning to a nurse standing at the side of his bed, taking his vital signs.

"What time is it?" he whispered.

Nurse: "It's 7:30. I am waiting on Dr. Patel to send me the orders, and we will begin checking you out."

Jordan: "Okay, thank you."

Nurse: "You know, Jordan, you are lucky you are who you are. You know we don't allow people to sleep in the bed together."

Jordan: "I know, thank you."

Nurse: "I will bring you the paperwork when I get it from Dr. Patel."

"Thank you," Jordan whispered.

Jordan looked over at Hayley. The two were still holding hands. Jordan did not want to let go of her hand or wake her. He liked the feeling of Hayley being so close to him. She looked so peaceful when she slept, like she felt safe and comfortable. Jordan let Hayley sleep, trying not to move much, watching TV, and periodically looking at Hayley.

The peace was interrupted 30 minutes later when the breakfast cart came in, ramming up against the wall. Hayley jumped and woke up.

Startled, trying to remember where she was. "It's okay, just an idiot with a cart," Jordan said, looking over.

Server: "Good morning, how did you sleep?"

Jordan: "Pretty good."

"Well, good," the server said, handing Jordan a tray and adding, "Have a blessed day."

Jordan: "You too, ma'am."

Hayley sat up as the server left the room, "I was sleeping, good."

Jordan opened the tray and grabbed the bacon, "Oh yeah."

Hayley: "Yeah, how long were you up before me?"

Jordan: "About 30 minutes, I was watching TV, going to let you sleep."

Hayley: "Why, you weirdo?"

Jordan laughed, "I figured you needed to sleep. Want some bacon?"

Hayley slides off the bed and into the chair, "Hell no. Did they get your orders yet?"

Jordan: "No waiting on Dr. Patel."

There was a knock at the door.

"Good morning, Jordan, Hayley." Both said good morning to Dr. Patel.

Dr. Patel: "You are good to go. They will need you to sign some paperwork, and they will get you checked out. They will bring a wheelchair up here, and you can go home."

Jordan: "Oh, I am not using a wheelchair," Jordan said with pride.

Hayley looked at Dr. Patel, "We are so using the wheelchair."

Dr. Patel smiled, "You guys take care." Dr. Patel walked out, and almost immediately, a nurse came in with paperwork for Jordan to sign. Jordan signed the paperwork, and the nurse said, "Let me get you the wheelchair, and you can go home."

"Okay, thank you," Hayley said before she left.

After the nurse closed the door, Jordan turned to Hayley, "I want to walk out of here. I don't want to use a wheelchair."

Hayley: "Jordan, don't be stubborn. You have to for now."

About ten minutes later, the nurse came back in and brought the wheelchair. Jordan sat down in the wheelchair, and Hayley grabbed all of the things sitting around the room.

Hayley began to wheel Jordan. Jordan said, "This is so embarrassing."

Hayley leaned over to Jordan, "You owe me, buddy."

Jordan smiled as Hayley wheeled him out of the room and down to the front lobby, where she parked him.

"Let your chafer get the car. I will be right back," Hayley said.

Hayley walked to Jordan's truck and pulled it towards where she had left Jordan. When she got close, she could see Jordan talking to a female. The female had her hand on Jordan's shoulder and was smiling. Jordan was smiling talking back to the female. Hayley pulled up and got out of the truck. The female looked over at Hayley and then at Jordan, "I'll talk to you later. I hope you feel better, Jordan."

Jordan said, "Thank you, Mary." With that, the female walked off.

Hayley opened the door, "One of your many women?"

Jordan smiled, which made Hayley jealous, "No, but why are you jealous?"

"No, I was just wondering," Hayley replied. The truth was it did bother Hayley a little. It bothered her in a way she did not understand. She didn't even like Jordan; why was it bothering her so much? Hayley helped Jordan get in the truck. Hayley began to drive; both were quiet until Jordan broke the silence.

Jordan: "You know what I can't wait for?"

Hayley: "What is that, Jordan?"

Jordan lifted a plastic bag and grabbed a book out of it.

Jordan: "To get to the house and start reading this book."

Hayley smiled, "Where did you get that book from?"

Jordan: "I bought it in the gift shop when you left to get the car."

Hayley: "What did you buy?"

Jordan: "Huh, The Notebook by Nicholas Sparks."

Hayley laughed, "You have never read the book or seen the movie?"

Jordan: "No."

Hayley: "Why did you choose that book?"

Jordan: "It kind of sounded like the other book, two people who liked each other separated and then got back together again."

Hayley: "Those are two totally different books, but I think you will love that book."

Jordan: "I don't know about that, but I figured I owed you."

Hayley smiled, "Yes, you do."

As the two pulled up to the house, they stopped in the driveway, just staring at the house and the damage around it.

Hayley looked at Jordan, "Are you ready?"

Jordan replied, "Yeah."

Hayley got out of the truck and opened Jordan's door. Jordan slid out of the seat, landing on his good leg. Jordan wrapped his arm around Hayley's neck, and Hayley wrapped her arm around his waist. The two slowly made it into the house, and Jordan sat down on the couch. Emma came up to Jordan, excited that someone was home.

"Hey girl, I know you missed me. I am home, don't worry. I didn't forget about you," Jordan said to Emma. Hayley rolled her eyes and walked back outside to get all of the items out of the vehicle before returning to the house. Hayley dropped everything by the coffee table where Jordan was sitting. Hayley sat down, and as she did, she heard beeping and the lights flicker. "Oh my God, we have power," Hayley said, excited.

Jordan: "Oh, thank God, it is going to be a really hot day."

Hayley got up and turned on the washer for the clothes that were wet. She could hear Jordan turn on the TV. When she walked back into the room, Jordan was staring intently at the storm damage and said, "It was pretty bad, Hal." Hayley sat down and watched with Jordan. There were places hit so bad, it was like they had been demolished.

"Wow, that looks pretty bad," Hayley said, looking at all of the damage being shown.

Jordan: "Yeah, it does. The boys are going to be busy for a while."

Hayley: "Who, Dan and the department?"

Jordan: "Yeah."

Hayley's phone began to ring. Jordan turned down the TV and Hayley walked to the kitchen.

Hayley: "Hey, Christian."

Christian: "Hal, have you made it home?"

Hayley: "Yep, we got home about 30 minutes ago."

"We huh?" Christian began to laugh.

Hayley: "Don't start. Are you still coming tomorrow morning?"

Christian: "Yes, that is what I am calling for. Do you guys have power, or do we need to stay somewhere close by?"

Hayley: "Yes, we do have power, but Christian, there is nowhere to stay even if you wanted to. You are stuck with me and Emma."

Christian: "Oh, let's not forget Jordan Hal."

Hayley: "Oh, stop it. Is Kelsey excited to come?"

Christian: "Yes, of course she is. She said she needs some female time."

Hayley: "Yes, we do, and you can have bromance time with Jordan."

Jordan heard Hayley, turned, and looked at her. Hayley smiled at Jordan.

Christian: "Hayley, bromance really? I think I will settle for liking him."

Hayley laughed, "Alright, we will see. What time in the morning?"

Christian: "Probably around 10 if you will be up. You know you have this casual life now."

Hayley: "Yes, Christian, I will be up by then. So, it's set, I will see you at 10. I am so excited."

Christian: "We are too. See you tomorrow, Hal. Bye."

Hayley: "Bye, Christian."

Jordan, hearing Hayley get off the phone, turned in her direction.

Jordan: "You don't think it will be weird for me to be here when they come? I mean, I can crash at Dan's house for sure. I don't want anyone to feel uncomfortable."

Hayley: "No, of course not. Why would it be weird?"

Jordan: "Come on, Hal. Eric's best friend, you guys used to do everything together."

"I never thought about that?" Hayley said as she stared off.

Hayley: "No, Christian and Kelsey are good people. They will like you; I know it."

Jordan: "They will like me? Like you liked me up until about 3 days ago."

Hayley laughed, "Well, we bonded during a traumatic experience."

"Yeah, and I don't want another traumatic experience, as you call it, anytime soon," Jordan said, smiling.

Hayley: "It will be fine, truly it will be. He's a cop, you're a cop. Kelsey deals with cops all the time."

"Just because I am a cop doesn't mean I like all cops, Hal", Jordan said, chuckling.

Jordan: "Just promise me something, if it gets weird, please tell me, and I will go to Dan's. I won't think any differently about you."

Hayley: "Okay, I promise."

Jordan did not want the situation to feel weird with Christian and Kelsey. He wanted to just go to Dan's house and stay away from the life that he knew very little about. He was torn between wanting to be there with Hayley; he knew it would be hard to see them, and he really did want to meet people from before Eric's death. He wanted to know who Hayley was, and he actually wanted them to like him.

Hayley jumped up, "What do you want to do? We have time to kill."

Jordan: "Well, I am not doing much. Want to read?"

Hayley: "Jordan Voss, do you really want to read a romance novel?"

Jordan: "No, not at all, but I will sit and listen to you read it and ask a ton of questions."

Hayley went to where she had dropped the stuff from the vehicle earlier and grabbed the book out of the plastic bag it was sitting in.

Hayley: "I will tell you, this is a tear-jerker."

Jordan: "Bring on the tears, let's do it."

Jordan laid back on the couch while Hayley laid on the other side of the L-shape couch. She began reading. Jordan sat quietly for a long time listening to every word that Hayley spoke. Hayley did her best to read every meaning of the words on the page.

As they moved through the book, an hour had passed before Jordan finally spoke.

"Hal, I got to pee," Jordan told Hayley. Hayley had not thought about that part of the arrangement the two had made.

Hayley asked, "Okay, what do I need to do?"

Jordan replied, "If you will help me up, I can do the rest."

Hayley put down the book and walked over to Jordan. She grabbed the crutches for Jordan, and he grabbed them.

"Hold that thought, I will be right back," Jordan said.

Hayley sat down, listening in case Jordan fell or needed her. After what felt like forever, Jordan finally reappeared in the room.

Jordan said, "I got it handled, but the crutches and washing my hands were not happening at the moment."

Hayley leaned over and opened a drawer, removing hand sanitizer from it. She held it up to Jordan, "Use this."

Jordan: "Are you a germaphobe, Hal?"

Hayley: "No, but that's gross."

Jordan made it over to the couch and sat down, holding out his hands for Hayley. Hayley places a glob of hand sanitizer in Jordan's hand.

Jordan massaged it into his hands and looked at Hayley, "Is that better?" "Yep, it is," Hayley replied, grabbing the book and lying back on the couch. Jordan laid back on the couch.

Once Hayley felt Jordan was comfortable, she began reading again. Jordan sat and listened to every word that came out of Hayley's mouth. He listened intently as if to decide whether the story could be true or not. Again, another hour had passed, and the only sound in the house was Hayley's voice reading and Emma breathing hard next to Jordan, deep in sleep. The knock at the door made Hayley and Jordan jump. "Gezzus, that scared me," Hayley said. "Right, who could that be, your boyfriend?" Jordan guessed.

"Ha, funny, probably one of your girlfriends," Hayley replied as she set the book down on the coffee table at the page they were at. Jordan turned the volume up on the TV, acting like he was watching TV.

Hayley opened the door. It was Dan. "Hi," Hayley said.

Dan: "Hi. Can I speak with Jordan?"

Hayley: "Yeah, come in, it's not like he can get up to you easily."

Dan pushed past Hayley, which irritated Hayley.

"Jordan, my man. How are you feeling?" Dan said while smacking hands and bumping arms.

Jordan: "I am good. What have you been up to?"

Dan: "Working not like you. You are laid up in this house just relaxing."

Jordan: "Yeah, exactly what I want to be doing right now."

Hayley could tell Jordan's character had changed from moments earlier. He was cockier; his ego was showing through, and Hayley wanted nothing to do with it.

Hayley: "Look, I am going to leave you guys to it. I have to get some stuff for tomorrow anyway. Do you want me to pick up anything for you?"

Dan, without turning towards Hayley, said, "No, I am fine."

"I wasn't asking you, Dan, I was asking Jordan."

Jordan looked at Dan; he knew the comment did not sit right with Dan.

Jordan: "What about some chicken Hal? I can cook it on the grill. I can sit down doing that."

"Okay, I will be back," Hayley said as she grabbed her things and walked out of the house.

Dan looked at Jordan, "Man, she is moody."

Jordan: "Well, dude, you came into her house and acted like you owned it."

Dan: "Are you defending her?"

Jordan: "No, I just know how much you can be a dick at times."

Dan started laughing.

Dan: "This is true, I will give you that one. What the hell do you guys do? I mean, she has no personality."

Jordan laughed, "She is not bad, Dan. She's actually pretty funny and interesting to talk to."

Dan: "So, what have you guys been doing then?"

Dan looked down at the coffee table, then picked up the book.

Dan: "You reading love stories?"

Jordan laughed, "No, but I do want to know how you know that book is a love story."

Dan: "Who doesn't? Every chic digs the story. What are you doing? Are you trying to move in on her? Take your shot?"

Jordan laughed, but the comment kind of irritated him.

Jordan: "No, Dan, not with her. She has been reading, and I have been watching TV."

Dan could tell by Jordan's comment that there was more than Jordan was telling him.

Dan: "What is it with her?"

Jordan looked at Dan, "Nothing. There is nothing to tell Dan. She is helping me while I am down. I mean, damn, she took me in, she helped me get free, she took me to the hospital, she stayed with me. The least I can do is be nice to her."

"You like her," Dan said, looking at Jordan.

Jordan: "Man, Dan, did you come over here to talk about her the whole time or what?"

Dan knew Jordan was not going to tell him what was going on.

Dan: "Okay, damn, I'll drop it."

Dan and Jordan continued to talk. Jordan wanted to hear about everything that was going on with work. He wanted to know all of the exciting things he was missing. It hurt not being out in the midst of it all. Jordan felt he was letting everyone down. It angered him that he had been hurt, and he felt he should have been more careful with his decisions and his surroundings during the storm.

The two talk about work, the new woman in Dan's life he met during the storm, and the rumors going around at work. The two were laughing when they heard the door open. Both looked towards the door. Dan had a blank stare on his face, and Jordan smiled at Hayley as she walked through the door, arms full of groceries. Jordan was the first to speak, "Hal, did you bring everything in at one time?"

"No, but close," she said as she set the groceries on the floor and went back outside to get the rest of them.

Dan turned to Jordan, "I'd better go."

"No, you don't have to leave. It's fine," Jordan said as Hayley barged back through the door, closing it with her foot.

Dan looked at Jordan, "No, I actually do."

Dan stood up and looked at Hayley, "Always a pleasure to see you, Hayley." Dan walked to the door, looking back at Jordan, "I will call you." Dan disappeared through the door.

"Well, that was fun," Jordan said, getting up from the couch and grabbing his crutches.

Hayley was putting away groceries silently.

Jordan: "What's wrong? Did something happen at the store?"

Hayley looked at Jordan, "No."

Jordan: "Was it Dan?"

Hayley: "Oh, there are so many things I could say about Dan, but I won't."

Jordan: "Look, Dan is my friend. He has been through a lot with me. He can be a dick; I do know this."

Hayley: "It's not so much Dan, it's you too."

"What did I do?" Jordan asked, confused and a little irritated at the comment.

Hayley: "As soon as he walked through the door, you could feel the cocky, egotistical person come right out of you. You were a totally different person."

Jordan: "Hal, are you serious right now? I am a cop; you know that is how we are. Hell, you were married to a cop, what made you think I was different?"

Hayley: "No, I guess not. You all are the same."

Jordan: "Hal, calm down."

"I am calm," Hayley said, still putting away groceries.

Jordan could tell she was still irritated. Jordan could see how Hayley could be irritated at Dan and the whole situation.

Jordan: "Hal, I appreciate you more than you know. Look, guys in this career field don't act soft. It is the persona, you know this, but it does not mean anything. I have enjoyed every minute spending time with you."

Hayley: "But just not for anyone to know?"

Jordan: "Look, I would have to quit if I told the guys, Dan, that I bought a romance book and we were sitting here reading it together. Are you kidding me Hal?"

The look on Jordan's face, explaining the severity of the situation, made Hayley smile.

Hayley: "I think you should tell them."

Jordan: "You have lost your mind. I still want my job."

Hayley thought about the sequence of events up to the point they were at.

Hayley: "I am sorry. I don't do the ego, and it irritates me."

"Well, obviously after that outburst," Jordan said with a surprised look on his face.

Hayley smiled.

Jordan: "I mean, can I still stay here, or do I need to go stay in my house, in a room without a tree in it?"

Hayley: "You're an idiot, Jordan. I am not going to throw you out."

Jordan: "Look, let's just decide right now that if we ever irritate each other again, we'll tell each other right away. We deal with it and move on."

Hayley: "Okay, but that is most of the time with you."

Jordan: "Well, we will have to deal with it for a little while. I'll be able to go home eventually."

"Okay but..." Jordan cut off Hayley, "No buts."

Hayley was silent.

Jordan: "Are we good?"

Hayley looked at Jordan, "Yes."

Jordan: "Are we good, like you want to finish our book, or are we good, you're not going to slit my throat if I fall asleep?"

Hayley: "Good that we can read, the jury is still out on the other."

Jordan: "You act like we are married."

Hayley: "You wouldn't know anything about being married."

"I can imagine," Jordan said, sitting back down on the couch.

Hayley grabbed the book and laid back down on her part of the couch. Jordan did the same. Hayley began to read again. Jordan listened to every word that Hayley spoke, looking off in the opposite direction.

Hayley read every word until she read the last words and closed the book. Jordan turned towards Hayley, "That was awful."

Hayley: "What do you mean?"

Jordan: "They freaking died."

Hayley: "Yeah, of course they died, but they were old, and they died together."

Jordan: "And why the hell did they have to make it where she didn't remember. That has got to be the worst of it."

"I think you liked the story," Hayley teased Jordan.

Jordan: "I mean, do you really think people stay together for that long. That seems hard to believe."

Hayley: "Your parents have been married forever. How can you say you don't believe people stay together forever?"

Jordan: "Well, my parents are different."

Hayley: "Well, they were different in the story as well."

Jordan: "Well, it's fiction."

Hayley: "Exactly—where you can have any ending you want, as long as you can draw people in for four and a half hours to read the book."

"Has it been that long?" Jordan looked at Hayley, surprised.

Hayley: "Give or take a few. We did have a break when I went to the store."

Jordan: "That was a waste of a day."

Hayley: "Oh, stop grouch, like what else were you going to do?"

Jordan: "This is true. You hungry? I am getting hungry."

Hayley: "Yeah, we can cook."

Jordan: "You going to eat some chicken?"

Hayley: "Huh, no, but veggie cabobs."

Jordan: "What the hell is that?"

Hayley: "You will see. You are going to try them."

Jordan: "Hal, I am not going to become a vegetarian."

Hayley: "I don't expect you to, you just need to open your eyes to other foods."

Hayley and Jordan got up from the couch. Hayley went to the kitchen to grab the food to go on the grill, and Jordan went outside to start the grill. Hayley walked outside and placed the food on the side of the grill for Jordan before walking back into the house, returning with a stool for Jordan to sit on.

"Thank you", Jordan said as he saw Hayley walking out with the stool.

Hayley sat down on the couch as Jordan began putting the chicken and veggie cabobs on the grill.

Jordan: "Is there anything special I need to do with these?"

Hayley: "No, just put them on the top rack to keep them away from the chicken and to not burn them."

Jordan: "Got it."

After Jordan had everything on the grill, he went over to where Hayley was sitting and sat down, "Let's drink some wine."

Hayley looked at Jordan, surprised, "You are taking medication."

Jordan: "Yeah, but nothing heavy, not taking the pain meds."

Hayley: "I am not agreeing to this."

Jordan: "Hal, I am a big boy. I'll be fine. I've done worse."

Hayley imagined there was no truer statement than what Jordan had just spoken. Jordan looked at Hayley, "One or two glasses, I am not getting drunk, Hal."

Reluctantly, Hayley disappeared into the house and came back with two glasses of wine. She looked at Jordan, "You don't even like wine."

Jordan: "It's growing on me, and I don't want anything hard. I just need to take the edge off a little, dealing with you."

Hayley: "You are such an idiot Jordan."

He sipped the wine Hayley had given him, "I know." Hayley took a slip of her wine, rolling her eyes at Jordan. The two sat and ate once the food was done.

"One of the best parts about this house is the sunsets", Hayley said, pointing to the direction where the sun was setting. The sky was a mixture of pinks and purples as night started to set in.

Jordan: "Yeah, they are pretty good ones. Not that I noticed."

Hayley: "Are you finished? I'll put these in the house."

"I'll help you", Jordan said, standing up on one leg.

"No, I got it, you can wash them later," Hayley said, smiling.

Jordan: "I guess that is the deal."

Jordan sat down on one of the couches on the porch. Hayley returned to the porch, sitting on the chair next to the couch Jordan was sitting on. Jordan had propped his leg on the table sitting in front of the couch.

Jordan: "God, that is uncomfortable."

Hayley: "Why don't you lie back on the couch? It has to be better than that."

Jordan thought Hayley's idea was perfect, and he laid down on the couch.

Both were quiet, listening to the sounds at dusk and the day winding down.

Jordan spoke first, "Have you only been married one time?"

Hayley: "Yeah, that was enough for me."

Jordan: "You would never do it again?"

Hayley: "I don't know. I would like to think I wouldn't, but I am not dumb enough to think I won't."

Jordan: "Do you always have to explain things so complicated?"

Hayley: "What. You asked a simple question, and I answered it."

Jordan: "You could have said maybe."

Hayley: "You could have not asked the question if you didn't like me to answer."

Jordan continued, "Did you want kids?"

Hayley: "Yes, we had spoken about it. It wasn't in our cards at the time. Why all the questions?"

Jordan: "I am just making conversation."

Hayley: "Well, it's my turn then."

Jordan smiled, "Ask away."

Jordan: "Why did you never get married?"

Jordan thought he would lie, thought about not telling her the truth, but he felt he had kept it from Hayley long enough.

"I was married", Jordan said, turning to Hayley's direction.

Hayley had a look of surprise and disbelief.

Hayley: "You were married?"

Jordan: "Yes, Hal, someone actually liked me enough to marry me. Don't act so surprised."

Hayley: "For how long? And where is she at now?"

Jordan: "She lives about an hour away. We were married for about a year."

Hayley: "Wow, do you still talk to her?"

Jordan: "Hell no. I didn't say it was a good marriage."

Hayley: "Was it at first? I mean, you did marry her."

Jordan: "Yeah, of course it was at first. I just married her for the wrong reasons."

Hayley: "What do you mean by the wrong reasons? Was she good in bed or something?"

Jordan laughed, "Yes, if you want to know, but I got her pregnant and we decided to get married and raise the child together."

The picture Hayley had seen must have been the child.

Hayley: "What happened to the child after the divorce, and was it a boy or a girl?"

Jordan: "It's a little girl, Miah. She lives with my ex."

Hayley: "Do you ever get to see her?"

Jordan: "No, my ex stays away, and sometimes I think it is better for Miah."

Hayley: "It is never better for Miah not to have her dad."

Jordan: "The ex has men in and out of her life. I am sure Miah has a lot of male figures in her life."

Hayley: "But they're still not her dad."

Jordan: "I know, maybe one day. It just hasn't been the right time."

Hayley: "How old is she?"

Jordan: "She will be 3 next month. I saw her for a little while after the divorce, but my ex; she is just so hard to deal with."

Hayley: "Where did you meet your ex?"

Jordan: "At a bar."

Hayley: "That should have been a clue, Jordan."

Jordan: "Well, yeah, but bars, alcohol, and the badge bunnies flow like water; all great decisions fly out of the window."

Hayley: "That is true. I'm sorry you had a crappy marriage."

Jordan: "You don't have to be sorry. It happens."

Hayley: "Yeah, it does, but it has shaped the way you view women and relationships."

Jordan: "Hal, I just don't have time to give to a person. I work all the time, and in the harsh times, you know, you dealt with it with your husband. It's a rough life to live, and the divorce rates are horrible in this field. I guess I figured, why try when I already know how it is going to end."

Hayley: "I get that, but you will never know if you don't try. There may be a better circumstance next time."

Jordan: "I am just having fun. I am still young enough. Maybe when I get older, we will see."

Hayley: "Oh, so you want all your options depleted before you choose who is left."

Jordan: "Hal, I am not saying that at all. I just am not in a hurry to rush into anything and have the cycle begin again with another female."

Hayley: "I get that."

The two were quiet. Hayley was trying to process what Jordan had just told her. Jordan was trying to process that Hayley was the only one besides Dan that knew the whole truth about his divorce and Miah.

After what seemed like an hour, Jordan finally spoke, "Well, do you hate me now for not telling you?"

"I always hated you, and that still hasn't changed. But no, you told me at a time that felt comfortable to you," Hayley said, looking at Jordan.

Jordan smiled back, "Hal, you are actually starting to sound like someone who is easy to get along with."

"Oh my friend, don't hold your breath. I am only helping you because I feel bad for you," Hayley said, smirking at Jordan.

Jordan was still looking away, "I'm scared I won't be able to go back and do the job." Hayley's face stopped smirking. She wondered what Jordan had thought about the job and his injury. "I mean, I am trying really hard, Hal. It just seems like the harder I try, the weaker I get. It seems like I have gotten nowhere so far," Jordan added.

"Jordan, it was the hospital PT, and geezus, it's only been a few days," Hayley said, trying to encourage Jordan.

Jordan: "I don't know what I am going to do if I can't do it, Hal. I can't go sit behind a desk at the department and watch while my old crew goes and does things. What career am I going to do besides this? I can't just sit at a desk. I am not smart; I can't go to school and get a degree in something."

Hayley: "Jordan, slow down. Give yourself time, and your body time. Be nice to yourself Jordan. This wasn't a small injury."

Hayley reached out and placed her hand on Jordan's leg. Jordan placed his hand on top of Hayley's, intertwining their fingers, looking down at their hands, "I know, but it is something I may have to think about."

"Well, for now," Hayley jumped up, letting go of Jordan's hand, "I am going to get some more wine. Want a glass?"

Jordan smirked at Hayley, "Are you trying to get me drunk and take advantage of me?"

Hayley replied, "That's wishful thinking, but no. I am trying to kill you."

Jordan laughed, looking at Hayley, "Yes, please. I will be fine."

As Hayley walked off, Jordan watched her. She had a half smile on her face, which made Jordan smile. Jordan thought, *"God, it felt good holding Hayley's hand. What is wrong with me? She is just a friend. Not even a friend or an acquaintance is helping me out. It must be one of those trauma responses, like when people experience something traumatic, they become attracted to their caretaker or capture. What is wrong with me!"*

Hayley reappeared at the door, asking, "What are you thinking about?"

Jordan: "Oh, nothing, it is a quiet night for everything that is going on around us."

Hayley: "Yeah, it actually is. You know, I bought this house because of the view over the back fence."

Jordan: "Oh yeah, why?"

Hayley: "It has the prettiest sunset, and at night, it looks like a painting, the way the moon shines through the trees."

Jordan got up and slid onto the couch Hayley was sitting on, looking in the direction Hayley was looking.

Jordan: "Yeah, I can see that."

Hayley was shocked when Jordan sat next to her, but at the moment, she was enjoying it. Both leaned back on the couch, resting their heads on the couch, placing their feet on the table in front of them, sipping on the wine Hayley had brought. Both were sipping it too fast, and both were equally nervous because they were sitting together.

Jordan: "What time are your friends getting here tomorrow?"

Hayley: "In the morning sometime. Probably around tenish."

Jordan: "I'll make sure I am up and everything is folded up before they get here."

Hayley: "It's okay, they understand the situation."

Jordan: "What do they know? Do they know you don't like me?"

Hayley laughed, turning her head to Jordan, "Yes, they know you frustrate me, and they know what happened and the situation."

Jordan: "How are they taking that?"

Hayley: "They have laughed and know it's typical of me."

Jordan: "Typical you?"

Hayley: "Just that I always try to help people no matter what."

Hayley wasn't going to tell Jordan that this was exactly how it started with her and Eric.

Jordan: "Typical, you let strange men you hardly know stay in your house?"

Hayley and Jordan had turned their faces towards each other. "Stop it," Hayley said, smiling.

"Hal, you said it!" Jordan said, taking his hand and pushing a piece of hair away from Hayley's face.

Jordan: "I am not that bad. I just don't trust people."

Hayley smiled, "And I am not that bad either. I just don't like people."

"Oh, you don't like people?" Jordan said.

"No, I don't like people. They are frustrating," she replied.

Jordan looked at Hayley and, without thinking, he leaned over and kissed Hayley. To his surprise, Hayley kissed him back. Jordan took his hand, placing it in Hayley's hair, holding the back of her head. Hayley placed her hands on Jordan's face, enjoying the moment.

The longer they kissed, the more intense it became—until Hayley pulled back. 'Okay, wait, wait,' she said.

"I am sorry. Did I do something wrong?" Jordan was confused as Hayley appeared to enjoy the moment.

"No, I just wasn't expecting that," Hayley replied as she was taken back; her heart was pounding out of her chest.

"I know, I kissed the shrew," Jordan said, sensing Hayley's confusion at the situation, trying to lighten her mood.

"The shrew!" Hayley said, smiling.

Jordan: "Yeah, that's what Dan calls you, but I think you are pretty cool most of the time."

Hayley: "You are such a jerk, you know that."

Jordan: "Yes, Hal, you tell me that almost every day. I won't forget that."

Hayley: "We need to go to bed. Christian and Kelsey will be here early, and we don't need any more wine."

Hayley stood up with the wine glass.

Jordan stood up next to Hayley, "Yes, you are probably right."

As Hayley turned to go inside, Jordan grabbed her again, pulling her into him, and began kissing her again. Hayley threw her arms around Jordan's neck, leaning in to kiss him. Jordan's hands slid to Hayley's back, pulling her in as close as he could. Both their hearts were racing, their breathing growing heavier. This time, Jordan was the one to pull back. "Okay," he said between breaths. "I'm trying to be good, but I can't hold out much longer before I lay you down on this couch and have my way with you."

Hayley, breathing heavy, looked at Jordan, "You are right, but you did start this."

Jordan: "I know, but I didn't think I would like it this much."

Hayley smiled, "Really?"

Jordan, still breathing heavy, "Yes, and I can't believe I am stopping this. Oh my God, what am I doing?"

Hayley: "Being respectful."

Jordan: "That gets people nowhere, ugh."

Hayley leaned in and kissed Jordan's lips before walking away.

Jordan stood in place; in shock, he had just stopped it. *What is wrong with me? I could have gotten laid. It's Hal, though. She is different.*

Jordan grabbed his crutches, his wine glass and went inside. Hayley was inside washing her wine glass out. Jordan handed her his wine glass. "Thank you," Hayley said. Jordan moved towards the couch, "No, Hal, thank you."

Hayley: "Thank me? For what?"

Jordan: "For getting me drunk and having me kiss you. You knew what you were doing."

"I have no idea what you are talking about," Hayley smiled, looking at Jordan.

Jordan: "Oh yes, you do. I have seen your type before."

Hayley laughed, walking over to where Jordan was. She handed him a blanket and leaned over, kissing his lips. She pulled back inches from his face, "Goodnight, Jordan."

Jordan didn't know whether to kiss her again or say goodnight. As he was thinking, he said, "Goodnight, Hal. I had fun tonight."

"Me too." Hayley stood up and walked to her bedroom.

Oh my God. What the hell is going on! What did we do, and why did that just feel so good and so right? Hayley thought to herself.

Jordan lay back on the couch, covering his face with the pillow. Hayley had got him excited, more excited than he had been in a long time.

Why didn't I take the chance? I could have had her. Why did I stop this? Well, probably because I can't even move my freaking leg. Ugh, I am so stupid. Oh, no one is going to know about this. I will never hear the end of this one.

Hayley lay down on the bed, putting her phone next to her. She rolled over with a smile on her face and fell asleep.

Chapter 15:

The Visit

Hayley woke to her phone ringing. "Hello", Hayley said in a sluggish voice.

Christian: "Hal, you are still asleep?"

Hayley sat up in bed, "No, what time is it?"

"Hal, it's quarter to 10. Remember, we were going to be there at ten?"

Hayley slid out of bed, "Yes, I remember. I'm up, just lost track of time."

"It must have been some kind of night. You are always up early," Christian laughed as he looked at Kelsey.

Hayley: "No, it wasn't, but there was wine, and we stayed up way too late."

Christian: "Who? You and Jordan?"

Hayley knew that after the words came out of her mouth, she said too much. Hayley: "Yeah, remember he is staying with me."

Christian: "Why would you stay up late with him?"

Hayley: "Christian, it's too early, stop interrogating me."

Christian laughed, "I was just calling to tell you that we were running about 30 minutes late. Someone in the car with me didn't want to get up."

Kelsey leaned over towards Christian's phone, "That's not true Hal! You know who doesn't like to get up in the morning."

"Yeah, I remember," Hayley said with a smirk.

Christian: "Well, we will be there soon. Clean the house and be presentable before we get there. Both of you."

Hayley: "Christian stop it."

Christian laughed, "See you soon."

"Bye," Hayley hung up the phone and raced into the other room.

Jordan was still asleep on the couch, "Jordan", "JORDAN".

Jordan sat straight up from a dead sleep, "What's wrong? Hal, what is it?"

Hayley: "We overslept. They are going to be here in 30 minutes."

"Hal, 30 minutes!" Jordan was still trying to wake up. He slid his legs off the couch.

Hayley: "I am going to run and take a shower."

Hayley walked off fast, making her way to the bathroom to take a shower. Jordan stood up on one leg and started folding the blankets up on the couch. Jordan stood on his good leg and fluffed the couch cushions before heading to the kitchen to finish the dishes in the sink. Afterward, he went outside to straighten the cushions on the patio furniture, stepping back to adjust one more before returning inside. Making his way back to the couch, he sat down, exhausted. He felt useless, but at least he was trying to help.

As he was in thought, Hayley popped around the corner in a towel, "You can get in."

Jordan stared at her, "Are you serious right now, after the night we had last night?"

Hayley: "What? I am just telling you, you can get it."

Jordan: "Hal, go get dressed. I am getting up."

Jordan was a little frustrated. *Is she serious right now? I have to act like nothing happened and we don't like each other, and she comes out in a towel.*

Jordan got up from the couch and made his way to the bathroom. He looked in the direction of Hayley's room. Her door was slightly cracked. *Boy, I am getting soft,* he thought before walking into the bathroom and closing the door.

Hayley finished getting dressed and raced out into the living room. She looked around and smiled at the sight of Jordan straightening up the living room. She walked into the kitchen; he had cleaned up everything that was out. Hayley walked outside, and it was also straightened up. She smiled and walked back inside. Hayley went to the mantle that contained Eric's shadow boxed flag and lit the candle sitting on the mantle. As Hayley turned around, Jordan was making his way back to the couch in his underwear.

Hayley: "Jordan, what are you doing?"

Jordan: "Hal, I need you to help me get clothes."

Jordan was shocked at the question.

Hayley: "They are in the room, where they have always been."

Jordan: "Hal, I can't bend down and get them dear."

"I didn't think about it," Hayley said, rushing back into her room.

Hayley: "Don't call me dear, I'm not a piece of meat."

Jordan smiled, knowing Hayley would have a smart comment for his words. Hayley came rushing back in, "Will this do?"

Jordan: "Hal, I don't care. These are your friends, not mine."

Hayley threw the clothes at Jordan.

Jordan: "Hal, calm down, it's going to be alright. I am not going to do anything crazy; you will barely know I am here."

"It's not that."

Hayley said as she thought to herself, *I just want them to like you. I want things to run smoothly.*

Jordan looked at Hayley; he could see the anxiety all over her face. He said, "Hal, it is going to be okay. Come sit here for a minute."

Hayley made her way to Jordan and sat down next to him. He then asked, "What are you freaking out about, Hal. Is it me being here? I can get Dan to come and get me."

Hayley: "No, you don't have to leave."

Jordan: "What is it then, do you think I am going to embarrass you, or are you embarrassed of me here? Hal, I will do what you need. I am not as hard as you think I am."

Hayley, without even hesitating and before thinking, said, "I want them to like you."

Jordan wasn't missing the opportunity this time; he leaned over and kissed Hayley's lips. Jordan pulled back, "I promise, it is going to be okay. They either like me or they don't. No matter what, it will be fine."

Hayley pulled away, "You are too much."

Jordan smiled, "But let's not forget the fact that you like me."

Hayley piped back, "Let's also not forget that I don't take any of your crap either."

Jordan kissed her again and smiled, "Enough said, Hal."

Jordan and Hayley sat on the couch for a few more minutes, stealing kisses from each other until they heard a car drive up.

"It's them", Hayley said, smiling. She walked to the door and flung it open.

Jordan got up from the couch, making his way to the door and onto the porch. As he was making his way to the door, he heard Hayley yell, "Hey ya'll."

"Hey ya'll?" Jordan thought. *"Is she serious? She's never talked like that. What kind of town did she live in?"*

Jordan stopped at the edge of the porch. Hayley was glowing and full of life. She hugged Kelsey, and Christian had his arm around Hayley. Christian said, "The crew is back together." Hayley smiled and hugged Christian. Christian looked over at the porch to where Jordan was smirking at the interaction they were having.

Hayley looked back to see Jordan and smiled at him. "Come on, you guys, grab your bags. Let's go inside, and I will show you around."

Hayley, Christian, and Kelsey walked towards the porch to where Jordan was standing.

Christian: "You must be the famous Jordan."

Jordan laughed, "Yep, I am the one she cusses every other day."

Christian laughed and stuck out his hand to shake Jordan's. Jordan shook Christian's hand, "It's nice to meet you, man. It will be good to have a brother in blue for a few days around." Christian glanced at Hayley while answering, "Yeah, we are far and in between now."

Hayley pushed past Christian, bumping him. "How long are you guys going to stay?" Hayley walked up the porch, walking past Jordan, who was turned in the opposite direction and mouthed to Christian, *"He doesn't know."*

Christian smiled, "Well, I have to be back at work Monday, so probably Sunday around noon, we should leave."

Jordan said, "Well, that stinks, but at least you are here."

Kelsey piped up, "Yeah, we have catching up to do."

Jordan waited for all of them to pass him before he turned around and made his way into the house. He stood by the couch listening to Kelsey and Hayley talk. Christian stood by Jordan.

"Oh my gosh, Hayley, this is so cute," Kelsey said before retreating into the next room. Christian and Jordan stood looking in the direction they had left for a moment.

They looked at each other. "They are going to be gone for a while", Christian said. "They know how to talk," he added.

"You want to sit?" Jordan asked Christian.

"Yeah," Christian said, not knowing how to take Jordan asking him if he wanted to sit down in Hayley's house.

"So, what do you do Christian? I know you are a cop, but where in the department do you work?" Christian looked at Jordan in shock. He was shocked that Hayley hadn't told him.

Jordan sensed the shock, "Come on, I am lucky I got out of her what you did and your name. I am not her favorite person most days."

Christian laughed. He liked Jordan's sense of humor, and he knew Hayley better than he thought.

Christian: "I am on the drug unit where we are from. I am a narcotics detective."

Jordan: "Oh wow, that is awesome. Hayley said you and Eric were close?"

Christian's heart was heavy hearing Eric's name, and he was also shocked that Jordan brought Eric up.

Christian: "Yes, he was my partner for many years. He was a really good guy, honorable."

Jordan could sense the uneasiness in the question.

Jordan: "That is awesome, I am a narc too."

Christian: "Yeah, Hayley told us you were a drug agent. She said she actually helped you on a case."

Jordan laughed, "Yeah, it was really weird, I was chasing one and there she was shopping. It was really weird. She was actually standing right next to the drugs, too. She didn't even know it."

Christian smiled, knowing Hayley knew exactly what she was doing to help him. Christian: "Yeah, she has the weirdest luck."

Jordan: "Yeah, about as weird as the time she almost shot me."

Jordan: "Shot you?"

Hayley had failed to mention the incident to him.

"Yeah!" Jordan said, chuckling. "I heard a noise outside the house, and I was coming around a corner and bam, there she was, pointing a gun in my face," he added.

Christian started laughing hysterically.

Christian: "I am sorry that is not funny, but it is."

Jordan: "I was about to piss myself that night. Was not expecting to have a gun pointed in my face, especially by her. Would have never guessed she had a gun. I guess you guys taught her how to shoot?"

Christian smiled, "I guess you could say that."

Jordan: "You've got to tell me more about her, I mean, I don't even know what she did back home, she won't say anything."

Christian looked at Jordan with a half-smile on his face.

Christian: "You really want to know?"

Jordan: "Yeah, she hasn't said anything. She should have been a detective, though. She would have been great at it. I don't know, maybe she learned because of you guys."

Christian looked at Jordan, "A detective?"

Jordan: "Yeah, did she tell you she found a body? She went right to it. I thought she was a killer at first. Nobody has those skills right off the bat, but she did. Hal did better than I did. I'm not a body person, but she did great."

Christian slid forward in his chair, resting his elbows on his knees, "Jordan, Hayley is more complex than you think, she…" Christian could hear Kelsey and Hayley walking back into the house. He slid back in his chair, looking in the direction of the voices.

Kelsey: "Oh, Hal, this place is amazing and so cute. Definitely different from the other house, but so you."

Hayley: "Thanks, I love it."

Hayley looked in the direction of Jordan and Christian, "What were you guys talking about?"

Christian smiled, "Boring cop stuff."

Hayley: "Can't you two put it down? You are on vacation."

Christian: "Hal, a few days out of state doesn't mean it is a vacation."

Hayley: "Well, it is for you."

Christian: "This is true."

Jordan was sitting in silence thinking *What did Hayley use to do? Hayley is more complex than you think. What did that mean? What did she do?*

Kelsey sat on the couch next to Christian and Hayley sat next to Jordan.

"So, how are you feeling, Jordan? How is your leg?" Kelsey asked.

"Well, I am not really sure yet. It's only been a few days out; I have a long way to go. Hal has been motivating me to take it day by day," Jordan said, looking at Hayley. Hayley smiled back at him.

Kelsey: "When do they think you are going to get back on the job?"

Hayley spoke, "They said 6 weeks at least, but he has to get through the physical therapy, and then they will know more."

Jordan began talking, "Yeah, it is up in the air. They want me to take it easy, but Christian, you know how that is; you can't sit still. It has killed me being like this with the hurricane damage."

Christian: "Yes, it looked awful on the way here."

Jordan: "Yeah, it was pretty bad. Obviously, a lot of houses were damaged."

Hayley smiled at Jordan's comment, "You think?" Jordan looked at Hayley, and the two smiled at each other. Kelsey and Christian stared; they could see the connection already.

"Do you think you will go back to the drug unit? Or are you done?" Christian asked Jordan.

"Well, I would like to think I could go back, but I don't know. My fear is not being able to go back. I don't know what I would do. This has been my life for many years. It is scary to think about," Jordan said sincerely.

Christian could tell that Jordan was being very open about his response, and he changed the subject, "So Hal, you failed to mention that you pointed a gun at Jordan."

Hayley looked at Jordan, "You told him?"

Jordan: "Well, yeah, it came up in conversation."

Hayley: "Because pointing a gun at someone's head comes up in random conversations?"

"When you're talking to cops, yes, sometimes," Jordan said, looking at Hayley.

Hayley looked at Christian, "Yes, he was sneaking around my house. I thought he was a Peeping Tom. He was in my yard."

Jordan: "I was trying to protect the neighbor, you were female. It was before I knew you had a gun and could hurt someone with your words."

Christian and Kelsey laughed. "You know her well already it sounds like," Christian said to Jordan. Christian couldn't help but smile. He liked Jordan.

The three sat and talked, learning about each other all over again. Kelsey and Christian were watching everything Hayley and Jordan said, watching their movements and reactions to one another. Before they knew it, 2 hours had passed.

Hayley: "Are you guys getting hungry? Jordan likes these greasy cheeseburgers and fries at a restaurant down the street."

Jordan looked at Kelsey and Christian and added, "They are the best cheeseburgers and fries. Hal smuggled me one in when I was in the hospital. Hal has no idea what she is missing."

"She seemed to forget to tell us that too," Kelsey said.

"Yeah, I have been living on the edge lately," Jordan glared at Hayley.

Christian: "Yeah, I could eat."

Hayley: "Kelsey, you want to come with me to get them?"

Kelsey: "Of course."

Hayley: "Jordan, you want your usual?"

Jordan: "You have got it once for me, do you even know what I want?"

"A cheeseburger with everything on it but mayonnaise," Hayley said proud that she remembered.

"Well, look at you, you like me," Jordan said, joking with Hayley.

"Don't get your hopes up," Hayley said, smirking back at Jordan.

Again, Christian and Kelsey just stared at the two. Wondering if the two even knew they had chemistry. Christian couldn't help but be reminded of Eric and Hayley. Jordan and Hayley were so similar.

Hayley grabbed the keys, and Hayley and Kelsey walked towards the door to leave.

Christian: "Hey Hal, you might want to pick up some more wine while you guys are out."

Hayley: "Got it, we will get some."

"Drive safe," Jordan said as they walked out the door.

Hayley: "We will."

Christian looked at Jordan. He had a half-smile on his face watching Hayley walk out the door. It was sweet the way Jordan looked at Hayley, but Christian knew cops and knew their motives.

Christian: "So, you have a girlfriend, Jordan?"

Jordan: "Oh no, I haven't had one of those in a while, and right now, it would probably be weird explaining being at a female's house while my house gets fixed."

Christian: "Oh yeah, it probably will be. Have you been married before?"

Jordan: "I have been once; it lasted about a year."

Christian: "What happened?"

Jordan: "I married the wrong person. Married her for the wrong reasons."

Christian: "Do you have any kids?"

Jordan: "Yeah, a little girl named Miah. She will be 3 next month."

Christian: "That is awesome, Kelsey, and I want kids, but with the job, we have been waiting for the perfect time."

Jordan: "I don't think there is ever a perfect time honestly."

Christian: "You are right, and I am not leaving my job anytime soon. I think Kelsey and I have been enjoying ourselves, too. That is part of it. We were always doing something with Eric and Hayley. I guess living up to young married life."

Jordan: "It sounds like fun. I didn't have that. My ex got pregnant, we got married and raised an infant until we couldn't stand each other anymore."

Christian: "So that is why you are living the single life?"

Jordan: "Pretty much. I have figured that it will always bring drama. There are very few people like Kelsey or Hayley out there."

Christian: "Yes, they are very rare."

Jordan: "What was Hayley like when she lived up there? How was she married? I am guessing she kept Eric on his toes."

Christian laughed, "They kept each other on their toes. They both were firecrackers."

Jordan laughed.

Christian: "Hayley was full of life. Free, I guess you can say a jokester. She loved to turn on music and dance, which would irritate Eric when she was goofy at times. She was always feisty, I'm sure you see that daily."

Christian and Jordan both laughed.

Jordan: "I get under her skin, I will admit."

Christian: "With how full of life she was, her heart was the most amazing part. She loved like no one I have ever met, more than Kelsey ever could. She loved Eric so much, and I haven't seen her heart in a long time. Maybe because I am not here with her, but I hear the defeat in her voice most days until recently."

"Until recently?" Jordan was curious.

Christian: "Yes, I could hear the spark in her voice, and the Hayley I once knew coming back."

Jordan hoped some of the spark was from him, "Well, I know she has been excited to see the two of you. All of you needed to see each other. It's good for all three of you."

Christian wanted to change the subject; he was still trying to feel Jordan out.

Christian: "So, what are they going to do about your house?"

Jordan: "Well, I have to call on Monday, being in the hospital kind of stopped that. Yesterday, when we got home, I just wanted to relax. I think Hal did too, she was sleeping in the hospital, in a chair until last night."

Christian: "What did she do last night?"

Jordan: "I felt bad for her, so I moved over on the bed and she slept in it."

Christian: "You slept in it together?"

Christian had so many questions.

Jordan could see the confusion in Christian's eyes.

Jordan: "No, it wasn't like that. I just didn't want her to sleep in a chair again. She wouldn't listen and go home."

Christian: "Sounds like Hayley."

Jordan: "Christian, I promise you, nothing happened, and I did nothing to Hal."

Christian: "Hal means the world to me; I don't want anything to happen to her. She is different, Jordan."

Jordan: "I know she is different. I would never do anything to hurt her. She is a part of the blue family; I will protect her, Christian."

Christian could tell Jordan meant exactly what he said.

Christian: "How long do you think it is going to take to fix your house?"

Jordan: "I have no idea. It depends on how many people come in to help with the hurricane. Most of the time, companies will come in, and it moves a lot faster. I can only hope the tree will be out of my house within a few months, and then maybe after that it will be a little faster."

Christian: "Is this the first time you have had damage to your house?"

Jordan: "To this extent, yes. I've never experienced this much."

Christian: "So, it might be a year before you can get back in your house?"

Jordan: "Yeah, but I may be able to live in it while they are fixing some of it. I haven't been back to my house since we left. My leg is a hindrance, so I can't really get in there and look."

Christian: "I can understand that. I hope it won't take too long. I know how it can be misplaced."

Jordan: "Hal has been great, but man, I can't wait to sleep in my own bed. The couch isn't too bad, but there is nothing like your own bed."

Christian: "What are you going to do if it takes longer than you expect?"

Jordan: "Well, I hope to be back at work soon, but I don't know. If Hal throws me out, I can go stay with Dan, I am sure."

Christian: "Who is Dan?"

Jordan: "Dan is my partner. We went to the mandate together and have worked together ever since. Both went the same path in the department."

Christian: "Ah, you have worked at the same department since getting mandated in the police academy?"

Jordan: "Yep, the same department. I figure if it's not broken, don't fix it. I've been able to go where I wanted in the department. If I ever couldn't, I guess I would look."

Christian: "That makes sense. What do you guys do together? Seeing how you two appear to have shaky waters."

Christian smiled, looking at Jordan.

Jordan: "I don't know. We stay out of each other's way. We watch TV. We have been watching a lot of the damage coverage. I haven't pushed football yet. I am not trying to be thrown out."

Christian laughed, "This is true. You like college, NFL, or both?"

Jordan: "I'm a college person. What about you?"

Christian: "Both, but it just depends on when I can watch."

Jordan: "What are your teams?"

Christian: "Well, Georgia and the Falcons, of course."

Jordan laughed, "Well, I should have figured."

Christian: "What about you?"

Jordan: "The Gators. Was born a Gator and will die a Gator fan."

Christian: "Man, it has been rough for them for years."

Jordan: "Yeah, I know, but that's my team."

Christian: "I get it."

"In fact," Jordan grabbed the TV remote, "I think there is a game on now. You want to watch some before they get back?"

Christian: "Yep, that sounds good."

Jordan: "Do you want anything to drink, Christian?"

Christian: "No, I am good right now, but thanks."

Jordan turned on the TV to the Gator game. Christian and Jordan sat and watched the game.

On the other side of town, Kelsey and Hayley were inside the grocery store, walking down the aisles with a cart.

Kelsey: "So, how has it been since the hurricane? It seems like it tore up the whole town."

Hayley: "It's been alright. Things opened pretty fast after; I guess they are used to it."

Kelsey: "How has it been with Jordan in your house? Doesn't that seem weird to you?"

Hayley: "Yeah, it has been different to say the least, but I couldn't leave him. I guess it is the job still in me. It hasn't been too awful. He is easy to live with. His friends are pretty bad, though."

Kelsey: "His friends?"

Hayley: "Well, before the hurricane, it was a party every weekend. Obviously, now they have found other places to go, or they are working. Dan is the only one who comes around now. He's just a typical male cop; he thinks he is a gift to people, women, everything. Just rude."

Kelsey: "Sounds like the way you describe Jordan."

Hayley: "Yeah, I guess. Jordan just has a mute button at times. Dan does not."

Kelsey: "Ah, I see. What have you and Jordan been doing? I know he can't do much."

Hayley: "Well, we haven't had too much time to run out of things to do. When we were waiting for the hurricane to pass, we laid on the couches and read. He was in the hospital for a few days, and then last night, we just hung around and talked. Read another book."

"Read?" Kelsey questioned.

Hayley: "Yeah, kind of. I read and he listens."

Hayley could see the confusion on Kelsey's face.

Hayley: "When the hurricane was coming, I went to the store and got a book and was reading it. When all the stuff happened at Jordan's house, he came over to my house, we had nothing else to do, so I read aloud the book. When he got out of the hospital, and he knew he was coming to stay with me for a while, he went to the hospital store and grabbed a book he thought I would like reading, and well, that's kind of how it started."

Kelsey was in shock but was intrigued, "What kind of books are you two reading together?"

Hayley didn't even look in Kelsey's directions; she continued grabbing a bottle of wine off the shelf.

Hayley: "Romance."

Kelsey: "Romance?"

You couldn't wipe the smile off of Kelsey's face.

Hayley grabbed the wine off the shelf and looked at Kelsey and her smirk.

Hayley: "Yes, romance."

Kelsey: "You guys are reading smut?"

Hayley: "God no, not that kind of romance novels. Whispered Promises, The Notebook, nothing graphic like that."

Kelsey could not hold her laughter, "I would never imagine that one."

Hayley: "Yes, and it stays between you and me because I'm sure Jordan doesn't want all his friends with over-inflated egos to know about it."

"Oh, your secret is safe with me," Kelsey held her hands up, still smiling, "So, like what do you do after you read these books?"

Hayley: "Nothing, we talk about the ending."

Kelsey: "Do you cuddle?"

Hayley: "Kelsey, no."

Kelsey could not help but laugh aloud at the way Hayley said no.

Kelsey: "Okay, I get it, but Jordan is not an ugly guy, Hal, he's pretty hot."

Hayley: "He also has a huge ego problem, and he's a cop."

Kelsey and Hayley made it to the counter and started placing things on the register.

Kelsey: "You were married to a cop, Hal, and one that had a huge ego problem. Did you forget that?"

Hayley: "No, it was just a different time. Things are different since Eric. I am a different person now; there is no getting around that."

Kelsey could tell that the conversation was uncomfortable for Hayley to talk about. She tried to lighten the mood, "But he still is nice to look at."

Hayley glared at Kelsey, "Yes, Kelsey, he is good looking. Can we drop it now?"

Kelsey: "Yes, we can drop it."

Kelsey and Hayley smiled and finished paying. They placed the groceries into the vehicle and started the drive home, stopping at the drive-thru to get the food they promised to bring home. Kelsey and Hayley talked on the way home about what was going on back home with Kelsey and Christian, and at the job. They pulled into the driveway. Before they got out of the vehicle, Hayley turned to Kelsey, "Not a word." Kelsey looked at Hayley, "I promise."

Hayley and Kelsey grabbed the groceries out of the car and walked up to the house. They opened the door and saw Jordan and Christian sitting in the living room watching football.

"How does that not surprise me?" Hayley said, walking inside with groceries in her hand.

Jordan jumped up, "Do you need a hand?"

"Yes, but what are you going to do?" Hayley said, smiling at Jordan.

Jordan: "I see you didn't lose your spice at the store."

Hayley: "I did not, but I brought you a greasy cheeseburger."

Jordan: "I am thankful, I am starving."

Christian, Kelsey, Jordan, and Hayley sat down around the kitchen table and ate. They talked, and surprisingly, the conversations weren't forced. Jordan being added to the threesome since Eric died was easy. As if Jordan stepped into Eric's place without even trying.

Jordan teased to find out more about Hayley from Christian and Kelsey.

Jordan: "So, tell me about Hal before she moved here. Was she wild? I have found the most conservative ones move when they are changing their wild ways."

Christian and Kelsey laughed, "She was not much different. She was feisty back then, had all the men wild. Hal only had eyes for Eric, or he was the only one who got to her."

Hayley laughed, "He did not get to me. I made the decision on my own to be nice to him."

Jordan was enjoying the teasing between Christian and Hayley.

Jordan piped in, "Ahh, so one did get to you whom you didn't make cry."

All of them laughed. As they finished eating, Hayley got up and started cleaning up the plates. Kelsey joined Hayley as Christian and Jordan still talked.

Kelsey: "I can see why you like him."

"What do you mean?" Hayley said, looking at Kelsey, who had grabbed a dish and was washing it.

Kelsey: "He is easy to get along with. I can see why you let him stay with you."

Hayley thought Kelsey had seen right through Jordan and her.

Hayley: "He's alright, he tries to act right and not make me mad."

Kelsey could see there was more to the story than what Hayley was saying.

Kelsey: "That sure is rare to find. I am glad he isn't making you mad."

Hayley could read through Kelsey's words.

Hayley: "What are you saying, Kelsey?"

Kelsey: "I am just saying, it is very rare to find someone willing to work with you. It's even rarer to find it twice. I am not saying Jordan is the one, I am not saying you two need to start a relationship but…"

Hayley cut off Kelsey, "Eric was my person, Kelsey. There will never be anyone who takes his place."

Kelsey piped back, "No, but there may also be someone not trying to replace Eric but trying to be his own person to make a life with you."

Hayley: "You don't know Jordan. He is not everything you are seeing right now."

Kelsey: "I know, and neither was Eric."

Kelsey looked at Hayley, and they didn't speak. Kelsey walked back to the table and sat down. Hayley was not ready to think about what Jordan actually meant and where his place was in her life. She was a widow, nothing more. Hayley turned and looked in the direction all of them were sitting, watching Jordan, Christian, and Kelsey interact. It was like they had known each other for years. It was natural; it was going better than she had expected.

Hayley wondered how Christian and Kelsey could be so open to Jordan. They were Eric's friends, not Jordan's. How could they be okay with all of this, and if they were, why?

Then Hayley came to the realization that maybe it was her. It was her feelings she continued to hold on to; her world stopped the day that Eric died, not Christian's, not Kelsey's. They had found a way to live without Eric. Not forgetting, honoring him while living their own life again.

Jordan looked over at Hayley, "You good, Hal?"

Hayley: "Yeah, I was thinking maybe we should go outside. It's a pretty nice day."

Jordan, Christian, and Kelsey all agreed and walked outside. Christian and Kelsey sat together on one of the couches, and Jordan and Hayley sat on another. Hayley was quickly brought back to just last night, kissing Jordan for the first time on the very couch where they sat.

Christian: "What kind of medication do they have you on, Jordan?"

Jordan: "Christian, there are so many things they want me to take. I am taking the antibiotic, of course, and the muscle relaxers as needed. I've stopped the pain meds. I am weird about getting addicted to them. I've seen too many people get addicted to them in this line of work."

Christian: "I agree with that."

Jordan looked at Christian and Kelsey, "So what is next for you two? Kids in the future or still enjoying married life?"

Kelsey answered, looking at Christian, "Well, I think we are both enjoying married life. The job kind of puts a damper on things. We will see."

Jordan asked the question because of the conversation Christian and Jordan had earlier.

Jordan: "The job will always be here. Don't wait too long. You guys need to have kids, and both of you are ready."

Hayley looked at Jordan, "Jordan, they will when they are ready."

Jordan put his hand on Hayley's leg and rubbed it without even thinking, "I know, but you know this job stops people at times. I just don't want them to wait too long."

Christian and Kelsey saw Jordan's hand on Hayley's leg, and the fact that Hayley was allowing him to keep his hand there. Hayley saw the reaction of Christian and Kelsey out of the corner of her eye and moved her leg. Jordan, realizing what he had done, pulled his hand away. As they were talking, the sun began to set. It was as if time was speeding up, and there was not enough time to be together and enjoy just being happy.

Hayley: "Wine? Does anyone want some wine?"

All agreed it was time for some wine.

Hayley: "I'll get it."

Jordan got up, "If you are getting the wine, I am going to use the boy's room before I get wine in my system."

Christian and Kelsey laughed. Hayley walked into the house, right behind Jordan. Jordan made his way to the bathroom as Hayley pulled out the wine.

Christian and Kelsey sat outside waiting for both of them to return.

Kelsey whispered, "Do you think they are messing around?"

Christian: "Hell, I don't know Kelsey. He seems sweet to her, but he hasn't said anything to me."

Kelsey: "Hal didn't say anything to me, but she said they read romance novels together."

Christian looked at Kelsey, "What?"

Kelsey started laughing, "Yes, they have read two books so far. It's been since the hurricane."

Christian: "They are reading dirty books together, that is just weird, Kelsey."

Kelsey: "No, not those kinds of romance novels, like PG-13 ones."

Christian: "It's still weird, Kelsey."

Kelsey: "You wouldn't read with me."

Christian: "I love you, but heck no, I wouldn't."

Kelsey laughed, she knew the answer before she asked the questions.

Kelsey: "I do like him, Christian. I know it is different for you."

Christian: "I like him too, Kelsey, it's just different but not a bad different, just different."

As Jordan was coming out of the bathroom, Hayley had her back turned to him. Jordan made his way to where Hayley was, coming within inches of her. He was so close, Hayley felt uncomfortable knowing that Christian or Kelsey could come in at any moment.

Jordan: "I really like them."

Hayley turned towards Jordan, "You've got to back up, they are going to see us."

Jordan: "Why does it matter Hal? They have to know."

Hayley: "I am not ready to explain anything to them or anyone right now."

Jordan backs away, "Okay, but Hal, what do you want then? Last night and this morning, was that just a thing for you?"

Hayley: "No Jordan, but it just happened really fast. I haven't had time to process it yet."

Jordan: "Process it? Hal, you kissed me this morning."

Hayley: "I know. I just don't know."

Jordan came close to Hayley again, "Don't run from this, Hal. We both know this doesn't happen often. The connection is undeniable."

Hayley: "Jordan, I am just not ready to tell them."

"Okay, enough said," Jordan felt defeated, and Hayley could tell.

Hayley: "You can't be mad at that."

Jordan: "No, I am not Hal. I just need to know that after the time you need that there are no more secrets, no more hiding."

Jordan made his way towards the door. Hayley watched as he went back outside. She could hear Jordan talking as if the conversation between the two had never occurred. Hayley knew Jordan was right. Eventually, if they allowed things to progress, she would have to be open with Christian and Kelsey. It was just too new for Hayley to be okay with telling them. It still seemed so new that Eric had died.

Hayley grabbed the glasses of wine and walked back outside. They began to talk again, but Christian and Kelsey could feel a little tension between Hayley and Jordan.

Christian looked at Hayley, ignoring the tension he felt, "Hal, how is your online store doing?"

Hayley: "It is doing pretty well. I make enough to pay the bills and have a little extra. I am hoping it will pick up a little more."

Christian: "That's good, it will, I am sure you will make it work."

Kelsey piped in, "Where are you taking me tomorrow?"

Hayley's spirits lifted, "It is an outdoor shopping market. They have some of the most unique stuff there. I found it by accident, but I am so glad I did."

Christian: "Isn't that the place where you helped Jordan find some dope?"

Kelsey and Hayley were shocked at the comment and looked at Christian. Hayley, after looking at Christian, looked at Jordan, "You told him about that?"

Jordan smiled, "It came up in conversation."

Hayley: "Me finding drugs came up in conversation."

Jordan: "Well, yeah, we are narcs. You didn't think we could go without talking about it, did you?"

The comment made Hayley smile.

Hayley: "No, but you found the drugs; I just happened to be standing in the right place."

Jordan: "With your foot pointed directly where it was."

Hayley laughed, "It was just luck, I guess."

She turned to Christian. It was a look that seemed to ask, *Does Jordan know?* Christian could sense it.

Christian: "Jordan said he was chasing a guy, and there you were. Just standing there. He was shocked to see you. Said you would have made a great detective."

Christian took a sip of the wine Hayley had given him. Hayley gulped the wine she had brought for herself.

Hayley: "I would have made the best detective. Too bad I chose the wrong field."

Kelsey laughed, "Yep. How interesting was that?"

Jordan looked at Hayley with pride, "I should take her to work with me. She is my good luck charm. He finally went to jail that day."

Hayley looked over at Jordan, and they both smiled at each other, as if to forget about the last conversation they had. The tension had subsided, and the foursome went back to laughing and talking.

As the night turned into early morning, Christian felt sluggish and could barely keep his eyes open from the drive. Kelsey was also resting on Christian's arm, about to fall asleep as Jordan and Hayley continued to talk. Christian finally broke the chatter, "Look, I know you two live in Florida and can party all night, but I've got to get to bed. We do have more time."

Hayley and Jordan looked at each other and laughed. The wine had loosened both of them up, and it could be seen. Both were just enjoying spending time with Christian and Kelsey.

Hayley smiled, "Christian stop it. It is getting a bit early in the morning. We'd better go to bed if we are going to get up in the morning."

All got up from the seats they were sitting in and walked inside. Jordan made his way to the couch and sat down. Hayley, Christian, and Kelsey were looking at him standing in the hallway.

"Do you need anything before I go to sleep? Haley asked Jordan.

"Nope, I got it, but thank you," Jordan replied, smiling.

Hayley: "Okay, see you in the morning."

Hayley walked to the left doorway, into her room, closing the door behind her.

Christian and Kelsey looked at Jordan. Christian smiled, "It was really good to meet you today, Jordan."

"Yeah, it was really good to meet you guys too," Jordan said while he slid his leg on the couch.

"See you in the morning Jordan," Kelsey said, smiling. Christian and Kelsey turned and walked to the doorway to the right, closing the door.

As Kelsey and Christian changed, Kelsey was the first person to talk.

Kelsey: "I actually really like him. I was expecting someone totally different."

Christian, whispering, replied, "Yeah, I know. He actually reminds me of Eric, some."

Kelsey: "Yeah, me too. Do you think those two have something going on?"

Christian: "I don't know, to tell you the truth. It is the way they look at each other. Like they have been living together as a couple for a while."

Kelsey giggled and whispered, sliding into bed, "Well, they have, babe."

Christian laughed, sliding into bed next to Kelsey, "You're right."

Kelsey: "When Hayley and I go shopping tomorrow, I will try to get more out of her."

Christian: "I doubt she will tell you, she is so headstrong. I will try to get something out of Jordan, too."

Kelsey: "Do you think he knows she was a cop yet?"

Christian: "He didn't mention it. I don't think he knows yet, Kelsey."

Kelsey: "Don't you find that strange she hasn't told him?"

Christian: "You know, Hal, she is secretive, and this was her escape plan. He could actually help her if she would let him."

Kelsey leaned over and kissed Christian, "I love you, I am going to roll over. You talk too much."

"Oh, I talk too much?" Christian said, wrapping his arms around Kelsey. He kissed Kelsey's head, "I love you too." As soon as the two closed their eyes, they were fast asleep.

Jordan was lying on the couch, staring off in thought. He could hear Christian and Kelsey talking and laughing, but he could not make out what they were saying. He was wondering if they actually liked him. He thought he played it "cool," but really hoped that they did like him.

Jordan grabbed his phone and texted, *"Hey, what are you doing?"*

Hayley was lying on her bed under the covers in her own thoughts. She thought Christian and Kelsey liked Jordan. She did not see any weird looks or smart remarks from either. She felt that there would have been if they didn't like Jordan. As she was thinking about it, she then thought, *What does it matter anyway? They are my friends, and Jordan is just well Jordan.*

As Hayley was deep in thought, her phone began to vibrate. It was Jordan, *"Hey, what are you doing?"*

Hayley smiled and picked up her phone, *"I'm lying in bed, what do you think I am doing?"*

Jordan smiled, receiving Hayley's message, *"Do you kind of feel like we are in high school again and are being separated by our parents for safety reasons?"*

Hayley saw the message and began to laugh softly, *"Yeah, in a way, but you can't be trusted."*

"I can't be trusted. You seem to forget who has pointed a gun at whom," Jordan hit send.

"You were the one sneaking around my house at night, if I remember correctly," Hayley hit send.

"There was a noise," Jordan hit send.

"I think it was more than that. You got busted as a peeping tom." Hayley hit send.

"This may be true, but don't tell anyone."

"I won't! Your secret is safe with me." Hayley texted with a smile.

"Hey Hal, do you think they like me?" Jordan asked.

Hayley was surprised at Jordan's question, *"Yeah, Jordan, I do believe they like you. Christian and Kelsey aren't afraid to hurt someone's feelings."*

"Good after you cursed so much about me to them, I didn't know if they would." Jordan typed, trying to lighten the mood from caring to joking around again.

Hayley knew what Jordan was doing, *"Well, it was touch and go for a while, but I told them you weren't that bad."*

Jordan smiled at Hayley's message, *"Oh you complimented me to them. I feel special."*

"Don't get a big head, Jordan, I don't like you that much. I just feel sorry for you, and I'm helping you," Hayley replied.

Jordan chuckled softly, *"I guess I'd better take it when I can, then huh?"*

"Yes, you know I don't say many compliments about you. Good night, Jordan, go to sleep," Hayley replied.

Jordan smiled at Hayley's message, *"Goodnight, Hal. I really like them too. I can see why you love them."*

"I am glad, and I am glad they liked you," Hayley texted.

Hayley kept her phone and closed her eyes with a smile on her face.

Jordan laid his phone down and closed his eyes, smiling at Hayley's last message. Jordan opened his eyes, picking up his phone, *"So what are you wearing?"*

Hayley heard her phone vibrate again. She grabbed her phone, reading Jordan's message. She smiled, knowing Jordan was joking with her.

"Go to bed, you idiot," Hayley smiled, putting her phone down and closing her eyes again.

Jordan read the message with a grin on his face. It was a typical Hayley answer. Jordan laid his phone down and closed his eyes again.

Both fell asleep smiling, thinking about each other.

Chapter 16

Help From Beyond

Christian woke in the morning and rolled over to Kelsey already gone. He knew Hayley and Kelsey would be gone early; he didn't realize he had slept so late. Christian got up, grabbed his clothes, and went to take a shower. He peeked in the living room, and Jordan was still asleep.

Jordan heard Christian get up and close the bathroom door. Jordan sat up, looking at his phone. Dang, it was late in the morning. He folded up the blankets on the couch and was sitting on the couch watching TV when Christian got out of the shower. Christian walked into the room, asking, "Did I wake you?"

Jordan: "No, I slept too late anyway."

Christian sat down on the couch next to Jordan, "Yeah, that wine kept us up."

Jordan laughed, "Yeah, it has a way of doing it, but it is Hal's favorite. I am going to take a shower real quick. Do you need me to get you anything?"

"No, I am good. If I need anything, I will get it," Christian replied.

Jordan made his way to the bathroom and closed the door. Christian picked up his phone, *"Hey, my lovely bride. Just checking on you."*

Kelsey and Hayley had made their way to the exact store where the situation happened with Jordan. "And this is the famous store you learned about last night" Hayley told Kelsey.

Kelsey laughed.

Kelsey's phone vibrated. She quickly grabbed it and read the message from Christian. "Well, obviously, the boys are finally up," Hayley said. Kelsey and Christian then texted.

Kelsey: *"We are doing good. Just finishing up. Did you just wake up?"*

Christian: *"No, we have been up for hours."*

Kelsey: *"You are a lie."*

Christian: *"Yes, dear, we just got up. I was just checking on you. Remember, I want to leave around 12 to miss traffic and to get back."*

Kelsey: *"I know, we won't be much longer."*

Christian: *"K, love you."*

Kelsey: *"Love you too."*

Kelsey put up her phone, "They are up. Christian was checking on us. You know him, he wants to get back so he can relax."

Hayley: "That is him. Understandable though."

Kelsey: "I really like it here. It's peaceful."

Hayley: "It is, it has been what I needed."

Hayley was still browsing in the store, Kelsey right beside her. Without looking at Hayley, Kelsey said, "I didn't mean to upset you last night, Hal. I just thought that I saw something between the two of you."

Hayley: "Kelsey, you didn't upset me. I just don't know if I am ready to deal with anything like that yet."

Kelsey: "I understand that."

Hayley: "Jordan has been great to me. He tries to appease me and not get in my way. He's a cop, Kelsey, just like Eric."

Kelsey: "And Christian and you, what's the big deal?"

Hayley: "He doesn't know me as a cop. He knows me as the neighbor who likes it quiet and thinks he is an ego-driven idiot."

Kelsey laughed, "He knows better. I can see it in the way he tries to get under your skin."

Hayley smiled, "He does do it on purpose sometimes."

Kelsey: "He's crazy about you, Hal. I can see it, and Christian can see it. My thoughts are out on you, though."

Hayley looked at Kelsey.

Kelsey: "I could see it sometimes, and then it was like you made yourself stop what was happening. You stopped what was naturally happening."

Hayley: "I just don't want to replace Eric Kelsey. I can't let him go."

Kelsey: "Girl, you know I love you, but the boy is crazy about you. Jordan is not trying to replace Eric. He is trying to be with you because of who you are. He wants to stand as a totally different person in your eyes. He knows he will never replace Eric; he just wants you to love him."

Hayley: "Kelsey, we are far from that."

Kelsey: "I know, but when that time comes, he doesn't want to be compared to Eric. He wants to be Jordan and Hayley. Does that make sense?"

Hayley: "It does, but there is so much I haven't told him. He doesn't know me, Kelsey."

Kelsey: "What he knows about you Hal, he likes. Tell him Hal, he will understand your reasoning for everything."

Hayley: "I will think about it. I just don't know."

Kelsey: "I mean, what could it hurt?"

Hayley: "How could it help Kelsey? I am not ready."

Kelsey: "I don't think Jordan is ready either, but that doesn't mean you guys can't experience things together and have fun together."

Hayley: "I know."

Kelsey: "Hal, let go of everything that is holding you back. Just let it come."

Hayley: "I have let go of some."

Kelsey smiled, "Oh, really?"

"Not ready Kelsey," Hayley said smiling.

"Oh, you can't do this to me, you've got to spill it."

Hayley looked at Kelsey, "I don't kiss and tell."

Kelsey smiled, "Okay, but eventually I want to hear about it."

Hayley looked at Kelsey, "That's a deal."

Kelsey and Hayley continued to shop; no more was said about Jordan and Hayley. Kelsey had enough information to know; there was something more than just friends, and Hayley was giving it at least a chance.

Christian was looking at the mantle when Jordan came back to the living room.

Christian: "I can't believe she still has that up."

Jordan looked over at Eric's flag sitting on the mantle, "I think it gives her a sense of peace. Kind of knowing he is still here. It's how I finally figured out she was married at one time."

Christian: "She was upfront with you about it."

Jordan: "Not at first. She didn't say anything about it, but I was here and we talked about it. She finally told me about it. After that, I felt a sense of family with her. I felt I needed to protect her because she was the wife of the blue."

Christian: "Eric and I always had a deal: If anything ever happened to the other, we would take care of the spouse. I don't remember a conversation about it, but it was just known. I hope I have done enough for Hal."

Jordan looked at Christian, "You have. Hal knows she can count on you for anything. You guys are family and always will be. How are you doing with everything?"

Christian did not expect Jordan to ask him, "It is okay. I mean, he was my partner, and we had many fun times together. We hung out at work, and then when we came home, it was the four of us when Kelsey came into the picture. I play the day over in my head a lot. I miss him."

Jordan: "You were there when he died?"

Jordan was shocked that Christian had been with Eric the day he died. Christian looked at Jordan. Jordan sensed that Christian didn't know what to say.

Jordan: "I am sorry if these are too personal questions. Please tell me."

Christian looked away from the mantle and back to Jordan.

Christian: "No, you are fine. We were serving a search warrant on a house. We had a search warrant for the house and warrants for the husband and wife for trafficking Meth. It was just a normal day; we had done this type of work weekly for years. Eric walked up to the residence, and they started shooting. He didn't have a chance; the first shot dropped him. We returned fire until we could finally get to Eric. I dragged him back, but there was nothing we could do.”

Jordan: “Man, I am so sorry. I am sure that is something that is ingrained in your mind.”

“That wasn’t the worst part,” Christian looked back at Eric’s flag.

Jordan looked at Christian, “What do you mean? What else happened?”

Christian looked at Jordan, “It was seeing Hal lose it.”

Jordan was confused, “What? She was there?”

Christian continued, “When she heard it on the radio, she came to the scene. She parked her car and started running to where EMS and I were with Eric. One of the Lieutenants stopped her. I was told she kept asking Lt. if Eric was dead, and he wouldn’t tell her.”

Jordan listened, confused still, “Hal broke free from Lt. and ran around the corner where we were. I heard her scream my name. It was a scream I will never forget. I turned around and shook my head no. She started screaming *No* and crying. Hal ran over to Eric and laid down next to him, putting her head on his chest, crying. Telling him that he couldn’t go, that he was going to be alright.”

Jordan, listening to the story, had tears in his eyes. He had slid himself to the end of the couch and had his elbows on his knees, listening intently.

Christian: “We had to pull Hal off of him. She wouldn’t let him go. She kept screaming.”

“Oh my God,” Jordan started running his hand through his hair.

Christian: “You know, I haven’t even told Kelsey that part. I just didn’t think she needed to hear the pure heartbreak I heard that day in Hal. It’s something I don’t want Kelsey to ever know. It was the worst day of my life in more than one way.”

Jordan: "God, I hurt for both of you. How the hell did Hal hear it over the radio? Did she have a portable scanner or something? Your agency didn't have a ban where no one could pick it up?"

Christian knew it was time for Jordan to know the truth. He could see the hurt he felt for what he and Hayley had gone through.

Christian: "Jordan, Hal was a cop."

Jordan's face went blank; he was shocked by the words that Christian had just spoken.

Jordan: "She was a cop? Like a beat cop or school resource officer."

Christian: "No, Jordan, she was a narc just like you and me. She only became a homicide detective after she and Eric got married. The agency wouldn't allow them both to stay in the unit. Hayley was bright, always was. She decided to go to the homicide unit because it would be easier if and when they decided to have kids. Hal could have gone anywhere in the department, and that is what she chose."

Jordan put his head down and his hands on his head. He was just in pure shock and disbelief, but things started to make sense; all of it.

Jordan: "Geezus Christ, she never told me. Why the hell didn't she tell me?"

Christian: "She came here to start over. To put law enforcement behind her. It was too much of a memory. Eric and Hayley worked together for years before they started dating and eventually got married. It didn't happen from day one."

Jordan: "I am just in complete shock; I just don't know what to say. I mean, everything makes sense now."

Christian: "I imagine it does now."

Jordan: "Was she good at the job?"

Christian: "One of the best. She was a good narc, could go undercover, and could buy just about anything. She was one of the best homicide detectives, if not the best I've ever seen. She can just put things together, and the details she can link; it was amazing."

Jordan's mind was spinning; she was a cop. He did not know whether to be angry at Hayley or feel for her on what she went through.

Jordan: "So, she and Eric worked together for years before they were married? Were they friends?"

Christian: "Oh hell no."

Christian said, laughing.

Jordan looked at Christian.

Christian: "They fought like cats and dogs. We always had to separate them. She nicknamed him ass hole and told him that he was not as irresistible as he thought he was. I will say Eric liked the dating pool of women, and he would date a lot of them. Hayley just got to him. I don't think they would have ended up together if they hadn't worked together for so long. I guess that's why it worked so well for them, they had seen each other at their worst."

Jordan laughed. It was the same thing Hayley had told him.

Jordan: "I can hear her saying that. When did it change?"

Christian: "You know, I really don't remember. I know that the year that they started dating, we had a bunch of crap go on in the city. We were all working overtime, and there was no way we could keep them apart. I guess the long hours together did it. It's like it changed a little at a time. We noticed them sticking up for each other and then laughing together, and then we all went out one night, and we just knew by watching them together. We all suspected it for a while, but it was evident that night."

Jordan: "Wow, what a story. It helps me understand Hal so much more. I just wish she had told me."

Christian: "I don't know how she has not. I don't know how she has managed to stay out of it for so long. She had loved the job so much. But it just changed after Eric. She wasn't the same."

Jordan: "Has she tried to date anyone since Eric?"

Christian: "There was a guy we worked with who was very sweet to Hal. She just wasn't ready, and I don't think she would have ended up with him anyway. He didn't have enough fire in him for her."

Jordan laughed, "Not enough fire?"

Christian laughed, "You know exactly what I am talking about. Hal has told me stories."

They both laughed.

Christian: "Hal is a special person to me, Jordan. I don't want to see her get hurt. She has been through enough."

Jordan sensed where Christian was going with his words.

Jordan: "Christian, Hal is a special person to me, too. I am so grateful for everything she has done for me, and in the middle of all of the chaos and confusion, she has made me want to do better and be better for me and for her. She's different from the other women, and I know that Christian."

Christian: "You like her?"

Jordan didn't know how to answer the question. A usual sarcastic joke would not have worked at the moment.

Jordan: "Yeah, I do. More than I've felt before. She has reshaped the way I view things."

Christian: "Look, you don't have to explain anything to me, Jordan. Just don't do cop shit. You know what I am talking about."

Jordan: "I wouldn't do that to her."

Christian: "I don't think you would. I can see it in the way you both look at each other. I've seen it one other time. Just don't screw it up."

Jordan: "I won't, Christian, I can promise you that. I will keep her safe."

Jordan's attention went to the driveway. Hayley and Kelsey had pulled up. Jordan and Christian slid back on the couches and began to watch TV again. Hayley and Kelsey burst through the door.

Kelsey: "Christian, we have to come back soon. This place has the best market."

Christian: "Do I want to know how much you spent?"

"Oh, Christian, it is fine," Kelsey said as she walked over to Christian and kissed him on the lips.

When Kelsey and Christian started talking, Hayley looked over at Jordan, who was on the couch. Jordan looked at Hayley, both smiled, and Jordan winked. Hayley only smiled and didn't react. It was as if the conversation between her and Kelsey had calmed her. She knew Christian and Kelsey were going to be okay, no matter what happened between her and Jordan.

Hayley looked over at Kelsey and Christian. Kelsey had sat in Christian's lap, and they were smiling and talking.

Hayley looked at them, "Why don't we eat one last time before you leave?"

Jordan spoke, "That would be perfect. We can put the chicken on the grill, and it won't take too long."

Christian looked at Kelsey, "That will be perfect. We won't have to stop."

All four of them got up.

Hayley: "Go ahead and sit outside. I will get everything ready."

"I'll help you Hal", Jordan said, moving towards the kitchen.

Kelsey got up from Christian's lap, and Christian grabbed Kelsey, holding her in his arms, carrying her outside. Kelsey laughed, and Christian smiled, walking towards the door. Hayley and Jordan just laughed, looking at the two of them.

Jordan: "They have a real good relationship."

Hayley was still looking towards the door.

Hayley: "Yeah, they do, it's been like that since they met."

Hayley grabbed the chicken out of the refrigerator and walked towards the sink.

Jordan: "How did they meet?"

Hayley: "She was a nurse at a hospital."

Jordan shot a smile at Hayley.

Hayley: "Yes, typical Jordan. It was just different with her from the beginning. He didn't try to play games. He knew what he wanted."

Jordan started toward the sink to help Hayley, "Did she play hard to get?"

Hayley giggled, "No, they both pretty much knew what they wanted from day one. They just had to figure it out."

Jordan was now standing right next to Hayley, inches from her, "Kind of like us?"

Hayley turned to Jordan. He was inches from her face, "Kind of like us."

Jordan leaned in and kissed Hayley. The denial both of them held onto was gone in that moment. Jordan pressed up against Hayley, and both in that moment did not care if they were caught. Hayley pushed Jordan, "Stop," she said, smiling.

"We got to cook," Hayley said as she grabbed the chicken and headed towards the door. "You've got to give me a minute," Jordan said, leaning on the counter, catching his breath. Jordan rested his arms on the counter and took a deep breath.

What is she doing to me? What is it about her that drives me so crazy? Jordan thought as he leaned over the counter for a few more moments before walking out to the back porch to join everyone. When he made it and sat down, Christian looked at him, "Are you alright?"

"Yeah, I got lightheaded for a minute. I am okay now," Jordan replied and smiled as the words came out of his mouth.

Hayley glared over at Jordan, smiling when he said it.

As the chicken cooked, the foursome sat and talked, waiting for it to finish. Once it was done, they all sat around the table talking. Hayley wanted time to slow down, but it seemed to be moving faster.

"Man, that is what I needed after all of that wine last night," Christian leaned back, rubbing his stomach.

They all smiled. Hayley grinned, "We did drink some wine last night."

Christian: "Kelsey, I know you don't want to go, but we have to get back."

Kelsey: "If we moved here, we wouldn't have to go."

Christian: "Oh here we go, you see what you did, Hal?"

Hayley laughed, "She is right, you know?"

Christian: "I know, but you know where I am with the department. I sure wouldn't want to start over again."

Jordan spoke up, "You know the good thing with the department here, you already know people that could make things happen."

Christian glared at Jordan, "Don't encourage this, trust me."

Kelsey and Hayley both laughed.

The four grabbed the plates and brought them inside, setting them in the sink. Kelsey: "Let me help you with the dishes before we leave."

Hayley put her hands up, "No, we got them, you are our guest." Kelsey hugged Hayley and said, "I don't want to leave you."

Hayley: "I will be fine, Kelsey. It just means you have to come back soon."

Kelsey let go of Hayley, "You hear that, Christian, we have to come back sooner."

"Next time, maybe I will be walking, and we can do more," Jordan hoped he wasn't out of line with the comment.

Christian: "Yes, we need to do man things when the girls go shopping next time."

Jordan shook his head, happy that Christian thought he would be around the next time they came and delighted that Christian would be good with it.

Christian disappeared into the room, grabbing their bags. Kelsey, Hayley, and Jordan walked outside. Kelsey hugged Jordan, "It was really good to meet you finally."

Jordan hugged Kelsey back, "The same. Please come back soon. Hal has really enjoyed you being here."

Kelsey grabbed the bags from Christian, and she and Hayley walked to the vehicle.

Hayley: "I hate you guys have to leave so soon."

Kelsey: "I know, but we will be back. I want you to do me a favor and enjoy yourself. Enjoy Jordan."

Hayley hugged Kelsey, "I will."

Christian shook Jordan's hand, "It was good to meet you."

Jordan: "It was good to meet you too."

Christian: "Take care of our girl."

Jordan: "With my life."

Christian (smiling): "For some reason, I believe that."

Christian walked down to where Hayley was standing. Kelsey had already gotten in the car. Christian got to Hayley.

Hayley: "I am going to miss you, Christian."

Christian: "I'll miss you too Hal."

They embraced in a long hug before letting go.

Christian: "Do me a favor and give Jordan a break. He cares for you, Hal."

Hayley looked towards Jordan's direction, "You don't know that."

Christian opened the car door and started to get inside, "Actually, I do."

As Christian got into the car, Hayley walked back to the porch where Jordan was standing. She stood on the step right below him. Both waved as Christian and Kelsey pulled out of the driveway. Jordan reached down and put his hand on Hayley's shoulder, "You okay?" Hayley reached up and put her hand on top of Jordan's, saying, "Yeah, I am good."

As they pulled out of the driveway, Christian and Kelsey looked back at Hayley and Jordan on the porch one last time.

"It's going to happen for them," Christian said, turning to Kelsey.

"My thoughts too. Both of them just need to stop fighting it," Kelsey replied.

Hayley and Jordan walked back into the house. Both were quiet. Hayley walked to the sink and started washing dishes and Jordan sat down on the couch. Jordan looked over at Hayley, "Why don't you come and sit over here on the couch and just relax for a few Hal. We have all night to wash the dishes."

Hayley turned off the water, wiped off her hands, and sat next to Jordan, putting her head back on the couch. Jordan followed and put his head back on the couch. Both were quiet for a few moments before Jordan said, "Man, it has been a crazy weekend starting Friday night, hasn't it?"

Hayley smiled and turned to Jordan, "You don't say."

Jordan: "I have enjoyed every bit of it. Kind of better than those loud parties I usually have."

Hayley: "Remember, you said that when you get better."

Jordan smiled, "I will get amnesia, I am sure, but I have you to remind me."

Hayley: "You do."

Hayley leaned over and put her head on Jordan's chest. Jordan wrapped his arm around Hayley and kissed her on the head. The two were silent in thought, enjoying each other's embraces.

Christian and Kelsey had finally made it home. Christian had been pretty quiet in the car, and she knew something was on his mind. They walked inside, and Christian placed the bags on the couch and started to unpack them.

Kelsey: "Babe, are you okay? You didn't say much in the car."

Christian smiled a little, "Yeah, hon, I am fine. Just a lot to take in."

Kelsey knew the weekend was rough for Christian. Seeing Hayley even hang around another male would be hard. Kelsey walked over to Christian, hugging him, not speaking a word.

Christian hugged Kelsey back, "I think I am going to run and get us something to eat."

Kelsey knew Christian didn't want to talk about it.

Kelsey: "Oh yeah, what were you thinking?"

Christian: "How about some Chinese food?"

Kelsey: "That sounds good. By the time you get back, I will have everything unpacked, and we can relax."

Christian: "That sounds perfect."

Christian grabbed the keys and started walking to the door.

Kelsey watched as Christian walked to the door, saying, "I love you."

Christian turned with a half-smile on his face, "I love you too. I will be back soon."

Christian got into the vehicle and backed out of the driveway. Kelsey watched from the window as he left. She knew the emotions from the weekend were overwhelming. Seeing Hayley again, seeing Hayley with Jordan, seeing the bond they had, even if it wasn't romantic. Kelsey knew Christian knew it was a matter of time. Tears welled in Kelsey's eyes as she watched Christian leave. She knew he had to go through the emotions on his own. She watched until she could see Christian no more.

Christian was in a dream-like state while driving. He replayed the whole weekend in his head, the interaction between Jordan and him, the way Jordan and Hayley looked at each other, and laughed together. His heart was heavy, missing Eric, knowing that eventually, in time, he would be replaced. It was the way Jordan looked at Hayley, how he interacted with Hayley; he knew Jordan was the perfect person for Hayley. Someone who could take over where Eric left off. Hayley would be happy, and it would work.

Christian pulled up to the drive-thru of Kelsey and his favorite Chinese restaurant and ordered their normal. His mind was racing still, this time with thoughts of Eric and Hayley and the four of them sitting around on a normal night laughing and talking. The memories became overwhelming to Christian as he waited for his order, and tears began to form in his eyes. His thoughts were broken by the drive-thru attendant opening the window, saying, "Here you are. "Do you need any sauce?"

Christian grabbed the bag, blinking his eyes to get rid of the tears that started to form in his eyes, "No ma'am, thank you."

Christian placed the food in the passenger seat, rolled up his window, and began to drive again. As he got down the road from his house, instead of turning right, he turned left, heading in the opposite direction. He rode for a few minutes before turning onto a driveway. He peered up at the wrought iron sign, which read Valor Cemetery. He drove down the path before stopping, looking over at the stone which read Eric Dolce. He had not been to the cemetery since Eric had been buried; he couldn't bring himself to do it. Christian got out of the car and walked to Eric's grave. He peered down at it for a while, staring at the inscription, "My husband, My friend." Tears started to form in Christian's eyes again.

Christian, choking back the tears and began to speak, "Why did you have to go, dude? How am I supposed to do life without my best friend? I miss you, man. There is not a day that goes by that I don't think of some crazy stuff you did. The job isn't the same with you being gone, man."

Christian crouched down next to Eric's stone, quiet for a moment.

"I know I told you I would take care of Hal. She is just as fiery as ever; that hasn't changed."

Christian smiled as he said it.

"She met someone and he's perfect for her. Hal is, of course, denying it, but I can see it, just like I saw it between the two of you. It hurts, man, it hurts knowing that one day you are going to be replaced." Christian was again quiet for a moment.

"They will be good together, just like the two of you were. I'm trying, Eric. I'm doing my best to accept that you're gone, but I can't let go of the thought that you and she were meant for each other. I need your help; I need your help, Eric."

Christian stood up, wiping away his tears, smiling, "I know, you would be telling me right now I am a pus." Christian reached into his pocket. pulling out a quarter. He touched the top of Eric's grave, "I love you, man." Christian placed the quarter on top of Eric's grave before walking away. Christian got back into the vehicle, looking one last time at Eric's grave before driving off.

As Christian pulled back into the driveway, he felt a sense of calm with his emotions. Like a relief that he was not expecting to feel, a peace with what he had witnessed this weekend and the future that would come.

As Christian walked inside, Kelsey looked at him. She could tell he had been crying, "Was it busy?" Christian smiled, "Yes, madam, but I am here." Christian placed the food on the table and walked over to Kelsey, hugging her, "I love you, Kelsey."

Kelsey hugged Christian back, "I love you too." She did not say anything else. She knew it was not the time. The two sat down and ate. Christian had become talkative again. Kelsey felt a shift from just an hour earlier on the car ride home. Whatever helped Christian, she was happy to see him return to the Christian she knew. She knew in time Christian would tell her what happened and why the shift took place.

Chapter 17:

Saying Goodbye

In the two months following the visit from Christian and Kelsey, Hayley and Jordan went back to how it was before that weekend. They were friends, and there was no conversation about the weekend. It was like it never happened. Jordan stayed busy with physical therapy and trying to get back to work, and Hayley worked on her business, trying to get it more profitable. At night, the two would sit down and eat together, mostly watching TV. They lived together, but there was nothing more.

Jordan's house finally had the tree off of it, and they had begun fixing the damage inside. Jordan, able to get around for the most part with a cane, would walk over several times during the day to watch. Jordan had also gone to the office some. He went and caught up on cases he had done before his injury. It was good to be back at work and see everyone, but it also hurt, knowing he still had a long way before he could join them again fully.

Hayley tried to keep herself busy with the business and spending time away in the city. She missed Christian and Kelsey, often wondering if she had made the wrong decision moving away. She also thought of her mom. She had not seen her mom since the move. Hayley felt it was probably time.

As Hayley sat down to eat dinner with Jordan one night, she said, "I think I am going to go home this weekend and see my mom."

Jordan was surprised as Hayley had not seen her mom or mentioned going back home since he had known her.

Jordan: "That will be good. You can see Kelsey and Christian when you are there, too."

Hayley: "Yeah, it will be good. Will you be okay with me gone for the weekend?"

Jordan: "Hal, I will be fine. We are on the downhill slope now. Go have fun, you don't have to take care of me. If I need anything, I will call Dan. Are you okay?"

Hayley: "Yeah, I am good. I just think it is something I need to do for me."

Jordan: "Do you want me to come with you? I don't mind."

Hayley: "No, I think I need to do it alone."

Jordan: "Are you sure you are okay?"

Hayley: "Yeah, I am good."

Jordan looked at Hayley. "Hal, what happened?"

Hayley looked at Jordan," What do you mean?"

Jordan: "Since the day after Christian and Kelsey left, you changed. Did I do something to upset you?"

Hayley: "No, Jordan, I guess we just needed to come back to reality. We were acting irresponsibly."

Jordan: "Hal, we were acting on passion and feelings. We weren't married, we didn't have kids, we were being responsible. I just don't understand."

Hayley thought about it for a long time and then answered, "It got too real. What were we going to do, play house and act like we both hadn't been through trauma?"

Jordan: "No, we would have seen where things went and gone from there."

Hayley: "And what would happen then, Jordan, when we decided it wouldn't work? Huh? We would live together without talking until your house got fixed. It was moving too fast."

Jordan: "Hal, we kissed, geezus christ, where do you think it was moving too fast?"

Hayley: "It just wouldn't have worked. We are two different people."

Jordan: "No, we are more alike than you want to admit."

Jordan said, snapping at Hayley.

Hayley: "What is that supposed to mean? I don't party; I don't have several women on my arm or messages every day."

Jordan: "Oh, Hal, that hasn't happened in months, you know that. Why are you bringing all of that stuff up anyway?"

Hayley: "It's going to happen again; you and Dan are going to go out and find what do you call them, badge bunnies?"

Jordan: "Oh, come on, Hal."

Hayley: "How do I know you aren't lying to me and hiding stuff from me?"

With that, Jordan lost it before he could contain his anger, "You mean like you being a freaking cop? Or no, maybe it was you being a narc or a homicide detective, or maybe it was moving here to forget your old life."

Hayley looked at Jordan in shock that he knew.

Jordan: "Yes, Hal, I know all of it. I thought, maybe just maybe, after Christian and Kelsey's trip, you would come out with it. That you would tell me all on your own, but instead, you pulled away. I know you felt something that weekend. I just wanted to be with you, Hal, and help you.”

Hayley: “I don't need your help, Jordan. I can handle myself.”

Jordan stood up from the table, “Hal, I know you can handle yourself, but you could have let me be there too.” Jordan turned and walked away, “Have a good weekend. Be safe while driving.”

Jordan walked into the bedroom he was now staying in and closed the door. Hayley closed her eyes; emotion had swept over her. How could he not tell her he knew? How could Christian tell Jordan and not tell her? Hayley took a deep breath and grabbed the dishes off the table and placed them in the sink.

Jordan lay down on the bed, *What the hell is wrong with her. She has snakes in her head. If one of us was lying, it was her. She told me nothing about her life. Damn it, Hal, why are you so hardheaded? I did nothing wrong; I could have, but I didn't. This is why nice guys always finish last.”*

Jordan jumped as his phone went off. He looked over, and it was Dan.

Dan: “Hey, bud, what are you up to?”

Jordan: “Nothing, just sitting around.”

Dan: “Where's the shrew?”

Jordan: “Man, I told you to stop calling her that, but I don't know, somewhere in the other room.”

Dan: “Some of the guys are off this weekend. We were going to hit the town. I figured you could hit the town with us since you are doing better.”

Jordan: “Yeah, Dan, I don't know if I am up for that. I still have a long way to go, and I am still using a cane.”

Dan: “Oh, come on, it will be fun and better than sitting another night in that house with the shrew.”

Jordan: "Dan, I don't think so. A cane doesn't scream desirable."

Dan: "Sure, it does. We can make up some shit that you got hurt in the line of duty. Get this whole story going."

Jordan laughed, "You are an idiot, dude."

Dan: "You know it will work; the girls are going to be popping this weekend."

Jordan thought about it for a moment, "You know, Dan, I will go. I don't know how long I will stay, but I will go. Can you pick me up?"

Dan: "That's what I am talking about. I'll pick you up tomorrow night."

Jordan: "Alright, these girls better be popping as you say."

Dan: "Oh, they will bud, maybe we will get you laid."

Jordan: "Bye, Dan."

Jordan could hear Dan laughing as he hung up the phone.

Jordan lay his head back on his pillow. He thought to himself, *Why not? I mean, he and Hayley weren't in a relationship. All they did was kiss.* Jordan's thoughts were just to get out and see what was out there. He had been so tied up in living with Hayley that he forgot he was single. He was not tied down to anything.

Early the next morning, Hayley packed a bag and left for her hometown. She did not want to even see Jordan, and she knew he would be asleep. As she began to drive, the weekend Christian came was in her mind. The Friday night before, when Jordan had kissed her, his smile, the way he looked at her. There was so much passion between the two of them, there was so much of a connection. She didn't understand why it just stopped. Like they woke up one morning and it was done. Jordan was a player, though; he probably was talking to several women. That is who he was; she couldn't change that in him. It didn't matter what she had to offer him.

Hayley picked up her phone, not wanting to think about it. She scrolled through her contacts before hitting call.

Mom: "Hello."

Hayley: "Hey, momma."

Mom: "Hayley! How are you, baby girl?"

Hayley: "I am good. I just wanted to let you know I will be there in a few."

Mom: "Oh, darling, I can't wait to see you."

Hayley: "I can't wait to see you either. Give me an hour, and I should be there."

Mom: "I will be waiting for you."

Hayley: "Bye, momma."

Mom: "Bye."

Hayley scrolled through her contacts and found Christian.

Christian: "Hal, what are you doing, girl? How have you been?"

Hayley: "I am good. I just wanted to let you know I am coming home this weekend."

Christian: "You are? When will you be here?"

Hayley: "In about an hour."

Christian was quiet, "Hal, why didn't you say something? We had no clue you were coming."

Hayley: "No, it was a last-minute thing. I haven't seen my mom in a while. I figured it was time."

Christian: "Well, what are you going to do tonight? We have a bunch of people coming over tonight. They are all from work, some new faces, but some old ones too. They would love to see you."

Hayley: "I don't know Christian, it has been a while."

Christian: "Yeah, but they would love to see you. Is Jordan with you? They would love to meet him, too, I am sure."

Hayley had not mentioned Jordan to Christian since the day they left.

Hayley: "No, Jordan is not with me."

Christian didn't like the way Hayley said that.

Christian: "Are you okay, Hal?"

Hayley: "Yeah, I am fine. Just needed to get away."

Christian: "Hal, come. I know there are a ton of people who would love to see you."

Hayley thought about it. It would be good to see everyone. Her mom would be asleep or close to it before the party started.

Hayley: "Okay, I will see you there."

Christian: "Perfect. I will let Kelsey know. She will be so excited to see you."

Hayley: "Yeah, I will see you there."

Christian hung up the phone.

Kelsey: "Who was that?"

Christian: "It was Hal."

Kelsey: "Oh, really, how is she doing?"

Christian: "She is on the way here. She is going to see her mom for the weekend."

Kelsey: "Is Jordan coming with her?"

Christian: "No, she said he didn't come."

Kelsey: "Hmm, is she alright?"

Christian: "I don't know Kelsey, but I think so. Something happened, though."

Kelsey: "Is she going to come to the party?"

Christian: "Yeah, she will be here tonight."

Kelsey: "Well, good, I'll get it out of her."

Hayley pulled up at her mom's house. Her mom walked outside, and Hayley met her on the front porch. "Hey, momma," Hayley said, hugging her mom.

"Hey, baby," she said, hugging Hayley.

Mom: "My lord, let me look at you, you look like you are straight out of Florida. You are so dark and skinny, are you eating enough?"

Hayley: "Momma, I am fine."

Mom: "Well, come inside, it's just you and me. I sent Charles away for the day. Tell me all about Florida."

Hayley smiled and walked inside with her mom, carrying the bag she brought. They sat down on the couch, and Hayley began to tell her mom the story of the house, the hurricane, and Jordan. Hayley's mom listened intently. When Hayley stopped, she said, "Well, at least you two have the cop thing in common. I am sure you two have made time pass."

Hayley: "Momma, he didn't know I was a cop until about 2 months ago."

Mom: "Hayley, you didn't tell him. Why?"

Hayley: "I don't know, momma. I just wanted to start over, and he was a typical cop, and I didn't want to deal with it. And I wasn't a cop anymore. I was just someone who ran an online store from home."

"Hayley Ann," Hayley hated when her mom called her by her middle name, "You can't hide who you are. It doesn't matter if you are not a cop anymore; you did it for years."

Hayley: "I know."

Mom: "Does he know about Eric?"

Hayley: "Yes, I did tell him about that. At first, he thought I was a badge bunny that got Eric caught up."

Hayley's mom laughed, "You had him fooled, I see."

Hayley smiled, "I did. And everything was going fine until the hurricane, and his house was destroyed, and him living with me because he was hurt."

Mom: "Why did you let him live with you for so long if you didn't want him there?"

Hayley: "That's present tense. He still lives with me. I don't know, I kind of got used to him being there, and he tries to appease me. He is funny."

Mom: "What's wrong with him then? Is he ugly?"

Hayley laughed at her mom's comment, "No, he is good-looking."

Mom: "Then what is it, Hayley Ann?"

Hayley: "I don't know, he likes women, I guess."

Mom: "I seem to believe you thought that was a challenge at one time."

Hayley: "It is just different now."

Mom: "Different now, Hayley Ann, you are young, bright, and beautiful. How could it be different?"

Hayley: "I was married to Eric. He was the one I picked."

Mom: "Yes, but Hayley Eric died a while ago now."

Hayley: "I know, but you didn't marry again for a long time after dad left."

Mom: "Hayley Ann, that was a totally different situation, and I also had you. I had to do my best for you, and I did what I thought was best until you went off and started living your own life. That was my choice, you don't have a child, Hayley Ann. No matter what, Eric isn't out there. He is gone, Hayley, and if I know Eric, he would not want you to be alone. He would want you to be happy and be who you always were."

Hayley: "I just can't let it go."

Mom: "You don't have to let it go, Hayley, you just have to move forward. He will always be with you. You take the love you had for him, and you find a new life with the same happiness. Different, yes, but that doesn't mean it will be less of a ride."

Hayley: "I just don't understand why this had to happen still. Everything was fine, we both were happy, we loved each other."

Mom: "You will never know why, and you are going to drive yourself crazy trying to figure it out. Some things in life we will never understand, and I don't think we are supposed to Hayley Ann. I don't know why all of the stuff happened with your dad. I thought my life was over, and I was okay with it as long as I had my Hayley. In the end, it turned out exactly the way it was supposed to."

Hayley: "I just miss him momma."

Mom: "Hayley, I don't think you will ever not miss him. It is always going to be there, but the right person won't try and erase that inside of you. They will only hope you love them with the same intensity that you loved Eric."

Hayley lay her head in her mom's lap and began to cry.

Mom: "Oh, Hayley Ann, you are going to be fine. Open yourself up and live, hon." Hayley's mom began rubbing Hayley's hair.

Mom: "Just live, Hayley Ann, that's why you moved, to start over again."

Hayley lay in her mom's lap, crying, talking about Eric and his death. She talked about Jordan and everything they'd been through—the weekend they shared, and then how it all suddenly stopped. It was like Hayley was a teenager again, telling her mom all of the stories of her younger years. Hayley felt relieved talking to her mom, as she always did when she was younger. Her mom never judged her, just listened until Hayley was done talking. This time was no different.

Back home, Jordan had just gotten out of the shower, getting ready for the evening with Dan and the other guys from work. His leg felt good, and he was hoping it would be fine. As he got ready, all he could do was think of Hayley, wondering what she was doing. He couldn't help but think going out was wronging Hayley. Jordan kept telling himself, they weren't together and that he was doing nothing wrong. Jordan stood back and looked at himself in the mirror. He hadn't put on nice clothes in a long time, and it felt good.

Jordan's phone rang; it was Dan.

Dan: "Dude, I'll be there in about 5 minutes."

Jordan: "Okay, I'll be waiting outside."

As Dan said, he was there in exactly 5 minutes. Jordan stepped off the porch and walked to Dan's truck. As he opened the door and started to get in, Jordan said, "Hey man."

Dan looked at Jordan, "Aww, look at you. Looking all fine tonight."

Jordan: "Dan, shut up, you already are annoying me, man."

Dan: "I am just saying. It's good to have my partner back. I've been worried about you."

Jordan closed the door, "Yeah, it is good to see you."

Dan: "Now, let's go find some hotties."

Jordan looked at Dan and joked, "That is why you are single. No one says let's go get some hotties. You are an idiot."

Dan laughed as they drove off.

Hayley began to get ready to meet Christian and Kelsey at their house. Hayley's mom came in, "Do you need anything before I go lie down?"

Hayley: "No, momma, I am good."

Mom: "Well, you know where the spare key is. Just make sure you lock up before you leave."

Hayley: "Okay, momma I will."

Mom: "I'll see you in the morning Hayley Ann, love you."

Hayley: "Love you too."

Mom: "Goodnight."

Hayley: "Night momma."

As Hayley's mom walked away, Hayley looked at herself in the mirror. The reflection staring back at her, she hardly recognized. Another year older, and she thought she would have things figured out, but she still didn't. She didn't know what she wanted. As she pondered what she wanted, Jordan flashed in her head. The memories of reading together, her rescuing him from the tree, and laughing together. Of course, the first kiss came to her mind, and in those moments, everything seemed like it was going to be okay. Hayley was in thought when her phone went off. It was Christian.

"Hal, when are you going to be here? People are asking about you."

Hayley set her brush down and picked up her phone, *"I am about to leave. I will be there in about 15 minutes."*

Christian replied, *"Okay, see you soon. Can't wait."*

"See you soon," Hayley texted as she set her phone back down, looking at herself in the mirror. She was going to be alright. She just had to figure out what she wanted and needed. Hayley walked out of the bathroom into the living room. She picked up her car keys and turned out the lights. Hayley got in her vehicle and began to drive to Christian's house. She thought that it was going to be a good night.

Dan and Jordan had made it to the restaurant they were all going to meet up before going to the bars. As Dan walked in and saw the other guys, he yelled, "Look who I got out of the darkness." The guys looked up and saw Jordan standing there. They began to yell; Jordan could tell some of them were feeling the effects of the alcohol already. Jordan smiled and did what guys do: fist bump, half hug, and smack hands. Jordan had to admit it felt good being out with the guys. He had not done it since before the hurricane.

Jordan sat by Mike and across from Nick. Mike turned to Jordan, "I heard you have been playing house with that neighbor of yours."

Jordan laughed, "I wouldn't call it playing house. More like a refuge until my house gets fixed."

Mike: "Oh, come on, Jordan, I know you are banging her."

Jordan laughed, "No, it's not like that. You have seen her personality."

Mike and Nick laughed. Nick looked at Jordan, "What the hell do you guys do all day? I mean, a brick has more personality than her."

Jordan: "Hell, I don't know, watch TV, or she is off doing something, or I am off doing something. The only time we really sit down together is when we eat."

Nick looked at Jordan with a surprised look, "You eat dinner together?"

Jordan: "Yeah, it is our peace offering since we do live together technically right now."

Mike looked at Jordan, "and you ain't hitting it?"

Jordan: "Come on guys, let it go. No, I am not sleeping with her."

Nick smirked, "How did you get out of jail tonight?"

Jordan took a sip of the Crown that Dan had gotten him. Jordan about choked; it was so strong.

Jordan: "She is out of town visiting her mom and her friends, Christian and Kelsey."

Dan yelled, "Party at the shrews' house tonight."

Jordan: "Oh no, we are not going back to her house. Get that out of your head. If you guys are going anywhere, it is one of your houses."

Dan said, "Respect, I get it."

The guys kept talking as they drank the Crown that Dan had brought to the table. Jordan was already spinning; he couldn't tell the guys, but he knew he had to slow down. Everyone was laughing and talking, Jordan sat there trying to wear off the effects of the Crown he had drunk.

"I am going to run to the bathroom. I'll be back," Jordan excused himself as he took his drink and his phone to the bathroom. As Jordan got into the bathroom, he locked the door. He turned on the water to the sink and dumped the rest of his drink down the drain. He put some water in his hands and splashed it on his face, grabbing a paper towel and wiping the water off his face. He picked up his phone, scrolling to Hayley's name.

He stared at his phone for a long time, wondering if he should call her. He began to think about it, *"Why am I trying to call her. She doesn't give a crap. I'm out with the guys, get over it, Jordan."* Jordan closed his phone, thinking, *No, tonight is for me and my buddies. I deserve this.* Jordan grabbed the empty glass that was still sitting on the counter.

Jordan walked back to the table; their food had arrived. Jordan was thankful, hoping that eating would help with the effects of the alcohol. Jordan had another full Crown glass sitting at the table when he got back. Jordan looked at the waiter, "Can I get some water, please?" Dan looked at Jordan, "What, are you done already? You are lightweight."

Everyone began to laugh. Jordan laughed, then said, "No, I am not knocking back drinks while I am trying to eat. Calm down." Jordan was trying to sober up a little; he wasn't going to tell the guys that, but it was way too early to feel buzzed. The guys ate and continued to talk before Dan announced, "It's about that time, gentlemen, let's go find the ladies." The guys got up, and Jordan drank the last of the water the waiter had brought.

The guys paid and walked out of the restaurant, walking towards one of the bars down the street. Jordan tried to keep up with them the best he could. Dan turned and saw Jordan struggling to keep up. "You alright?" Jordan turned to Dan, "Yeah, man, just takes me a little longer."

Dan looked at Jordan, "You worried about it."

Jordan looked at Dan. He could tell Dan was close to being drunk, but he was being sincere.

Jordan: "Yeah, of course I am worried about it. It's been two months."

Dan: "What is the doctor saying?"

Jordan: "After 6 weeks, he said to wait for 12 weeks; we aren't there yet."

Dan: "Well, you have 4 more weeks to not worry about it then."

Jordan looked at Dan, laughing," I don't until times like these when I can't keep up."

Dan: "They will slow down by the middle of the night."

As they reached the bar, there was a line. When they finally got inside, Jordan looked around. It was so loud and there were people everywhere. Dan was right, it was popping. Jordan looked at Dan and yelled, "I am going to sit at the bar."

Dan walked off, "Alright, see you in a bit." Jordan watched as he disappeared into the crowd.

"What are you having?" The bartender asked.

Jordan: "Can I get a glass of water and a Coke?"

Bartender: "Just Coke?"

Jordan: "Yes, please. One of us has to be sober."

The bartender laughed, picking up a glass and pushing the button for Coke, "Here you go."

Jordan picked up the Coke, "Thanks."

Jordan sat at the bar, watching everyone in the room. People came and went from the bar as Jordan sat there. Finally, Dan popped up, and he wasn't alone. "Jordan, look who I found," Dan said as Jordan looked. It was Michelle. He hadn't seen Michelle in months. Michelle was your typical girl who chased the badge. Jordan looked her up and down. Her long blonde hair was down past her shoulders. She had a full face of makeup, a tight-fitting top, and a skirt that barely covered her butt. The last time he had seen her was at his house, the day he kissed her in front of Hayley to make her mad.

Jordan: "Michelle, what a surprise."

Michelle was half-wasted, hugged Jordan, "Why didn't you call me?"

Jordan could smell the liquor on Michelle. "I've been kind of busy."

Dan stepped in, "Yeah, he got hurt in the line of duty. He is still recovering."

Michelle looked surprised, "Oh no, are you okay?"

Jordan looked at Michelle, "Yeah, I am good."

Dan: "Jordan, what are you drinking?"

Jordan was not going to tell Dan he was drinking just Coke, so he replied, "Crown and Coke."

"Hey bartender, give me another round of Crown and Coke," Dan said as Jordan cringed, knowing he was about to be buzzed again.

Michelle: "So, Jordan, Dan said that we are all going back to his place when we leave here. Will I see you there?"

Jordan: "I am sure I will be there, Michelle."

Michelle: "Good, maybe we can catch up."

Michelle and the girl she was with walked off. Dan sat down next to Jordan, smiling as they walked away.

Jordan: "Don't you get tired of that shit?"

Dan looked at Jordan, "What shit?"

Jordan: "Girls like that. They are thrust traps."

Dan: "That's why you have to outsmart them, Jordan. What the hell, man? What is wrong with you?"

Jordan: "Nothing, I just get tired of the same girls, doing the same things."

Dan: "We can get you another girl if you are finished with Michelle."

Jordan knew there was no talking to Dan. He was too far gone. Mike and Nick walked up, "Let's do a shot."

Dan: "Make it brown, Jordan is drinking Crown and Coke."

Nick came back with 4 shots. Jordan took his shot from Nick, it was brown, maybe it was Crown, or Jager. He was hoping it was nothing too strong. Nick raised his shot, "To us. The first night back together." They all said, "To us." Jordan lifted his shot glass and drank the brown liquid inside. Jordan felt it going down, and he began to cough, "Holy hell, man, what was that?"

Nick laughed, "We had Jagar. I got you a Mind Eraser." They all laughed. Jordan was still trying to catch his breath.

Jordan: "Nice, Nick, thanks a lot."

Nick hugged Jordan, "Loosen up a little bit." Nick and Mike were off again. Dan laughed and looked at Jordan.

Dan: "You alright?"

Jordan: "Yeah, I just haven't drank like this in a while. I am fine."

"DAN!" Jordan and Dan turned in the direction they heard Dan's name called.

Dan: "Shelly! Wow, girl, you look great."

Shelly: "Dan, you didn't call me."

Shelly had her hands on her hips with a sad face.

Dan: "Oh, girl, you know we have been busy with work. You remember Jordan." Jordan smiled and waved.

Shelly: "Yeah, I remember him."

Dan: "Look, we are going to get out of here in a little bit. You want to come back to my house?"

Shelly: "You aren't going to get me back to your house again."

Dan smiled, "It is going to be a bunch of us, come on, it's safe."

Shelly looked at Dan, who was making a pouty face. Jordan rolled his eyes, grabbing what he thought to be his Coke. It was not, though; it was the Crown and Coke that Dan had ordered earlier. Jordan just could not taste the liquor in it any longer.

"Okay, I will come. You are so cute," Shelly said as she walked off smiling.

Jordan looked at Dan, "You've got to have your options open, Jordan."

Jordan looked at Dan, trying to concentrate, "And what if both of them come?"

"I just have to keep them in separate rooms," Dan said, laughing. Jordan sat back in the chair, watching Dan walk off again. Jordan looked back at the bartender, "Can I get some water?" The bartender looked at Jordan, "Are you okay?"

"Yeah, I am going to be. I just need some water," Jordan replied as he grabbed the glass from the bartender and started drinking the water. He watched Dan, Mike, and Nick mingle. The whole bar was spinning at the moment.

Hayley arrived at Christian's house. She knocked on the door, and Christian opened the door. "HAL!" Hayley could tell Christian had already been drinking.

Christian: "Girl, it is good to see you."

Christian pulled Hayley inside. Kelsey grabbed Hayley from Christian.

Kelsey: "Hey Hal, sorry they have gotten a little carried away already. It was a long week."

"What happened?" Hayley asked worriedly.

Kelsey sensed tension in Hayley's tone, "Nothing like that. Just been really busy, and they have been working really long hours. You know the criminal never sleeps."

Hayley relaxed a little and smiled, "Yes, all too well."

Kelsey threw her arm around Hayley, "It's really good to see you." Kelsey shut the door behind Hayley before yelling, "HEY EVERYONE, LOOK WHO I FOUND!"

People turned to see who or what Kelsey was yelling about and saw Hayley walking with Kelsey. People began to say, "HAL!" People came toward Hayley, hugging her and asking her how she had been. For the time, it felt as if no time had passed, as if Hayley was still working at the department and it was just another night with everyone. Hayley thought the bond would have long been gone, like she wasn't a part of the team she once worked with, but they had not forgotten her, and they did miss her.

As Hayley was talking, out of the corner of her eye, she saw Steve approaching her.

"Hey, Hal," Steve said as he hugged her.

"Hey Steve," Hayley replied.

Hayley: "How have you been?"

Steve: "Been good, Hal. Man, you look great."

Hayley: "Thanks, Steve."

Steve: "You want a drink? Rum and Coke? Or what did you use to drink Amoretto Sours?"

Hayley: "Oh no, I am good right now but thank you."

Kelsey heard Steve and knew the history of what happened the last time he saw Hayley.

Kelsey: "She drinks wine now, Steve. She has moved up to classy adult life."

Hayley laughed, "That is not fair, Kelsey. You and Christian didn't mind when you came."

Kelsey: "Tasted like Kool-Aid, but we sure paid for it the next day."

Kelsey, Hayley, and Steve all laughed.

Steve: "Hey, Hal, you want to sit and talk?"

Steve motioned to the chairs a few steps away.

"Sure," Hayley said as she looked back and winked at Kelsey. Kelsey knew that Hayley was fine with it by the wink, and she went on talking to others around her.

Steve and Hayley walked over to the chairs and sat down.

Steve: "So what have you been up to? You kind of disappeared after you moved."

Hayley: "Nothing much, just working with my online store and enjoying the city. We had that hurricane come through, so the city is still rebuilding from that."

Steve: "I didn't think about that, you are talking about Hurricane Sarah?"

Hayley: "Yeah, it came right through and tore up the city pretty bad."

Steve: "Did you help with the cleanup?"

Hayley: "No, I have just stayed out of the way. I figured the best way to help is to stay out of law enforcement's way."

Steve: "You still aren't back in, huh?"

Hayley: "No, I gave it up when I left here, Steve."

Steve: "You were so good at it, Hal, I don't understand."

Hayley: "After Eric died, it just changed everything."

Steve: "I know, but it may have helped."

Hayley: "No, it wouldn't have, I just was done."

Steve, wanting to change the subject, said, "Are you dating anyone, or is there someone you're interested in back home?"

Hayley thought about whether she should mention Jordan.

Hayley: "No, it is just Emma and me still. We don't have much time to do anything else."

Steve: "Hal, I am sorry about what happened between you and me before you left. I was out of line, and I should not have come on to you the way I did."

Hayley didn't even want to talk about the kiss between the two, "Look, don't worry about it. It's in the past. I am sure we both have moved on from it."

Steve laughed, "I don't know about moving on from it, but I am still sorry for everything. If you ever do decide to take me up on my offer and go out with me, though, I am willing."

Hayley laughed, "Thanks, but I think I am going to pass. I kind of like the way my life is going right now." She knew that was a lie but wanted to let Steve down easily. No matter what, he was a nice guy.

Steve: "Well, you, my dear, have many people to see. Get your butt out there and mingle."

Hayley got up and hugged Steve, "Thank you."

Steve: "Anytime, Hal."

Hayley walked off, and Christian grabbed Hayley and hugged her, "Hal, where have you been?" Hayley could tell Christian was drunk.

Hayley: "Boy, Kelsey is going to have a time with you tonight."

Christian: "She loves me, though. You know she is my person."

Hayley: "Yes, she does. The only way she would put up with you." Hayley and Christian started laughing and talking. Kelsey joined them, joking about Christian being drunk. It was always the three of them, it would never change.

Meanwhile, Jordan, Dan, Mike, and Nick made it back to Dan's house. There were several people who had come along, including Michelle and Shelly. Jordan found a chair and sat down with a bottle of water. He watched how Dan, Mike, and Nick mingled, looking for the women they would be with for the night. He thought about the lines they would tell them and how the women would eat every bit of it, hoping for a chance to be their girlfriend.

Those women were always different; they weren't real, they were after the chase to catch an officer, just like the officers were after their next "victim". It was a sad cycle that always continued, drinking and women, about the only way to not think about all of the stuff they have seen. It was a way to try and forget, even if it was only for a night. The next day, they would wake again with a hangover and their trauma still there. It was only temporary, but in those drunken nights and endless women, there was a happiness they remembered.

"Jordan, what are you doing, man?"

Dan had come stumbling over to Jordan and sat down next to him.

"Nothing, Dan. How are you feeling, bud?" Jordan said, smiling at Dan.

Dan: "I am doing great. What are you doing? You haven't found Michelle yet?"

Jordan laughed, "No Dan. I am working on that Minderaser one of you guys gave me earlier."

Dan: "Oh, come on, Jordan, you need to loosen up. You have been hanging around the shrew too long. This is who you are, dude."

Jordan knew Dan was drunk, but he took offense to Dan calling Hayley a shrew again.

Jordan: "Look, Dan, I've asked you not to call her that. You don't know her, man, knock it off."

"Whoa, easy, Jordan." Dan laughed, "What is wrong with you? She got to you."

Jordan: "Dan, right now isn't the time to talk about this, bud. Just go have fun and enjoy yourself."

Dan: "You love this stuff, Jordan, come on. I'll go find Michelle for you."

Jordan: "No, I am good, Dan. I think I am going to head out here soon. But I had fun tonight with you guys. This just isn't really my thing anymore."

Dan sensed something was going on with Jordan.

Dan: "Okay, man, how about I come by and check on you tomorrow?"

Jordan: "Yeah, sure. That will be good."

Jordan stood up, hugged Dan, and said, "You guys don't burn it down too late."

Dan smiled, holding his drink up, "There is no such thing as too late, only early morning Jordan."

Jordan smiled and watched Dan walk away, disappearing into a sea of people. Jordan walked to the door and looked back one more time. He did not recognize the life he had lived only a few months ago. He had grown and didn't really know who he was, but he knew this wasn't it anymore. Jordan waited outside for his ride to come.

As he waited, Michelle came out the door, "You are leaving?"

Jordan turned to see Michelle walking towards him. "Yeah, I need to get home."

Michelle: "I thought we would spend some time together."

Jordan turned to Michelle, "No, I need to be getting home."

Michelle tried to hug Jordan, and Jordan grabbed her arms, "No, Michelle." Michelle was taken back by Jordan's resistance. She looked at Jordan, "What is wrong with you?"

Jordan knew that would come from the way he had treated Michelle in the past. Giving her hope in a future that he knew would never happen.

Jordan looked around and sat down, patting the seat next to him for Michelle to sit down.

Jordan: "Michelle, why do you do this every freaking weekend?"

She looked at Jordan in shock.

Michelle: "Damn Jordan, you are acting like a parent."

Jordan: "You don't have to do this and be like this. I've been around you long enough to know you are better than this."

Michelle: "Because it is fun and I get to meet people like you and be with people like you." Michelle reached out to touch Jordan, and Jordan flinched. Michelle pulled her hand back.

Jordan was silent for a moment, "Michelle, I am sorry for what I did to you. For making you believe that it would ever be more than what it was. I was wrong, but you have to stop this, too. This is no way to live. There are a lot of guys out there that would be happy to be with you and treat you right."

Michelle stood up, "I like this life, Jordan. I want to be around the guys; I want to feel a part of something more, and hopefully one day be married to this life. There is nothing wrong with this Jordan. What has gotten into you?"

Jordan: "I know there is nothing wrong with this life, it is why I got into it in the first place, but sometimes people change. There is good and bad with it all. The wild parties and drunken nights, we are all getting older, Michelle."

Michelle: "Yes, we are. That's why the party awaits."

Michelle got up and started walking to the door. She turned around to Jordan, who was watching her walk away, "How do I look?" she said, smiling. Jordan smiled, "You look amazing, Michelle." Michelle turned around and kept walking. Jordan's ride pulled up, and he started walking to the vehicle to get inside.

Michelle turned around as Jordan was getting in the cab, "Hey Jordan."

Jordan turned to look at Michelle. Michelle said, "I don't know who she is, but she is a lucky girl."

Jordan smiled, "Have a good night, Michelle." Jordan got in the vehicle, and it drove off.

The night was winding down for Hayley. She was sitting on the couch across from Christian and Kelsey, who were snuggled up together. Christian was forbidden earlier to drink anything else.

"What's up with you Jordan?" Kelsey finally asked.

Hayley: "Nothing, we argue like we always do."

Kelsey: "I just knew something was going to happen between you two. I could see it."

Hayley was looking down as she answered Kelsey, "I don't know. We just stopped, like when you guys were there, things seemed so real. After you left, we both got busy doing our own thing. We have always eaten dinner together, but we just started doing our separate things. Jordan went back to work, and we are just roommates."

Christian, still drunk, looked at Hayley, "Hal, you sure some of it isn't you? I sure saw the same thing I saw with you and Eric before you guys made it official. I think you won't get out of your own head. Hal, Eric's gone girl." Kelsey broke in, "Christian!" Christian looked at Kelsey, "What, babe, it's the truth." Hayley was looking at Christian in shock. Christian turned back to Hayley, "You are too stubborn to get out of your own way, girl. You think it was easy to see the two of you together, hiding your emotions. You could read through both of you." Kelsey broke in again, "Alright, Christian, it is time to go to bed."

Christian: "No, Kelsey let me get this out. Hal, I had a hard time with it. But what I had to realize is that you deserve to be happy again. Eric was my boy, he always will be, but I had to get out of my own way. I went and talked to Eric; maybe that is what you need to do. Get out of your own way, Hal. He's a good dude. Okay, I'm ready to go to bed now."

Christian got up from the couch.

Hayley got up and hugged Christian, "Good night, Christian."

Christian looked at Hayley, "We good?"

Hayley smiled, "Of course we are."

Christian: "Good cause I don't want Eric's ass to come haunt me because I pissed you off."

Hayley giggled, "Good night, Christian."

Christian: "Night, Hal."

Christian walked off and down a hallway heading to his bedroom. Kelsey and Hayley watched as he disappeared.

Kelsey: "He had a really hard time when we got home. I didn't know he had gone to see Eric. He didn't know how he was going to react to seeing you around another guy, but he really liked Jordan."

Hayley smiled, "He only liked Jordan because he was a cop."

Kelsey: "This is true, but Jordan is a really nice guy. I don't know how he acts at times, but it was the way he would look at you. You can see it."

Hayley: "It's just not like that with us. I think we have both just become numb to that part of our lives. We don't know what either one of us wants anymore."

Kelsey: "Maybe talk about it?"

Hayley: "There is no talking with us. It's just not worth it."

"Kelsey!" Christian was yelling from down the hall.

Kelsey: "I'd better go get him. Give me a few minutes."

Hayley: "No, go ahead, I'd better get going anyway. I will stop by and see you guys before I leave."

Kelsey hugged Hayley, "Alright, drive home safe?"

Hayley: "Yeah. I'll lock the door behind me."

Kelsey: "Don't worry, I'm sure the others who are still up will crash and won't wake until morning."

Hayley got up, hugging Kelsey, and both walked in different directions. Hayley got in her car and drove home. When she made it home, she walked to her mom's room, peering inside. Her mom was still fast asleep. She walked to her room door, closing it, undressing, and slipping into bed. Thoughts of Jordan rang in her head as she fell asleep.

After Jordan got home, he lay down on the couch and fell asleep. He woke to banging on the door. Jordan picked up his phone; it was 11:30 in the morning. Jordan got up from the couch and walked to the door; his head was pounding. He opened the door to Dan barging in.

Dan: "Good morning, princess. You still sleeping?"

Jordan closed the door behind Dan, "Come in, Dan. Yes, I was still asleep. Did you even go to bed?"

Dan: "Yeah, I went to sleep. You are just out of practice, boy."

Dan plopped down on the couch. Jordan walked over to the other couch and sat down.

Jordan: "I guess; my head is killing me."

Dan: "You left too early last night. Things got wild. Old Michelle?"

Jordan: "Yeah, what about her?"

Dan: "She ended up all over Nick last night. I think the two actually hit it off. I don't know, I was with Shelly."

Jordan smiled, "Those two would be perfect together. Shelly? Do you even like Shelly?"

Dan was lying back on the couch, "Yeah, she is alright."

Jordan: "You don't ever want more than that."

Dan: "Never really thought about it."

Jordan: "You should want more than that."

Dan sat up, "I don't need a speech from you, Jordan. My parents aren't the happy-go-lucky fairy tale marriage your parents had. I don't want to be stuck 20 years down the line with someone I grow to hate."

Jordan: "It doesn't have to be like that, Dan."

Dan: "How in the hell are you even talking about this right now? Your marriage was a flop."

Jordan: "I know, but I am starting to believe there is more out there."

Dan: "Dude, what is wrong with you? You are acting like a pus."

Jordan: "Just this accident has me thinking."

Dan: "It's her, isn't it? I freaking knew it."

Jordan: "No, we barely talk. I just want something different. Last night just showed me, I am not built for that life anymore. I liked hanging out and seeing everyone, but the bars, the partying all night, I just don't want that."

Dan: "You know you are my partner and I'm with you in anything you do, but don't get soft on me."

Jordan laughed, "You're an idiot. I am not getting soft."

Dan: "What is it about her?"

Jordan: "I don't know. Maybe she's just a pia more than the rest and doesn't put up with my crap."

Dan chuckled, "I don't know if that is healthy, but it has to be better than your last one."

Both chuckled.

Dan: "I am happy for you in a straight way."

Jordan: "Let's talk about something else. You are starting to make me think you actually care about me and have feelings."

Dan laughed, and the two talked for hours, catching up, something they hadn't done in a long time.

Hayley got up and said her goodbyes to her mom, promising to come back soon. She left her mom's house and drove to Christian and Kelsey's as she promised she would. As she got there, the once loud and exciting house was now quiet. Hayley knocked on the door. Christian answered the door. He looked like he had just woken up.

"I can tell you feel like crap," Hayley smiled.

Christian: "Let's not talk about it. Come in. Kelsey is in the shower."

Hayley walked into the house. The smell of alcohol could still be smelled throughout the house.

Hayley: "What time did everyone leave?"

Christian: "Well, when I got up, there were a few people passed out on the couch. So, probably about 30 minutes ago."

Hayley: "I don't know how you guys do it anymore."

Christian: "Hal, we are still young, you are still young."

Hayley: "Yeah, I know, I just figured it would slow down by now."

Christian: "Nah, it will be soon enough, though."

Hayley looked at Christian, "What do you mean?"

Christian smiled, "Kelsey and I are going to start trying to have a baby. We decided it is time."

Hayley: "Oh, Christian, I am so happy for you guys."

Christian: "Seeing you and thinking about everything, it had us thinking. We don't want to wait for a better time anymore. I think we have figured out, there is never going to be that perfect time."

Hayley: "That is a big step."

Christian: "It is probably why I was drowning in sorrow last night."

Hayley: "Oh, is that what it was?"

The two laughed before getting quiet.

Christian: "I am sorry for saying what I said last night, the way I said it. But I did mean all of it, Hal. You get in your own way sometimes."

Hayley: "I know I do. I just don't know if I can do it, Christian. I just feel like I am turning my back on him."

Christian: "Hal, he was my partner and my best friend. There is a lot of history between the three of us. I thought it was going to be harder than it was, but it wasn't with Jordan. I did have my thoughts about it when I left, and I went and talked to Eric. I know that sounds crazy, but it really helped me. Have you even been back out there since?"

Hayley: "No, I can't go out there. It would be too hard."

Christian: "You need to do it. Trust me."

Kelsey entered the room.

Kelsey: "Hey, Hal. When did you get here?"

Hayley: "Oh, just a few minutes ago."

Kelsey: "Did you get all your stuff packed and ready to go?"

Hayley: "Yeah, I was just stopping by on my way out."

Kelsey: "What's the plan next week?"

Hayley: "Oh, I don't know. I guess we will wing it. Jordan has some therapy, not sure if he wants me to take him. He still doesn't drive much."

Kelsey: "What has he been doing this weekend?"

Hayley: "I don't know. I haven't talked to him."

"Oh, well, maybe you guys should talk more. You two do live together, even if it's just because of odd circumstances."

Hayley smiled, "Maybe."

The three talked for a little longer before Hayley told them she had to go. Christian and Kelsey walked her to the door. She hugged both of them goodbye before pulling out of the driveway. As Hayley was waiting to turn, she thought about what Christian had said. She turned off her turn signal and went straight. She drove for a while and pulled into a driveway. She looked up, and she immediately had tears in her eyes looking at the wrought iron sign that read Valor Cemetery. She pulled up the road until she recognized the name on the stone, Eric Dolce.

Tears had already started to stream down her face, "I can't do this." She sat for a long time gathering up enough courage to get out of the car. Hayley took a deep breath and opened the door. She walked to Eric's grave and dropped to her knees. She began wailing out loud. Every bit of emotion she had held in since the funeral came pouring out. "Eric, I don't know if I can do this without you. This isn't how it was supposed to be. I was supposed to go before you. That was the deal."

Hayley continued to sob uncontrollably. She cried until there were no more tears left in her, and then she sat in silence.

Hayley sat in her thoughts about everything that had happened since Eric's death. "I couldn't do the job anymore. It wasn't the same, but I guess you know that. I bet that was a shocker for you."

Hayley smiled, remembering Eric had said he would never be able to pull Hayley away from policing. "I moved too. I wanted to start over again, and I thought somehow that would help me, but all it did was make me miss you more. I am doing good, but I feel sometimes that I don't know who I am at times. I was so sure of who I was with you here, I felt safe, I knew whatever happened, you were here."

Hayley was silent again in her thoughts. It was so quiet out in the cemetery. The only sounds were a few birds chirping in the distance.

"I met someone. His name is Jordan, and he is a bigger pain in the ass than you were," Hayley smiled. "I can't let you go, though, Eric. I feel if I let him in, I will have to let you go, and I can't let you go. The thought makes me sick to my stomach. I know you are not here, but I just can't. I know you would be telling me to move on and be happy. We talk about you; it's not like I must hide what I am feeling. It is just within me. I made a promise to you that it would always be you and me. I know, the promise doesn't mean anything now, but I just can't." Hayley became quiet again, holding back the tears, trying not to cry again.

"I don't know what I am going to do, Eric. I know he does make me laugh, and I do feel safe with him. I guess a part of me fears that it will happen all over again. If I give in and love someone, they will die along with you. Hello Eric, he does exactly what you did. Maybe that is why I like him; he understands the life we lived. He understands. I guess I will have to get back with you on this, but a sign from you would really help me out right about now."

Hayley stood up and walked to Eric's stone and touched it. "I will always love you and carry you with me." Hayley placed the dime she had been holding in her hand on the top of Eric's stone. There were several coins on top of the headstone, but one quarter. It had to be the one Christian placed on it when he came to visit Eric. Hayley walked back to the car, looking in the direction of Eric's grave one more time before pulling off. She didn't know how going out to Eric's grave would help her, but she did it; she had to see him one more time.

Chapter 18:

Just You and Me

As Hayley made it back home and pulled in the driveway, she looked at the house. She knew Jordan was inside. Her thoughts had been on Jordan throughout the ride home. She didn't know what to say to him; she didn't know what the next few days would hold. She wanted things to be right; she wanted things to go back to how they were before Christian and Kelsey had gotten there.

As she walked into the house, Jordan was sitting on the couch.

Jordan: "Hey, how was your trip?"

Hayley: "It was good. I forgot how long the drive is. How was the weekend?"

Jordan: "It was alright, went out with Dan and the guys. It got a little wild."

All Hayley could think about was the drunken parties that she remembered from Jordan's house.

Hayley: "Oh yeah, I am sure that was fun for you."

Jordan laughed, "No, not at all. It was great seeing the guys and going and eating with them, but then, it got a little loud and a little much. I ended up home in bed. Woke up with a splitting headache with Dan banging on the door."

Hayley: "He came here?"

Jordan: "Yeah, we talked for a long time. He was wasted last night, and there was no point in talking to him."

Hayley: "Well, that's good."

Jordan: "So, what did you do?"

Hayley sat down on the couch by Jordan.

Hayley: "I saw my mom. I hadn't seen her since I moved. It was good. I then went to see Christian and Kelsey, too. They were having a get-together at their house. I got to see a bunch of the people I worked with. It was good seeing them."

Jordan: "How are Christian and Kelsey doing?"

Hayley: "They are good. I think the get-together was kind of a farewell. They have decided to try for a baby."

Jordan: "Oh wow, I am happy for them. That is so good, they will be great parents."

Hayley: "Yeah, they will be."

Hayley got quiet.

Jordan: "Are you okay, Hal?"

Hayley: "I went to see Eric."

Jordan leaned forward, "How was that? Are you okay?"

Hayley: "Yeah, I will be. I hadn't seen him since his funeral. Christian actually encouraged me to go out there. He said that it helped him."

Jordan: "Did it help you?"

Hayley: "I don't know yet. I told him I needed a sign from him, a sign that everything is going to be okay."

Jordan: "Has he given you one yet?"

Hayley, worn out, looked at Jordan and smiled, "No, not yet." Hayley got quiet for a moment and then spoke.

Hayley: "I apologize for snapping at you before I left."

Jordan cut off Hayley, "No, don't be, I was out of line."

Hayley continued, "It's not you, Jordan. Yes, you are a pia at times," Jordan smiled, "but I still am having problems believing that my life is not turning out the way I planned it to. I thought that if I started over and moved, I could forget. I could not remember what got me here in the first place. Is that dumb?"

Jordan: "No, not at all. You can't forget where you came from, Hal, as much as we would like to forget sometimes. You just have to learn how to live with it."

Hayley: "I was going to be okay being alone after Eric. I was okay just going to be alone and to live away from everything. Not that I was giving up, but just with peace. But then you were my neighbor, and the hurricane and the reading."

Jordan stared at Hayley, "I know, I am sorry for putting all of this on you."

Hayley: "It's not that Jordan, I started to care about you, I started to think about you. And then the day before Christian and Kelsey got her, and while they were here, it felt right."

Jordan got up and sat next to Hayley and put his arm around her.

Hayley: "When it stopped, I didn't like it. I missed it."

Jordan didn't speak; he just looked at Hayley.

Hayley: "You know, right now would be a good time to say something, Jordan."

Jordan: "I am lost at what to say. I wasn't expecting this to come out of you."

Hayley, wanting more from Jordan, was upset, but she said, "I understand." Hayley went to move, and Jordan held on tight to Hayley's shoulder with the arm that was around her.

"Hal," Jordan smiled, "I didn't say anything bad. I just wasn't expecting you to want to talk about it. I'm just a little thrown off. I wondered why things just stopped, but I would rather have you in my life as a friend than push the subject with you. I have missed every minute of what happened that weekend. I felt the same thing you did, and when it stopped, I thought I had done something wrong. I already thought I was a pus when I let you walk away after you had come to me and kissed me."

Hayley smiled and laughed.

Jordan: "Hal, I know I am a pia, but I want to try. You are the only person I want to try with. There is something here."

Hayley: "You wanted to sleep with me?"

Jordan: "Huh, yeah, I am a dude."

Hayley smiled.

Jordan: "I don't want to rush you, Hal, I don't think I could rush either. I just want to do life together and see where it goes. Just you and me. I don't expect you to forget Eric Hal. I know he was your life for a long time and your friend. I just want a chance to try and make you happy."

Hayley: "I want that too, Jordan, but I just don't know how."

Jordan: "Why don't we just agree to be me and you against the world, and we will go from there. Just doing what feels right. Just go back to nights sipping wine and talking for hours. Just laughing and enjoying each other's company."

Hayley: "I can do that."

Jordan: "Good, because I just laid it out there for you."

Hayley laughed.

Hayley: "You laid it out there for me and I didn't?"

Jordan: "Oh no, you did. You had me speechless. I didn't know what to say."

Hayley: "So, what do we do now?"

Jordan: "I guess try to act like this conversation never happened and not feel awkward anymore."

Hayley slapped Jordan's chest, "You're an idiot."

Jordan: "Yes, that I am, but you like this idiot."

Hayley: "Don't think you're special."

Jordan smiled, "You want to cook on the grill? I know we have some wine."

Hayley: "That sounds perfect."

Hayley and Jordan got up and walked to the kitchen to start getting things ready to cook. They started chatting about their weekend. Jordan looked at Hayley. She had a sparkle in her eye when talking about being home and seeing her mom. She talked with excitement when she saw Christian and Kelsey. Jordan realized in that moment; he had fallen in love with Hayley. He loved every part of her.

Hayley: "Why are you looking at me like that?"

Jordan: "I am not looking at you anyway, I am just listening."

Hayley continued to talk, and Jordan listened to Hayley.

As Hayley went to grab something out of the refrigerator, Jordan grabbed Hayley, pushing her up against the wall. Hayley stared at Jordan. Jordan leaned down and kissed Hayley. Hayley wrapped her arms around Jordan. The passion came pouring out of both of them. Everything that the two held back poured into their bodies. The two pulled apart, placing their foreheads together. Jordan spoke first, "I missed that." Hayley replied, "Me too."

The two finished getting things ready and walked outside to start cooking. Hayley sat down on the couch as Jordan placed the chicken on the grill.

Hayley: "It looks like your knee is doing good."

Jordan: "Yeah, it was hurting last night walking so much, but it is getting better, little by little."

Hayley: "You walked on it?"

Jordan turned and looked at Hayley, "Well, yeah, you know they didn't stay in one place."

Hayley smiled, "What happened last night?"

Jordan walked over to Hayley and sat down next to her, "Lots of drinking, lots of man talk."

Hayley: "Lots of women?"

Jordan laughed.

Jordan: "Yes, lots of women. In fact, Michelle was there."

Hayley: "Who is Michelle?"

Jordan smirked, "She is kind of historical with us. She is the one I was trying to irritate you at one party. She was the one in the front yard."

Hayley had a look of not knowing on her face.

Jordan: "The one I kissed and was staring at you."

Hayley: "Oh yeah, I remember now."

Jordan laughed.

Hayley: "How is she?"

Jordan: "Still trying to find a police officer to sink her teeth into. I don't think she will stop until she does."

Hayley: "Did she sink her teeth into you?"

Jordan looked at Hayley, "No, Hal, she did not." Jordan jumped up from the couch to check the food on the grill.

Jordan: "Dan did tell me after I left that Nick and Michelle were cozy."

Hayley: "How can women be like that? It makes no sense to me."

Jordan: "They just want to belong to something more. A brotherhood. You are lucky. Hal, you were part of it, and you married into it. It's just different, kind of like the military."

Hayley: "Yeah, I guess."

Jordan: "So, now that you know I know you were a cop, are you going to share some stories?"

Hayley: "Stories about what? You have the same stories I have."

Jordan: "I just want to know about you as a cop, Hal. I know you as you are now, but not then. It's like a missing piece. How was it being a homicide detective?"

Hayley began to tell Jordan about her days as a homicide detective and why she made the switch. Jordan was amused listening to her stories and how she solved cases. Jordan would periodically get up and check the food before sitting back down, listening to Hayley intently.

As they sat down to eat, Jordan asked, "How was it being a narc?"

Hayley: "It was alright, once I learned how to do it, it is pretty easy, pretty repetitive. It had its place in my career. I didn't miss it when I left."

Jordan: "You left when you and Eric got married, right?"

Hayley: "Yeah, it was decided before we got married, but when we did get married, I moved over to the homicide unit."

Hayley then quietly picked her food. Jordan looked at Hayley and grabbed her hand, "Hal, it is okay to talk about him. You don't have to stop. He was a part of your life, and I want to know all of it."

Hayley: "I know, it is just weird talking about him. I don't want to hurt you."

Jordan: "Hal, how about this? I will tell you if it is too much for me to handle. I just don't want to know about you two kissing, stuff like that. You will give me a complex with that."

Hayley laughed, "I got you." Hayley looked down at her food and was silent before speaking again.

Hayley: "I didn't want to believe he was dead that day. I thought if I just talked to him, he would have been alright. Doesn't that sound dumb?"

Jordan had looked up at Hayley once she started talking, "No, it isn't dumb, you had hope. We all have hope that it's never as bad as we think."

Hayley: "I can still see him lying there. I can still see the way his face looked, the look Christian gave me. It's like it happened yesterday."

Jordan: "Hal, I don't think things like that just go away."

Hayley: "I know, but I thought changing everything would help. It hasn't, I still have it all with me, and I miss my mom and my friends."

Jordan's stomach kind of dropped at Hayley's comment, "Are you wanting to move back, Hal?"

Hayley: "No, not at all, but I miss them."

Jordan couldn't help but feel relieved by the comment.

Jordan: "Well, maybe you should go see them more. You really don't get out much."

Hayley got quiet again; Jordan stared at her. Hayley finally said, "I fear that if I get close to you, it will happen all over again. That I will have to go through everything."

Jordan was shocked by Hayley's comment, "Hal, I mean, it is the job, but I will always do anything and everything I possibly can to come home. I promise you that."

Hayley: "Yeah, you are right. "

At this point, Hayley and Jordan were finished eating.

"Let me take these inside," Hayley said as she started grabbing for the plates.

Hayley: "Need some wine?"

Jordan: "Yeah, but I can help too now, Hal. I am not on crutches anymore."

Jordan got up, grabbed some of the plate, and walked inside with Hayley. They stood side by side talking and washing the dishes. Hayley went to the refrigerator and grabbed the wine and two glasses. She poured the wine and handed Jordan a glass.

They walked outside, sitting on separate couches, and talked more about Hayley before the move. It was always easy for the two of them to talk for hours once they both had calmed down. They had talked so long, again like other nights, it was early in the morning.

Hayley: "Eee Jordan, it is early in the morning."

Jordan looked down at his phone, "Damn, it is. I guess we should probably go to bed."

The two walked inside and placed their wine glasses in the sink. Jordan hugged Hayley before kissing her on the head.

Jordan: "Night, Hal! I will see you in the morning."

Hayley looked at Jordan, "I was hoping you would sleep in the bed with me tonight."

Jordan smirked and looked at Hayley, "I will tell you right now, there is no way I can pus out again, Hal."

Hayley looked at Jordan, "Maybe I don't want you to this time."

Jordan pulled Hayley towards him and began to kiss her. The two embraced while passionately kissing each other. Jordan picked Hayley up, and Hayley wrapped her legs around Jordan's waist. Jordan walked to Hayley's bedroom and closed the door behind them.

In the morning, Hayley woke up and looked over. Jordan was still sleeping. Hayley smiled before getting out of bed to take a shower. As Hayley was sliding out, Jordan grabbed her hand, "You're not trying to sneak out on me, are you?"

Hayley smiled, "No, but I have things to do, and I know you like to sleep." Jordan smiled and grabbed Hayley, pulling her onto the bed next to him. He kissed her, "I won't sleep much longer."

Hayley got up and walked out of the room. Jordan smiled and fell back asleep.

Chapter 19:

The Sirens

In the months to follow, Hayley and Jordan formed a bond, a bond that was woven in trust and healing for both of them. Hayley continued to heal from the loss of Eric, and Jordan continued to heal from a marriage and a life he never wanted again.

Both had picked each other, and there was nothing that could break them apart. They chose each other when everything else seemed bleak in the beginning.

Jordan's leg did get stronger, and he was able to go back to the drug unit. Jordan could not do everything that he once could do, but he could do enough to stay in the unit and continue his career in law enforcement.

His house was beginning to look like a house again. The roof was fixed, and they were almost complete with the drywall. After that, it was painting, and he could move back in. Something Hayley and Jordan hadn't thought about.

Jordan had also made amends with Miah's mom enough to see Miah once or twice a week. Miah would come and stay with Hayley and Jordan. Both had grown attached to Miah and enjoyed their time with her. It was like they were a family. Secretly, both hoped they would have a child together one day, but they both weren't ready to admit it.

Hayley continued with her online store. It began to pick up, and it was busier than she ever expected. Hayley never thought about going back into law enforcement. She lived it through Jordan's story when he would come home and tell her how his day went. She was still afraid when it came to the job Jordan did, but she had faith he would come back every night.

Christian and Kelsey did not waste time; Kelsey had gotten pregnant, and they were going to be expecting a little girl in a few months. Hayley and Jordan talked to them often, getting updates and living their experience. Christian and Kelsey had come down a few times since, but it was getting harder for Kelsey, so Jordan and Hayley agreed to come up soon.

Dan had warmed up to Hayley once learning that she was a cop and, in fact, not a badge bunny. The two could sit and talk without hatred, and they both learned Jordan needed both of them. Dan was still Dan, no end in sight of slowing down, but he respected Jordan's decision to be with Hayley. He could see the connection between them.

It seemed that the past would never haunt the two again. The days seemed to fly by, like time would not slow down. Both had admitted to each other that they loved each other; both knew they had a bond beyond love. Maybe because of their past, maybe because they understood each other on a deeper level through the job that Jordan now worked.

Hayley walked by the bathroom and saw Jordan getting dressed.

Hayley: "Hey, sexy."

"Hey, you," Jordan said, looking at Hayley.

Hayley: "It's pretty early. Where are you headed today?"

Jordan: "Court this morning and then that case we are working on. We may have some leads. What are your plans today?"

Hayley came into the bathroom and sat on the counter next to Jordan.

Hayley: "I am going to complete some orders today. I don't know, it's a pretty day. I may head out to the shops."

"Must be nice to just do what you want," Jordan said, smirking at Hayley.

Hayley smirked back, "Well, if you could give up the job, you could do what I do every day."

Jordan leaned over and kissed Hayley, "Never." Hayley smiled at Jordan.

Jordan: "I shouldn't be too late tonight unless those leads pan out."

Hayley: "Alright, just let me know."

"I will," Jordan said, sliding in front of Hayley to hug her. They hugged for a few seconds before Jordan pulled back, "I love you."

Hayley: "I love you too, have fun today."

Jordan pulled away and started walking off.

Jordan: "You know I will."

Hayley: "I'm still a better cop than you ever will be."

"I beg to differ," Jordan popped his head back in the bathroom, "But I still would love to see you in a uniform."

Hayley smiled, "Not a chance, go to work."

"I'm gone," Jordan smiled, walking out of the house.

Hayley jumped down and went to the computer to begin her day. It turned out to be a busy day for Hayley, orders coming in and going out were more than she had thought. As she was immersed in the paperwork, her phone rang.

Jordan: "So, are you on the beach in one of those sexy bikinis you have yet?"

Hayley smiled, "You know you really are an idiot."

Hayley could hear Dan laughing in the background; Jordan had her on speaker phone.

Hayley: "What are you two up to?"

Jordan: "We are headed to talk to someone, follow up on these leads. We are going to do this and call it a day. I should be home in about 2ish hours."

Hayley: "Okay, I'll plan after 4."

Jordan and Dan both laughed.

Jordan: "Hal, you act like you know us."

Hayley: "I know men and all of ya lie."

Jordan and Dan laughed again.

Jordan: "Well, my untrusting girlfriend, I will see you soon."

Hayley: "Alright, I am going to head out to the shops. I'll be home before you get here."

Jordan: "Okay, sweetie, I love you."

Hayley: "I love you too, you two have fun."

Jordan: "Bye."

"Bye Jordan," Hayley hung up the phone, smiling. She finished backing up the last orders and got ready to leave. She grabbed her purse and her keys; Emma was sitting, looking at Hayley.

"I'll be back in a few, daddy will be too," Hayley said to Emma as she wagged her tail. Hayley walked out the door to her car.

Hayley went to her favorite shops, the ones she had taken Kelsey to, the ones that she once saw Jordan chasing someone by. Hayley beamed with the memories she had made with those whom she loved the most. As Hayley was shopping, her phone rang.

Christian: "Girl, I don't know how much I can take of these pregnancy hormones. The girl has lost it."

Hayley started to laugh at Christian's comment, "It is only temporary, she will be back to normal, in about 4 months."

Christian: "That is 4 months too long, Hal. My God, she has the devil in her."

Hayley continued to laugh, "You did it to her. That devil is about to be your child, that is going to have you wrapped around her finger."

Christian: "You are kinda right. What are you up to today?"

Hayley had walked out of one shop and was standing outside.

Hayley: "Well, I did a bunch of orders today, and now I am at my favorite shops. Jordan said he would be home early tonight, so I guess when he gets home, we are going to relax. He had court this morning."

Hayley began to hear sirens and started looking in the direction it was coming from.

Christian: "Oh, well, that is good. Where are the sirens coming from?"

Hayley: "Someone riding down the road hauling ass somewhere. What are you and Kelsey's plans?"

As Hayley asked Christian, more police cars came flying past Hayley. Then two ambulances. Hayley's stomach dropped. It brought her back to the day Eric died.

Christian: "Hal, what is all that?"

Hayley: "Oh my God, Christian. Jordan was going to talk to some people about leads in his case."

Christian: "Hal, he is fine."

Before Christian could finish, Hayley started running towards her vehicle, "No Christian, something is wrong. I know it."

Christian: "Hal, calm down, it's nothing."

Hayley: "I've got to go Christian."

Hayley hung up the phone on Christian and screeched out of the parking lot. She was following in the direction of where the police cars and ambulances went. Hayley's phone began to ring; it was Christian trying to call her back. Hayley just let it ring. Hayley could not see the police cars and ambulances any long. She rolled down her window and followed the sirens. She followed until she pulled down a street and saw nothing but blue and red lights. She drove until she couldn't drive anymore. She grabbed her phone and got out of the vehicle and started running in the direction she could barely see people walking around. Hayley's heart pounded harder and harder the closer she got.

As she reached where people were standing, she saw Dan's vehicle. She pushed past the people who had gathered around. She was stopped by an officer whom she did not know. "Ma'am, you can't go any further."

Hayley, out of breath, "What happened?"

Officer: "Ma'am, it is a police investigation. You have to stand back."

One of the individuals standing by said, "There were some gunshots and then everyone showed up."

Hayley waited for the officer to walk to the other side of the crowd, trying to push them back. Once the officer was on the other side, Hayley went under the police tape and ran. She ran as hard as she could until she saw where EMS was working on someone on the ground. She ran towards EMS, trying to see who was lying on the ground. Tears started to form in Hayley's eyes; those were Jordan's shoes. It was him, she knew it was him. Hayley had tunnel vision running towards EMS. She was grabbed right before she reached EMS.

"Hal, stop."

She turned, and it was Dan.

"That's Jordan Dan," Hayley shouted.

"I know it's Jordan. Hal, let them work on him, Hal. Stop, please," Dan replied. Hayley didn't care what Dan was saying at the moment. She pushed away from Dan, running the rest of the way to Jordan. Hayley's phone kept ringing.

Dan finally picked it up.

Christian was surprised to hear Dan answering Hayley's phone.

Christian: "Dan, what the hell is going on?"

Dan: "Christian, it's Jordan. He's down, dude. It's bad, it's really bad."

Christian was in shock. Every bit of memory he had of Eric's fatal day came back to his mind.

Christian: "Where is Hal Dan? Where is she?"

Dan: "Man, I tried to stop her, she is running over there towards him. Christian, it's bad, man."

Christian: "I'm on my way, Dan. Tell Hal I am on my way."

Hayley made her way to where Jordan was. She could see him gasping for air. She dropped down next to Jordan, holding his head. "Jordan, I am here, I am here, baby. Please look at me. Please," Hayley began to cry.

EMS, who was working on Jordan, began to yell at Hayley, "Ma'am, you've got to get out of here."

Hayley refused to leave, talking to Jordan, "You promised me, Jordan. You have to fight Jordan."

Dan had made his way back to Hayley and grabbed her, "Hal, come on."

Hayley began to scream as Dan picked her up, dragging her away from Jordan, "NO. STOP DAN NO." Dan pulled Hayley away from Jordan far enough that EMS could work on Jordan. They both could see Jordan gasping for air. Dan held on to Hayley tightly. Hayley continued to sob uncontrollably. This wasn't what was supposed to happen. This isn't how it was supposed to end. Dan and Hayley watched as they put Jordan on a stretcher and put him into the ambulance before pulling out and stomping the gas heading towards the hospital. Dan stood Hayley up, "Let's go."

Hayley was numb; she just couldn't believe this was happening again. She screamed, "He's dead, Dan."

Dan grabbed Hayley forcefully, "No, he's not Hal. If he were dead, they would not have him in the back of the ambulance headed to the hospital. He would still be lying on the ground waiting for the coroner to get here. Get your shit together, Hal."

Dan walked with Hayley in the direction Hayley had come from. The officer started walking fast towards Hayley, but Dan put up his hand to stop the officer. The officer stopped and continued to hold the other people who had gathered back. Dan walked to where Mike and Nick were.

Nick spoke, "Where the hell did she come from?"

Dan, irritated, said, "I don't know Nick. Where the hell were you guys?"

Nick: "We were with the other two jack asses that had to be arrested."

Dan: "How the hell could you let her get past you?"

Nick: "You aren't listening Dan. We were inside with the…"

Mike broke in.

Mike: "You two knock it off. Where are they taking him?"

Dan: "Emory."

Dan muttered.

Mike looked at Hayley, "Hal, you think you can drive your car?" Hayley didn't answer; she was in shock, and the images of watching Jordan gasp to breathe were in her head.

Mike looked at Nick, "I'll grab our car, you drive Hal's, and Hal will ride with Dan to the hospital."

Dan walked with Hayley to the car. Hayley still had not spoken. Hayley got in the passenger seat of Dan's car, and they pulled out heading to the hospital. Hayley could smell Jordan's cologne he wore. Tears ran down her face as she looked out the window. Dan reached over and handed Hayley her phone saying, "Christian is on his way." Hayley looked over at Dan, grabbing her phone and trying to understand what he had just said. Hayley held onto her phone and looked out the window again, "What happened?"

Dan didn't look towards Hayley; he kept his eyes on the road.

Dan: "We went to follow up on those leads. We were standing in the house, and they were sitting on the couch. Everything was fine, Hal."

Hayley was looking at Dan. Dan continued, "Some bastard came out of the back room and damn started shooting. Jordan and I both hit the ground, and we started crawling towards the door as we were shooting in the direction that it came from. I didn't even know he was shot until we got outside and were behind cover. I turned to him, laughing about how close it was, and he was bleeding. He couldn't say anything, but he just kept looking at me."

Hayley: "He never said anything?"

Dan: "No. I called it in and started to try and figure out where he was shot at. I know in the stomach, in the arm. I don't know where else. They were there pretty quickly and started working on him. I was standing there watching them when I saw you running towards him. Where did you come from?"

Hayley looked over at Dan, "I was huh, I was shopping. I heard the sirens and then more. I knew. You said Christian is coming?"

Dan glanced at Hayley and then back on the road, "Yeah, your phone kept ringing. I answered it when I saw it was Christian."

Hayley looked out the window, "I can't do this again."

Dan: "Hal, right now is not the time to think like that. Don't give up, Jordan is a fighter. He always has been. If I know Jordan, he is going to do anything he possibly can to make it. He needs you not to give up on him, Hal."

Dan and Hayley sat in silence until they made it to the hospital. Dan parked at the exit where law enforcement and the ambulances can go in.

"Come on, I can get you in," Dan said to Hayley as they got out of the vehicle. Mike and Nick were running up as Dan and Hayley made it to the doors. The guard at the door held his hand up, "She can't go in there. Law Enforcement only."

Dan looked at the guard, "She is a cop, you idiot. You don't know her?" Dan shuffled Hayley passed the guard. The guard, still confused about how he did not know Hayley. As they made their way in, it was pure chaos. Staff were running around, and Dan, Hayley, Nick, and Mike stood staring, trying to figure out which room Jordan was in.

Someone yelled, "DAN." They walked towards an officer, "They just wheeled him into surgery. Two in the lower stomach, one in the shoulder. Stomach ones are the worst."

Dan: "Why the hell couldn't he breathe if that is all?"

Officer: "The doc said something about the diaphragm, I don't know. He also said that when you guys got here, you could wait in here until they figured something out."

Dan Hayley, Nick, and Mike walked into the room. Dan let Hayley sit in the only chair in the room. Hayley looked around the room. There was blood all over the sheets, and the blood ran down to the floor where it had pooled up. All Hayley could do was stare; no words could come to her; all she could think of was that it was Jordan's blood.

As they waited, it felt like forever. All they could do was wait until a familiar face finally showed up. It was Doctor Patel, the one who had treated Jordan that first day. Hayley sat up when she saw the familiar face.

Dr. Patel: "Dan, Nick, Mike, oh, Ms. Hayley, it is good to see you again."

"Doc," Hayley said.

Dr. Patel: "The bullet that went through his shoulder was not bad. He has some damage, but nothing that I anticipate will hurt him in the long run. The bullets that went through his abdomen, hit his diaphragm, liver, and intestines. That is why he was gasping for air the way he was; that is where the blood from his mouth was coming from. Those were the only three bullet holes. The diaphragm, we don't think there is any nerve damage, but we will monitor and go from there. If no nerve damage, we are talking a few months, knowing Jordan, probably less. His intestines, we didn't see any major damage, we will monitor to make sure, but we are expecting a couple of months. His liver, I give it a few weeks, maybe a month. Overall, considering, he was lucky. He will be monitored to make sure he doesn't have blood clots, and everything is healing."

Dan shook Dr. Patel's hand, "Thank you, Doc. Thank you so much."

Hayley was listening but didn't know what to say. She wasn't comprehending what was just told to her.

Hayley: "Is he going to die?"

Everyone looked at Hayley, lost on what to say.

Dr. Patel looked at Hayley, "Yes, one day Jordan will pass away like all of us, but from this injury, no. Any complications that could arise, we will monitor him until I feel comfortable with releasing him. You need to tell him to be more careful, though. I've been seeing him too often."

It finally stuck in Hayley's head; he was going to be alright.

Hayley: "Thank you, Doc."

Dr. Patel: "He is in recovery right now. As soon as he is in a room, they will come and get you guys. Don't expect him to be up and talking. He probably will be out for a while."

Dan looked at Dr. Patel, "Thank you." Dr. Patel walked out. Hayley was still sitting, staring at the ground.

Dan bent down next to Hayley, "Hal, he is going to live."

Hayley looked at Dan. Dan said it again, "Hal, he is going to be okay, girl." Hayley reached out and hugged Dan. Dan rubbed Hayley's back to comfort her and said, "It's going to be alright now. He will be up before you know it."

Nick and Mike watched as Dan comforted Hayley. It was unlike Dan.

About two hours later, they came and got them. They brought them to Jordan's room. As they were told, Jordan was not up. He was hooked up to monitors. Hayley grabbed a chair and sat next to Jordan. She grabbed his hand, kissing it as she began to cry. Hayley stayed by Jordan's side while Dan, Nick, and Mike talked about the turn of events and chatted about other unimportant topics. They were hoping Jordan would wake up before they needed to leave. All of them had work in the morning, but they doubted whether anyone would question if they didn't show up.

As night drew on, Mike and Nick decided they would head home. "You guys go ahead. Hayley and I will stay," Dan said.

Mike and Nick left. Dan and Hayley were silent in the room, listening to the monitors, hoping Jordan would wake up just so they knew he was alright. As they sat in silence, Christian came walking fast into the room. Both Dan and Hayley jump with the fast movement.

Christian: "Is he alright? Is he going to be good? They wouldn't tell me shit."

Hayley jumped up, hugging Christian.

Dan got up, "Yeah, he is going to be fine, he just wanted to scare us."

Christian looked at Hayley, "Hal, you okay?" Christian grabbed Hayley's face, making her look at him. All she could do was shake her head no. Christian grabbed Hayley and hugged her.

Dan, looking at them, "I think I am going to grab some coffee and make a few phone calls. I'll leave you alone for a few." Dan walked outside the room. Hayley sat down by Jordan again and grabbed his hand. Christian grabbed another chair and sat by the foot of Jordan's bed. Both Hayley and Christian were silent. Christian was waiting for Hayley to say something; she still had not spoken since he had been there.

Finally, Hayley spoke, "It was worse this time." Christian just looked at Hayley.

Hayley continued, "He was gasping for air, and there was blood coming out of his mouth. I flipped out."

Christian looked at Hayley, "Well, considering the circumstances, I can imagine why."

Hayley had tears in her eyes, "That wasn't like me. I have always been able to be calm. I flipped out."

Christian replied, "Hal, you lost Eric the same exact way. I can't imagine what you were going through. It's why I am here. I knew you couldn't go through this again."

Hayley then asked, "Where's Kelsey?"

To which Christian replied, "She stayed. I told her I would call her and let her know what was going on. I just left Hal. I told Eric a long time ago I would take care of you if anything happened to him. I knew this was one of those times."

Hayley looked at Christian, "I am glad you are here."

Christian: "Hal, it's not always going to be death. You've got to let that go."

Hayley: "I just knew he was dead, I knew he was going to die."

Christian: "That's fear Hal. That is all fear."

Hayley was quiet for a moment before speaking, "You know what scared me the most?"

Christian: "What?"

Hayley: "Knowing that I was hurting just as much—if not more—than when it was Eric."

Christian smiled, "I told you, you liked him."

Hayley half smiled, "I don't want to lose him, Christian."

Christian: "Well, you're not. Old Jordan is going to be fine when he wakes up. Good luck on keeping him still again."

Hayley smirked, "I just had a feeling, Christian, a gut-wrenching feeling that he was gone too. That I was going to live it all over again. I can't explain it."

Hayley and Christian talked for a while. They discussed everything but what was in front of them.

Christian finally stood up, "Hal, I've got to go lie down."

Hayley looked at Christian; she could tell he was tired.

Hayley: "You want to crash at my house? My keys are right there. Just take them and bring them back to me in the morning."

Christian: "You don't mind."

Hayley: "No go, call Kelsey. I will see you in the morning."

Christian hugged Hayley.

Christian: "I love you, girl. I will see you in the morning. Are you going to be good with Dan?"

Hayley: "Yeah, it will be fine. I don't even know where he went. He probably found a room and is sleeping."

"Alright, see you in the morning," Christian said before walking out.

Hayley and Jordan were alone. Hayley sat down and grabbed Jordan's hand. As she sat there, she began to talk to Jordan.

"I need you to go ahead and wake up Jordan. You scared me today. It was like it happened all over again."

Hayley continued to rub Jordan's hand.

"Please wake up, Jordan. Please."

Hayley laid her head on Jordan's hand. She closed her eyes. She was exhausted from everything that had transpired. As she dozed off, thoughts of Jordan ran through her mind. At some point, she fell asleep. She woke up to fingers running through her hair. She looked up and saw Jordan watching her. She sat up, "Jordan."

Jordan: "You didn't think that was really going to take me out, did you?"

Hayley jumped up and kissed him.

"Oh my God, Jordan," Hayley exclaimed as she began rubbing his face, "Are you hurting?" she asked.

Jordan half smiling, "Well, Hal, considering that I was just shot, yes."

Hayley: "Stop joking. I thought you were going to die."

Jordan: "I know, I could hear you. I was gasping for air at the time and couldn't tell you I was good."

Hayley: "Jordan, you weren't good."

He smiled, "I told you I would do anything I could to always make it home to you. I promised you."

Hayley smiled with tears in her eyes. She kissed Jordan again.

"It's me and you, Hal," Jordan said as he squeezed Hayley's hand.

"You're up finally."

Hayley turned to the door. Dan was smiling walking in.

Dan: "Man, you gave me a scare."

Jordan: "You are always scared."

Dan laughed. Jordan could tell Dan wanted to tell Jordan something.

Jordan: "Hey, Hal, can you run and get me some Gatorade? That purple one?"

She knew what was up as she said, "Yeah, I will be back in a little while." Hayley got up and left the room. "Thank you," Jordan said as Hayley walked out of the room. He watched until he couldn't see her anymore.

Jordan looked at Dan and asked, "How bad was it?"

Dan sat down where Hayley was sitting. "It wasn't good, Jordan. It was pretty bad."

Jordan: "Does she know?"

Dan: "Christ Jordan, she was there. She came out of nowhere. You don't remember?"

Jordan: "No, I don't remember any of it."

Dan: "I had to pull her off of you. She kept telling you to open your eyes and look at her. It was bad. She flipped out, Jordan. She has barely said three words since. When Christian got here, she finally started talking more."

Jordan: "Christian is here?"

Dan: "Yeah, apparently she was talking to him on the phone when she heard the sirens."

"Geezus," Jordan put his head back, "I know it was bad for both of them."

Dan: "It wasn't good for any of us. It was really bad, Jordan. You can't do that to me again."

Jordan laughed, "Well, I wasn't trying to do it this time. Shit, I didn't even feel it until we were outside. I guess I was just trying to get out of there."

Dan: "Yeah, you were trying to leave me."

Dan laughed.

Jordan: "I need you to do something for me, Dan."

Dan: "Okay?"

Jordan lay his head back on the bed, looking up at the ceiling.

Jordan: "I need you to go to my house and get something for me."

Dan: "Okay, where at?"

Jordan: "It's in the top drawer of my dresser."

Dan: "I'm not digging in your dresser. Hell no. Not touch your bikini panties."

Jordan laughed, "Stop, it hurts to laugh. I'm being serious."

Dan stopped laughing and smiled, "What do you want me to get? I'll get it for you."

Jordan: "Just grab it, you will know when you see it."

Dan: "You are not convincing me to get whatever this is for you."

Jordan: "Dan, it's important for me, please."

Dan: "If you are screwing with me, Jordan."

Jordan: "I'm not, just get it for me, Dan."

Dan: "Okay, I'll bring it for you tomorrow."

Jordan: "Please remember."

Dan: "I'll remember, you have gotten weird."

Jordan: "I'm not weird, I almost died."

Dan: "According to Dr. Patel, you are fine. Just a few months off from work, milking this again. First, the leg, now bullets."

Jordan started laughing again, "Dude, you've got to stop."

Dan and Jordan were laughing when Hayley walked back in.

Hayley: "What's so funny?"

Dan stood up, "Your boyfriend is a little strange."

Hayley looked at Jordan, smiling, "Yeah, can't believe you are just now seeing this."

Jordan: "Hey, you two are supposed to be nice; you could have lost me."

Dan: "I'm leaving; it will be just Hal picking on you. I'll see you tomorrow, Jordan."

Jordan: "Alright, thanks for coming, Dan. I'll be out of here soon."

Dan walked out of the room.

Hayley stood up and bent over and kissed Jordan, "I never thought we would be alone."

Jordan smiled, "Oh yeah?" Hayley smiled, "Yeah."

Hayley pulled the chair closer to Jordan's bed. "So, who was your movie star crush when you were younger?" Jordan smiled at Hayley. The two played their own little game, trying to ask questions that the other didn't know about each other. It was their thing now, as this was the second time Jordan had been in the hospital.

Chapter 20:

Forever Isn't Always

In the morning, Dan did what Jordan asked. He had his own key to Jordan's house from years ago. He got to Jordan's house early enough that the workers had not come. Dan entered Jordan's house and looked around. It was about done, and Jordan would be able to move back in. Dan wondered how different it would be since both accidents and since Jordan was with Hayley every moment he could be. He selfishly wished it would go back to the way it was before the hurricane that shook their city, but he knew everything was exactly how it should be.

Dan walked to Jordan's room and started to open his dresser. He hoped Jordan was not messing with him, and he would find something horrid. That was Jordan's way. As he opened the drawer, there was a small square box. Dan smiled as he pulled the box out and sat on the bed. He opened the box and smiled, wondering how long Jordan had held onto it, how long he had known. Knowing Jordan, he was just waiting for the perfect moment. Dan shook his head, never thinking this day would come again. Dan put the box in his pocket and walked out of the house.

Hayley and Jordan were awake, talking when Christian walked into the room. Hayley turned and smiled, "Did you sleep well?"

"Yeah, I was out. The stress of you two, I guess."

Hayley and Jordan smiled.

Hayley: "How is Kelsey feeling?"

Christian looked at Hayley, "I am to get home as soon as possible now that Jordan is okay. I also have to pick up a few things and go through a drive-thru and pick up fried pickles. The cravings sometimes."

Hayley smiled, "You love her and will do anything she asks."

Christian: "Of course, I will, and I must leave before my stuff is on the front lawn when I get home."

Hayley stood up and hugged Christian, "Thank you so much."

Christian: "I always have your back, Hal."

Christian turned to Jordan, "Jordan, let's not do this again."

Jordan smirked, "Not for a while. Seriously, thank you for coming."

"Anytime," Christian said as he started walking towards the door, "I'd better see you guys in a few months. You have to see the most beautiful baby girl ever."

Jordan and Hayley smiled.

Hayley: "Of course, we will be there."

Christian walked towards the door, "I will catch you two later."

Hayley and Jordan were alone again. Jordan looked at Hayley, "I guess it's game time again."

Hayley smiled, knowing Jordan was going to start asking her random questions again, as they had the first time Jordan was in the hospital.

Jordan: "So, Hayley Dolce, what are you looking for in a relationship?"

Hayley, in a sweet, innocent voice, said, "A nice guy that likes to take walks on the beach."

Jordan laughed, "I am serious, Hal. We are supposed to be telling the truth."

Hayley: "Well, I would like you to take long walks on the beach with me."

Jordan: "Come on, I am serious."

Hayley laughed but thought about the question.

Hayley: "I want a guy who smiles when he thinks of me. Someone who knows I am their person, their ride or die. A person who knows that no matter how hard it gets, it is better to go through it together than apart. I want a best friend that I can laugh with but also challenges me intelligently. I want a secret keeper, someone I can tell all my deepest, darkest secrets and know they are safe. Someone I feel safe with and can relax because I know they've got things. Ummmm."

Jordan was looking at Hayley, "Ummm? That's not everything."

Hayley laughed, "I guess. I just want to know."

Jordan: "Know what?"

Hayley: "I want to know that we will be together until one of us takes our last breath. But the person has to agree that I go first because I don't want to live without the person one day. That's how I will know."

Jordan lifted his eyebrows, "You are going to know a person is for you if you want to die before them. It was so sweet, Hal, until it was morbid."

Hayley laughed, "I didn't mean it like that."

Jordan smirked, "I know."

Hayley: "Same question. What are you looking for in a relationship, Jordan?"

"That's a tough one," Jordan said as he began to think, but before he could answer, he heard Dan.

Dan: "How is my favorite partner doing?"

Jordan looked up, and Dan was walking into the room.

Jordan: "Funny how you only have one partner."

Dan: "I know that is why you are my favorite.

 How are you feeling?"

Jordan: "I feel alright. I think the knee hurt worse, actually, but I am just lying here, so I don't know."

Dan: "You would be the person to say that. When are you getting out of here?"

Jordan: "I don't know, they haven't even mentioned it. When are you going back to work?"

Dan: "I am going today, trying to get some of the paperwork done. Nothing big. Mike and Nick are back, too. They are doing more follow-ups."

"Alone?" Jordan was surprised.

Dan: "They will be alright; they have been in the unit long enough."

Jordan: "You are getting soft."

Dan "Never, but after what we all just went through, I think they have earned it."

Jordan: "True."

Dan: "Well, you know I got to get to work, but bring it in."

Dan opened his arms, walking towards Jordan.

"Dude, get the hell on," Jordan said as Dan continued towards Jordan in a joking manner, reaching into his pocket and grabbing the box. He hugged Jordan, placing the box under Jordan's pillow. Jordan pushed at Dan, "Get off of me." Hayley laughed at the whole situation. Dan swayed Jordan back and forth, "I love you, man."

"Dan, get off of me," Jordan shouted as he pushed Dan.

Dan whispered in his ear, "It's under your pillow." Jordan understood Dan's obsession with wanting to hug him, finally. Dan stood up, "Hal, is he this temperamental with you?" Hayley laughed. Dan said, "I am hurt, Jordan."

Jordan smiled, "You aren't right."

Dan started to walk towards the door. "Alright, I am gone. Jordan, we need to guy talk soon."

After Dan was gone, Hayley turned to Jordan, "He really is weird, Jordan."

Jordan laughed, "Yeah, he is, but he is a good guy."

Hayley: "But a more serious question, where were we? Oh yeah, what are you looking for in a relationship, Jordan Voss?"

Jordan: "You were waiting for him to leave to ask me that question!"

Hayley smiled, "No, I wasn't! I was picking up where we left off. Now answer it."

Jordan: "So pushy, Hal. I don't know."

Hayley: "That's not an answer, Jordan Voss."

Jordan chuckled, "You know this risks taking every bit of my masculinity away from me, right?"

Hayley: "Well, luckily, I am the only one who gets to hear it."

Smirking, Jordan said, "I want a badge bunny."

Hayley: "JORDAN!"

Jordan dropped his head, smiling.

Jordan: "I want someone I can laugh with. Someone who understands me for who I am and doesn't want to change me. Someone who accepts me and all of my quirks and smiles at each one. I want someone who will send me a message just because, not needing anything specific. I want to know that she is the one and that there is no one who will replace her. I want, I guess, the old school love where it lasts forever. She has to be smart to outwit me at times, but willing to compromise. I want a best friend, a person that I can sit around and talk with or go out and do things with. I want a ride or die, too. Just knowing we are in it together."

Hayley: "Interesting."

Jordan: "I know pretty boring stuff."

Hayley laughed, and so did Jordan. They played their game for hours. The two already knew everything about each other, but it seemed that there was always something new that was discovered. As night fell, the two were still talking. Hours always seemed like minutes.

Hayley: "I have a question for you, Jordan."

Jordan: "Oh yeah, what could you possibly not know about me?"

Hayley: "It's a two-part question. When was the first time that you knew there was something about me, and secondly, when did you know you were falling in love with me?"

Jordan: "Eww, that's dirty, Hal."

Hayley laughed, "Why is that dirty! It's just a question or two."

Jordan: "So low, Hal."

Hayley: "Can you tell me why that is low? Because you have to be vulnerable?"

"Oh, another blow," Jordan said, chuckling, "Those two questions don't bother me Hal. I'm just going to give you a hard time."

Hayley: "Okay, then tell me."

Jordan: "I knew there was something about you the first day I met you."

Hayley: "No, you did not!"

Jordan: "Oh yes, I did. I thought you were a little feisty and not my type, but there was something about you. The more you pushed away and were rude, it made me wonder. I could catch glimpses of who you were; I could tell there was more than you wanted people to believe, and that was what kept me wanting to know more. The day of the hurricane, when we were locked in the house, I knew that I couldn't get you off my mind. I was worried about you. Obviously, when the tree fell and you came and helped me out, I knew your heart was huge. I knew you were hiding it."

Hayley: "And when did you know that you were falling in love with me?"

Jordan: "In the hospital."

"What? You didn't love me before this?" Hayley was so confused.

Jordan: "No, you twit, the hurricane hospital visit. You came and you stayed with me through the whole thing. You put the animosity towards me away and just wanted to help me, so I wasn't alone. The night you climbed into bed with me, and we fell asleep. I remember waking up next to you, not wanting to move. It felt right, it felt like that was how it was supposed to be. I knew I was falling for you then. The weekend that Christian and Kelsey came, it sealed it for me. I knew I was in love with you."

Hayley: "You hardly knew me, Jordan. That is crazy."

Jordan: "Yeah, it is, I know now how much of a whack job you are."

Hayley: "Oh, hush your mouth, Jordan. I am completely lovable."

Jordan looked at Hayley in disbelief.

Jordan: "That cute innocent face isn't going to get you out of this question. Same questions, but now you answer."

Hayley opened her eyes wide, "Well, okay, but I am cute, and I am innocent. Wow, that was so soon. I did not know that."

Jordan: "I just knew. I am guessing you are wasting time so you can think about this, huh?"

"No," Hayley giggled, "I know both questions."

Jordan: "Do you?"

Hayley: "Yes, it wasn't as soon as you, but yes. We know you annoyed the piss out of me at first."

Jordan beamed with pride at Hayley's comment.

Hayley: "When you bought the book when we were leaving the first time at the hospital. That was so sweet, and I don't know, just sweet. I knew that I liked you. The hospital and the weekend, Christian and Kelsey were here, I realized you were different. Different from my perception of you the first time I met you, and I knew there was something about you. Me teasing you the day before Christian and Kelsey came, I didn't expect that to feel so comfortable. When they got here, and we all sat around talking, it was just so natural. That's when I knew."

Jordan: "You only knew you liked me at that time. Holy crap, Hal. You had just spent a lot of time with me in the hospital."

Hayley: "Yeah, but I think in a way I went back to my law enforcement days. Just trying to help. I didn't think of much more."

Jordan laughed and threw up his hands, "You really did feel sorry for me."

Hayley rolled her eyes, "It wasn't like that, Jordan. I wanted to help you; I just didn't see much past that."

Jordan: "Well, I will say, you have been the best nurse I could have asked for."

Hayley: "Whatever, Jordan."

Jordan: "No Hal, I am serious. You have changed my life more than you will ever know. I never thought it was possible to love someone the way I love you. You have been my light."

Hayley's eyes started to water, "Jordan, you are going to make me cry."

Jordan grabbed Hayley's hand, "I know we are always full of jokes, but I truly want you to know that."

Hayley: "I love you, Jordan."

"Love you too Hal," Jordan got a smile on his face, "You are a pain in the butt though."

Hayley smirked, "Now there is my Jordan, for a moment, I thought you had hit your head."

Jordan: "My head is killing me. Did you beat me when I was sleeping?"

Hayley laughed, "No, but I probably should have."

Hayley and Jordan continued to joke and talk like they always had. They just were being them, as doctors and nurses came to check, run vital signs, and continued their normal routines. As night fell, Hayley and Jordan continued to talk.

As they were talking, Dan popped in.

Dan: "Hey, I am heading to a call, but I wanted to pop in really quick to see how you were."

"I am good, my arm is a little sore, tingling," Jordan said while rotating his arm.

Dan: "Of course it is sissy, you were shot in it."

Jordan: "Yeah, I know."

Dan: "Anything interesting going on?"

Jordan: "No, just the norm."

Dan: "They give you a day when you are breaking out yet?"

Jordan: "Nah, I think they like me here."

Dan: "I doubt that. I have to run; I will stop by in the morning."

Jordan: "Alright, Dan, thanks for popping in."

"See you, bud," Dan turned around and walked out of the room.

Hayley looked at Jordan, "That was nice of him to check on you. I know you get bored with just me."

Jordan smiled at Hayley, "No, not at all, but what I do want is for you to climb up in this bed with me and snuggle."

Hayley: "Jordan, we were told last time that wasn't allowed."

Jordan: "Oh, come on Hal, no one will be back for a while, and rules are made to be broken."

Hayley rolled her eyes, getting up and climbing into the bed with Jordan. It was still early evening, but both were exhausted from the whole incident.

Hayley got into bed with Jordan and snuggled in close to him. Jordan wrapped his arms around Hayley, "Now this is better."

Hayley asked Jordan, "How is your head?"

Jordan kissed Hayley on her forehead, "It feels much better now because of you."

The two closed their eyes. Jordan was almost asleep, and he opened his eyes, looking at Hayley. She had fallen asleep. Jordan smiled as he brushed some of Hayley's hair away from her face.

Jordan reached under his pillow and took out the box that held the ring he'd bought for Hayley months ago. Carefully, he removed the ring and slid it onto her finger, moving slowly so he wouldn't wake her. When he was done, he looked at her again and smiled.

Tears came to his eyes, wondering how he was picked to be so lucky. He kissed Hayley on the forehead one more time before closing his eyes and falling asleep.

Christian had made it home to Kelsey. Kelsey hugged Christian, "Is he going to be okay?"

Christian: "Yeah, he is good. You can tell his body had a bunch of trauma, and he was pale. Jordan was in good spirits, though."

Kelsey: "I can't imagine going through that. I would not be as strong as Hal." Kelsey began to cry.

Christian: "Look here, my lady, that is something you never have to worry about; you or the princess that we get to meet in a few months. Now you stop crying, I brought you your favorite, fried pickles."

Kelsey: "You know a way to a woman's heart."

Christian: "At the moment. I'm sure I will piss you off soon."

Kelsey: "It's the hormones, Christian."

Christian: "I know, and I will be fine with the lashing I will get. You are carrying my princess. I can't wait to see our little girl. Our family will be complete. What have you been doing since I have been gone?"

Kelsey: "Just looking at more baby names."

Christian: "Oh, really, what have you decided on?"

Kelsey: "Well, I want you to be okay with it as well, Christian."

Christian: "Kelsey, I don't care what we call her. She will be known as a princess to me."

Christian: "Well, I was thinking, Ericka. I want to name her after Eric."

Christian couldn't fight the tears that came to his eyes. He hugged Kelsey, "I think that will be perfect. I'll call Hal later and tell her. Now let's eat." Kelsey and Christian sat and began talking about the sequence of events with Hayley and Jordan, and what Kelsey had done for the day.

As Dan made it to his call, Mike and Nick were already there. "What took you so long?" Dan looked at Mike, "It's not like it mattered if I was 10 minutes late. They weren't going anywhere. I went to see Jordan. I felt I needed to go see him. You know, he got Hal a ring?"

Nick looked at Dan, "You are kidding me?"

Dan: "No, I brought it to him this morning. Maybe that's why I felt like I needed to go see him. He hasn't asked her yet. I didn't see it on her finger."

Mike was speechless at first before saying, "Damn Jordan. I can't believe he is going to do it again."

Dan smiled, "Me either, but I am happy for him."

"Don't get soft on us, Dan," Mike smirked.

Dan replied, "I'm not, I love the ladies, but it is good for Jordan. It was his time to settle down. He was always different anyway; you guys know that."

The three began to help with the call, joking among themselves with their inside jokes that many did not understand.

Hayley and Jordan remained deep asleep. The sequence of events had drained everything within them. Hayley woke up, startled, and looked around. Jordan's machines were going off.

As Hayley turned to Jordan, she could tell something was wrong. "JORDAN, JORDAN", Hayley screamed. As Hayley was shaking Jordan, his room door barged open, and several individuals came rushing in.

"Get back," one of them shouted.

Hayley jumped off the bed, backing away into the corner. She began to cry as she watched doctors and nurses tear Jordan's shirt away and begin CPR on him.

Hayley could hear the crack of Jordan's ribs as they pressed down harder and harder on his chest. "Clear!" someone shouted, and they shocked him. "Clear!" the voice called again, and they shocked him a second time.

Hayley slid down the wall with her hands over her ears, crying hysterically. "JORDAN, come on. Try it again", Hayley could hear from the hospital staff. Finally, she heard, "Time of death 1:11 am.."

And in that moment, Hayley's world turned dark and numb for the second time.

Loving someone in law enforcement takes a special kind of strength. It means standing by them through the ups and downs, enduring the long hours apart, and weathering the strain that the job inevitably puts on a marriage or relationship.

It is a lifestyle, usually a change from the way the person was living. It is new friendships/family that last a lifetime; knowing sometimes that the lifetime is taken away too soon. It is missed moments together and with children. To some, it would seem to be an abnormal life, but for these select few, the abnormalities are outweighed by the love shared.

For those special people, it is everything they have ever asked for. It is the trials and tribulations that make the heart grow fonder; it is a bond between two that never fails. It's love shared and not taken for granted that grows with each day. For each of these people, it's the unspoken understanding that as long as they breathe, they will keep choosing each other—through everything.

Life doesn't always promise us happy endings, but it promises us that with each experience, we have two choices. We can either live in the darkness, or we can learn to live again, taking the love with us into our next journey.

Hayley: "Hey, Mark."

Mark: "So, where are we at this week?"

Hayley: "Well, my book will be published in 2 weeks, and my editor has already set up a few book signings. Oh, and I have been working with C.O.P.S. too. I am going to start out by donating 100 copies of my book to them, attend their survivor's week in October to speak, and do some peer support for the survivors."

Mark: "Hayley, you are going to be a busy girl."

Hayley got quiet for a moment and smiled.

I know. I owe it to Eric and Jordan to live.

Appendix

In 2024, 167 officers lost their lives in the line of duty. This year, as of today, while I'm writing this, 73 have lost their lives in the line of duty. This does not account for those officers who have taken their own lives by suicide, due to the mental anguish the job places on these officers every day.

If you or anyone you know is struggling with a line-of-duty death (a law enforcement death) or is struggling mentally coping with the job, please reach out to one of these groups. We owe it to our families and friends.

Concerns of Police Survivors (C.O.P.S): Provides resources, training, and support for families of officers.

- https://www.concernsofpolicesurvivors.org

International Association of Chiefs of Police (IACP): Has a National Consortium on Preventing Law Enforcement Suicide and the One Mind Campaign to address mental health and suicide prevention.

- https://www.nami.org

CopLine is a confidential 24-hour hotline with retired officers who help law enforcement officers and their families with psychosocial stressors.

- https://www.copline.org

- 1 (800) 267-5463

Author Bio

June Kraholik, is an author who believes every story — whether nonfiction or fiction — carries a heartbeat: a pulse of love, hope, and second chances. Blending emotional depth with relatability, she writes non-fiction and contemporary romantic fiction that explores the quiet strength found in "healing" and the beauty of beginning again.

June's stories are grounded in themes of resilience, redemption, and the human capacity to overcome. She believes that even in the darkest moments, there's always a path back to light — and that every story is worthy of its own redemption.

When she isn't writing, June enjoys spending time with her daughter and their many animals, finding joy in the everyday chaos that fills their home. The beach is her favorite place to recharge, a setting that often makes its way into her stories — a reminder that peace can always return, no matter how strong the storm.

Get social:

authorjunekraholik.com

Email: hello@authorjunekraholik.com

Instagram: @authorjunekraholik

Facebook: @authorjunekraholik

Tiktok: @theserenitydreamer

Pinterest: @authorjunekraholik